Shy, unworldly and penniless, Zaria Mansford had never known the delights of love. Now, suddenly, she found herself a passenger on her own luxury yacht, disguised as another girl, with danger all around her. Would the mysterious American, Chuck Tanner, protect her? Zaria knew the thrill of love as she was plunged into intrigue and incredible adventure!

Books by Barbara Cartland

BARBARA CARTLAND

58
SWEET ENCHANTRESS

A JOVE BOOK

SWEET ENCHANTRESS

A Jove Book / published by arrangement with
the author

PRINTING HISTORY
Six previous printings
Jove edition / May 1979
Second printing / April 1982

ISBN: 0-515-06214-6

Jove books are published by Jove Publications, Inc., 200 Madison Avenue,
New York, N.Y. 10016. The words "A JOVE BOOK" and the "J" with
sunburst are trademarks belonging to Jove Publications, Inc.

PRINTED IN THE UNITED STATES OF AMERICA

Chapter One

'What a sight!'

The younger partner of Patterson, Dellhouse and Patterson rather fancied himself as a judge of women. And the girl opposite looked very different from the usual client who sat in the leather armchair in his comfortable office.

"I came as soon as I got your letter enclosing . . . the ticket," she was saying in a low, melodious voice with just a little hesitation before the last two words.

Mr. Alan Patterson coughed in a somewhat embarrassed manner.

"My partners thought it wise to include it," he said. "We did not know if, after your father's death, you might have been finding it a little difficult to make . . . er . . . ends meet."

The girl on the other side of the desk smiled. Only a fleeting smile, but somehow just for an instant it transformed her face.

"It was nice of you to think of it."

"And now, to get down to business," Mr. Patterson said, opening a large file which had been laid ready at his hand by his attentive and very smartly turned out secretary.

'Where do people get such clothes?' he wondered, still occupied with the spectacle that his client presented in her ugly, badly cut tweed suit, which was worn at the elbows, while the natural coloured wool jumper seemed to make the pallor of her face even more noticeable.

'She looks as if she might collapse,' he thought. 'I suppose she's been ill.'

He noticed how tightly the skin was stretched over the prominent cheekbones and the harsh line of her jaw. Her eyes were sunk in her head and dark lined behind spectacles with steel frames.

A sudden movement and a dropping of her eyelids told him that he was staring, and once again he coughed apologetically.

"I was just wondering," he said quickly, "whether your journey was comfortable and if you managed to get breakfast on the train."

Even as he said the words he saw what seemed to him a sudden glint in the eyes opposite and he realised why her face, although it repulsed him, was somehow vaguely familiar.

He could still see the pitiful creatures who had run from their huts in the concentration camps to greet the Allied armies as they marched in. They had been nothing but skin and bone; he could still hear their hoarse cries, smell that indescribable odour of rotting, decaying flesh.

Hunger!

Sharply, because he was disturbed and yet at the same time utterly incredulous, he asked:

"Did you manage to get breakfast?"

The girl opposite him shook her head.

"No . . . I . . . I didn't have . . . enough money."

Mr. Patterson put his thumb down hard on the bell fixed to his desk. His secretary opened the door.

"Send out immediately for sandwiches," he commanded. "Chicken, ham—anything they've got—and coffee; plenty of it."

The secretary raised her eyebrows. Mr. Patterson was usually very careful of his figure. Then she glanced at the girl sitting opposite him and seemed to understand.

"Very good, Sir," she said with a little flounce of her black skirt.

"And quickly!"

The secretary shut the door with a decisive bang, which told Mr. Patterson far better than words what she thought of commands being barked at her as if he were still in the Army.

But as if she, too, understood the urgency of what was needed, coffee and sandwiches were brought into the office from the café next door in what was astoundingly quick time.

"Ah! Here it is!" Mr. Patterson exclaimed in a voice which seemed over hearty. "Put it down in front of Miss Mansford so she can help herself. I see you have brought two cups. Good! I can do with a coffee myself."

The secretary left the room. Zaria Mansford stared at the tray for a moment as if she didn't know what to do with the gleaming plated coffee pots.

"Black or white?" she asked at length.

"Black, please," Mr. Patterson replied.

She poured it out for him and passed the cup across the desk. And then, when he had refused the sandwiches, her hand went out towards the plate—the fingers very thin, blue veins showing against the whiteness of her skin.

'The old devil must have left some money,' Mr. Patterson said to himself, while aloud he asked:

"I think I am right in saying your father died three months ago. We did not have the privilege of handling his estate."

"No! It was a firm in Inverness," Zaria Mansford replied. "Mackenzie and McLeod."

7

"I think I've heard of them," Mr. Patterson said. "Your father left you the house?"

"Yes," she answered. "But I do not think I shall be able to sell it. It is such an out of the way spot, and it can only be reached by a private road across the moors. And then we're five miles from the post office or the telephone."

"I see," Mr. Patterson remarked.

"Not only that," Zaria Mansford went on, eating with what he felt was deliberate slowness, as if only a definite effort of will power kept her from gobbling, "my father left a lot of manuscripts behind. In his will he instructed me to finish them. I am hoping when they are completed that I can find a publisher."

'In the meantime, you have had nothing to live on,' Mr. Patterson thought.

"Well, all that is changed now," he said aloud. "If you wish to finish your father's last book, that, of course, will be up to you. But there is no need to do it in any discomfort. You realise that your aunt had two houses? A villa in the South of France and another in California. The latter is, I may say, a particularly valuable property."

Zaria Mansford stopped eating for a moment and stared at him.

"I can't quite believe it's true," she exclaimed. "I read your letter and I thought you must have been mistaken. Of course, I remembered Aunt Margaret, but it is over eight years since I last saw her. I was eleven at the time. My father and I were passing through Paris on our way to Africa. She asked him to bring me to see her, and while I was there they had a bitter row. My father stalked out of her hotel, dragging me behind him. He never spoke to her again."

"I am afraid your father had . . . er . . . differences with a great number of people," Mr. Patterson said firmly. "I understand that when he died he was in the process of litigation against two fellow archaeologists, his publishers, a firm of land agents and the Director of one of our big museums."

"Yes, that's true," Zaria agreed in a low voice.

'A man of strong, impetuous temper,' Mr. Patterson mused to himself, remembering what someone had once told him about the late Professor. And then, looking at the shrinking figure of the girl opposite, he wondered how much she had suffered personally from that temper.

"Well, your aunt certainly remembered you," he said in an effort to strike a more cheerful note. "She has left you practically everything she possessed. There are a few legacies to her staff, some thousands to her favourite charities; otherwise it's all yours."

"About how much does it come to?" Zaria Mansford's voice was breathless.

Mr. Patterson shrugged his shoulders.

"A little over a hundred thousand pounds, I should think," he said. "It is difficult to tell until probate has been agreed and the death duties provided for."

Zaria said nothing. He gathered that she was stunned by the information, and it was not surprising.

'It will be wasted on her,' he added to himself a little enviously, and thought that even smart clothes, provided she had the taste to buy them, would not be able to alter the sharp angles of that skull-like, bespectacled face.

Her hair was lank and lifeless, dragged back from her forehead to fall, straight and uneven, behind her ears to her shoulders.

"I wonder what you will do now?" he said aloud. "Would you like to go out to America to inspect your property there? Or perhaps a trip to the South of France would be easier."

"I don't know. I . . . must think."

There was a sudden flutter of Zaria's hands and a decided falter in her voice.

"There is no hurry, of course," Mr. Patterson said soothingly. "My partners have booked you a room for tonight and for as long as you feel inclined, at an hotel. Unless, of course, you have friends in London."

"No! No friends."

"Very well, then. We tried to find accommodation at the Dorchester or the Ritz, but unfortunately they were full up."

He saw the sudden panic in her face and realised that as far as she was concerned it was fortunate rather than the reverse.

"Therefore, seeing you are alone," he went on, "we have got you into the Cardos Hotel—a pleasant but quiet family hotel in Belgravia. You will be comfortable there, I think."

"Thank you," Zaria said gratefully.

"And now to continue your aunt's will," Mr. Patterson went on.

He read it through in a well-modulated, deep voice which he assumed for these occasions. Glancing up when he had finished, he felt that the girl opposite had not understood a word of it.

"I'm afraid the legal jargon is rather difficult for a layman," he said with a smile. "But you will understand that briefly it means that you inherit the sum of money I have already mentioned and Mrs. Crawford's two properties."

He paused and then said:

"Oh, but I have forgotten one other thing! There is your aunt's yacht. It is, at the moment, under charter. It would be difficult to cancel the transaction which was agreed some months ago and I feel sure you would not wish it."

"No, no, of course not," Zaria Mansford agreed.

"We managed to get quite an advantageous sum—or, rather, our agents did—from an American millionaire, Mr. Cornelius Virdon. He arrives in Marseilles, where the yacht is to meet him, in two days' time. I understand he will be cruising along the coast of Africa. He is extremely interested in archaeology and wishes to do some personal excavations.

"Of course, he has the money to indulge his hobby! The charter, by the way, comes to an end in approximately three months. That is, of course, provided you are agreeable and do not wish to ask him to terminate it sooner."

"Of course," Zaria Mansford answered. "Is it a large yacht?"

"Very reasonable size, I believe," Mr. Patterson replied vaguely. "It's called *The Enchantress,* by the way."

Mr. Patterson paused, then looked down at a number of letters held together by a paper clip which had been placed on his desk beside the file.

"Ah!" he said, as if they brought something to his memory. "There was something I particularly wanted to ask you. Mr. Virdon, this American millionaire—tycoon is, I believe, the right word these days—made one stipulation in renting the yacht. He asked us to engage on his behalf a secretary who had a knowledge of archaeology and who could speak Arabic.

"Now, you would think that was an easy thing to find and my partners and I agreed without realising what difficulties we were to encounter. We had always handled your aunt's periodic chartering of the yacht and we were delighted to be able to tell her that on this occasion we had obtained a very substantial sum indeed."

Mr. Patterson looked smug, then changing his tone, went on:

"But at one moment we feared the whole transaction would fall through owing to the fact that, despite innumerable advertisements, we could not find anyone who fulfilled Mr. Virdon's requirements."

"Why was it so difficult?" Zaria asked.

"I have no idea," Mr. Patterson replied. "We could find archaeologists by the hundred, of course. We could find people who spoke Arabic. But the two never seemed to be combined.

"Then, only ten days ago, when we were getting desperate, we had an application from a Miss . . . let me see . . . a Miss Doris Brown. She seems an excellent young woman who has worked at the British Museum and privately for some leading archaeologists. I think Mr. Virdon will be pleased with her."

"That's settled then," Zaria said, a little surprise in her voice as if she wondered why this long explanation was necessary.

"You are wondering why I am bothering you with all this," he smiled. "Well, the fact is we are still a little anxious and we would be most grateful if, as you happen both to be an expert on archaeology and to speak Arabic, you would have a word with Miss Brown."

"I think my modern Arabic is rather rusty," Zaria replied. "I haven't been abroad with my father for the last five years. I went several times before that, of course, and then he . . . decided to go alone."

There was something in her voice which told Mr. Patterson there was a story behind this, but aloud he said:

"I am sure that all you will need to do is just to ask

Miss Brown a few questions. You see, we have our reputation to consider and we would rather send no-one at all than send someone who was utterly useless."

He rustled through the papers in front of him.

"I have, indeed, taken up Miss Brown's references with great care. But Professor Johnson, whom she was with last, is somewhere in the Sahara and cannot be reached; while Sir Mortimer Greaves, whose book *Fragments of Tiles* was typed by Miss Brown, says she was an extremely efficient young woman but that he could not in any way vouch for her knowledge of Arabic."

"When would you like me to see her?" Zaria asked.

"I will send her to your hotel this afternoon, if that will suit you," Mr. Patterson said. "She has to catch the Night Ferry leaving Victoria at seven o'clock. Shall we say three o'clock at the hotel? And as it's Saturday I am afraid I shall not be here should you telephone us to say that she is not as proficient as we hope."

He glanced at his wrist-watch as he spoke.

"Actually, I shall be playing golf," he said with a smile. "It is my one relaxation at week-ends."

"Then supposing Miss Brown can't speak Arabic at all well, what am I to do about it?" Zaria asked.

"First of all," Mr. Patterson replied, "until you are perfectly satisfied about Miss Brown's Arabic, do not give her the tickets and the passport necessary for her journey. I will, with your permission, entrust them to your care now."

He picked up a large envelope as he spoke and held it out to Zaria.

"We may seem unduly cautious, but we have kept back everything until we obtained your approval of our selection. Mr. Virdon is a very important man—

13

very important indeed, and I would not think of letting him down in a matter of this sort."

"I've never heard of him as an archaeologist," Zaria said.

"No?" Mr. Patterson did not seem surprised. "Well, I assure you, he has taken up the subject very seriously to judge by his letters. He can afford to indulge his fancies, of course.

"He inherited a great deal of money from his father, played the Markets for a few years, being fantastically successful, and then started to be interested in the far off past. Not that it would be my choice of a pastime."

Mr. Patterson appeared to preen himself before he added:

"But every man to his taste—as I'm sure you will agree, Miss Mansford."

"Yes, of course," Zaria answered. "And if Miss Brown is unsuitable . . . I . . . I am to tell her so?"

"If you would be so kind," Mr. Patterson replied. "Then perhaps you would ring my secretary at her home number. She says she will be in all the afternoon—or, at least, until five o'clock. If she hasn't heard from you by that time, she will assume, and I hope very much that this will be the truth, that Miss Brown is as proficient as she appears."

As he spoke, he wrote a number on the back of the envelope.

"I've put down my secretary's number," he said. "But do not trouble to ring her unless anything is wrong. And now, Miss Mansford, if you will excuse me, I have another client waiting."

"Yes, yes, of course."

Zaria Mansford got to her feet in a flurry, dropping crumbs on to the floor as she did so and rattling the cups on the coffee tray as she bumped awkwardly against it.

"There is only one more thing to say," Mr. Patterson went on. "My partners have opened a bank account for you to tide you over until the estate is settled. They have, for the moment, deposited a thousand pounds in your name. When that is spent, you have only to come to us and we will make further provision."

"Th . . . thank you," Zaria faltered.

"In the meantime," Mr. Patterson continued, "as it is the week-end and you might be short of ready cash, here, with a cheque book, is fifty pounds in notes. I hope it will be enough, but you will find the hotel will only be too willing to cash a cheque for any reasonable amount."

He held out a long envelope as he spoke. Zaria took it from him with fingers that seemed to tremble.

"Thank . . . you," she said. "You are . . . quite sure . . ."

He waited and as she said no more, prompted her.

"Quite sure of what, Miss Mansford?" he asked.

"That the money is really . . . mine?"

"Quite sure," he answered.

"Then could you send some money to Sarah—the old woman my father employed at our house in Scotland?"

"Of course. Do you wish to retain her services?"

"No, because she wants to retire, but I think I ought to give her a pension."

"I'll see to the matter at once," Mr. Patterson promised. "You can safely leave all these problems to us—goodbye Miss Mansford."

He said the words aloud as the door shut behind Zaria and almost as if he held only bones between his own warm fingers. Then she turned and walked from the room.

He somehow had the impulse to laugh. It was ridiculous to think that scarecrow of a girl was worth so much money. More money than he was ever likely to earn if he worked until he was a hundred.

"What a waste!"

He said the words aloud as the door shut behind Zaria and his secretary escorted her through the outer office to the lift.

"What a waste!" he repeated.

He thought of the Bentley which his wife had been nagging him to buy for the last two years; of the house they had always wanted at Virginia Water and which would cost at least twenty thousand more than they could possibly afford.

"What the hell will she do with it all?" he asked aloud, then settled himself at his desk once more and rang the bell for his secretary to show in his next client.

Outside the office Zaria Mansford, carrying a suit-case, stared up and down the quiet street. Then she set off in the direction of the main thoroughfare. She had no idea how she got to the Cardos Hotel, but she supposed a 'bus would drop her somewhere near it.

She walked slowly up the street feeling inexpressibly weary. She had not slept the night before, despite the sleeper which had been provided for her with her ticket. She was also conscious that the sandwiches and coffee, though she had been ravenously hungry for them, had given her indigestion.

'I shall have to be careful what I eat,' she told herself, and even while she craved for food, she felt suddenly nauseated by the thought of it.

Oatmeal and potatoes—that had been her staple diet for the last six months and the years before, except when her father had been home. She could remember the row now when the butcher's bill had come in at the week-end before he died.

"Do you think I'm made of money, you little cannibal?" he had shouted. "How dare you order all this amount of meat? Ten pounds nineteen and three! Do you think I'm a millionaire?"

"It's for two months, Father," Zaria had answered.

"Excuses! Always excuses for extravagance," he shouted.

Then he had hit her—as he had hit her so often before—slapping her across the face, raining blows on the back of her head until she had crumpled up before him.

He had kicked her before he left the room, but even then she had realised that he was not hitting her as hard as he used to do. He was growing feeble, and the disease from which he had suffered for the last two years was eating into him.

Soon he would be so weak that his blows would no longer hurt her. She had not guessed then how soon deliverance would come.

She had reached Oxford Street by now and the roar of the buses, taxis and lorries tearing past seemed suddenly to send her dizzy.

'I can't faint here,' Zaria thought; and even while she looked round wildly for some form of support or help, she remembered that she could afford to take a taxi.

There were fifty pounds in her bag! Fifty pounds besides the few pence which were all she had left in the world when she had arrived at St. Pancras that morning.

A taxi stopped in the traffic almost opposite her and somehow she managed to crawl into it, giving the address of the hotel. Then she sat back and closed her eyes.

It was true, really true! She was rich! She never need be hungry again.

She never need be afraid of that shouting voice, those paralysing blows, that terror of going down to the village to buy what she was afraid would never be paid for. She was rich! Rich!

It seemed to her that the traffic was repeating the words over and over again, roaring them at her.

"Rich! Rich! Rich!"

Miss Doris Brown arrived at the Cardos Hotel at three o'clock and was taken by a page-boy up to the second floor. He walked down the corridor and knocked on the door of a room.

Then, as a faint voice said, "Come in," he turned the key and invited Miss Brown to enter.

Whatever sort of person Doris Brown had imagined to find, the reality was a surprise. Her reaction was very much the same as that of Mr. Patterson.

'Good Lord! What a freak!' she said to herself, and then aloud asked in an almost incredulous tone:

"Are you Miss Mansford? Miss Zaria Mansford?"

"That's right," the girl she had addressed answered softly. "Won't you come and sit down?"

Zaria had taken off the coat of her suit and the hand-knitted, faded and darned jumper that she wore above her baggy, ill-fitting tweed skirt, made Miss Brown very conscious of her own elegant black suit, stiletto-heeled shoes and jaunty velvet beret.

"Fancy you being Professor Mansford's daughter," Miss Brown said. "I saw him once—oh, a long time ago—and thought how good-looking he was. Of course, it isn't everyone who likes beards, but he was a fine looking man."

"Yes, very fine," Zaria agreed.

"When they told me I was to come along and see you because you owned the yacht to which I was going. . . ."

She stopped suddenly, her eyes fixed on a darn at Zaria's elbow.

"It is you who owns the yacht, isn't it?"

"Yes, that's right," Zaria said. "But I only heard about it for the first time today. In fact, until two days ago I had no idea that I was ever likely to have anything except what I earned."

"Well, fancy that!" Miss Brown exclaimed. "It must have come as a surprise. Not, if it comes to that, that I should like to own a yacht myself. I'm not such a good sailor as to care for the sea. But still, a job's a job, and when they offered me this one I accepted because it seemed a bit of a change."

"Yes, of course," Zaria answered. "And I expect you'll enjoy it."

"That's just the point, I shan't!" Miss Brown said.

Zaria looked at her in surprise.

"I'm afraid I don't understand."

"That's what I've come along to tell you. When they telephoned me just before lunch, I wasn't certain, you see, so I said O.K. I'd come and see you, because I still thought I was going. And then at lunch. . . . Well, to put it bluntly, he popped the question. I've accepted him and we're going to be married at the end of the week."

Zaria began to see daylight.

"You mean that you're not going on the yacht with Mr. Virdon after all?"

Doris Brown shook her head decidedly.

"No, as a matter of fact I'm going up to Yorkshire tonight to meet my future in-laws. My boy's father is in the wool trade. Very comfortably off he is, I believe. Not that that matters, of course. I'm in love with Ted and he with me. I'd marry Ted if he hadn't got a penny."

"Yes, of course," Zaria murmured.

19

"But it's nice to think that if anything did happen we wouldn't starve. Well, it gives one a sense of security, doesn't it?"

"Yes, it does indeed," Zaria agreed.

"Well, that's really what I came to say," Doris Brown said. "I'm awfully sorry and all that sort of thing, and I would have told that Mr. Patterson so myself if I could have got him at the office, and not bothered you. But as it's Saturday I knew there would be no-one there and so the only thing to do was to come to see you and explain."

"I'm afraid they will be very disappointed," Zaria said. "I understand they had great difficulty in finding someone like you."

"Oh, well, there's just as good fish in the sea as ever came out," Doris Brown said philosophically. "They'll get someone else, you'll see. And after all, sometimes one has to think of oneself, doesn't one? Especially when it's a case of love."

She smiled at Zaria disarmingly and then added:

"To tell the truth, I wasn't quite certain Ted was going to come up to scratch; and now he has, I'm not going to let him out of my sight."

"I'm sure you are wise," Zaria said a little hesitantly.

"Well, that's that, then," said Miss Brown, rising to her feet and holding out her hand. "Good-bye, Miss Mansford. Nice to have met you. I wish you all the luck in the world owning a yacht. If you like the sea, I should take the trip yourself."

She walked across the room, turning at the door to wave. For a moment Zaria stared after Doris Brown and then she sat down in a chair and picked up the big envelope that Mr. Patterson had given her.

His secretary's number was written clearly on the back of it—Kensington 0275.

'I must ring her,' Zaria thought and remembered with embarrassment that she didn't know the girl's name.

Then she noticed that the envelope was not sealed, but that the flap was folded in. She pulled it up and emptied out the contents onto the small table beside her.

There was a new passport with Doris Brown's name on it, a book of tickets—Victoria to Dover, Dover to Calais, Calais to Marseilles—a small wad of *franc* notes, and two letters. One was addressed to Mr. Cornelius Virdon and the other was from Patterson, Dellhouse and Patterson to Miss Brown, obviously giving her full instructions for her journey. This was not sealed either and out of curiosity Zaria opened it.

Miss Brown was to catch the 7 p.m. train from Victoria and when she arrived at Marseilles, to go to the Hotel Britannia where a room had been engaged for her until the yacht should arrive in harbour.

Then she was to report to the Captain and hand the enclosed letter to Mr. Virdon should he be aboard.

It was all very straightforward and business-like. It would be impossible, Zaria thought, for anyone to make a mistake as to what they were to do.

There was a knock and before Zaria could say "come in," Doris Brown put her head round the door.

"Sorry to disturb you," she said, "but I found when I got to the lift that I must have left my gloves behind."

Zaria looked and saw them tucked down the side of the chair where she had been sitting.

"So you have," she said. "There they are."

"Thank goodness! I'm always losing gloves," Doris said, picking them up. "And it comes expensive, I can tell you that, because I think good gloves make such a difference to a suit, don't you . . .?"

21

She stopped abruptly as if she realised that, looking as she did, Zaria was not likely to have good gloves, even if she had gloves of any sort.

"I see my passport," she went on, looking at the pile of things on the table beside Zaria. "In a way I'm sorry not to be going. I should like to have had a peep at Cornelius Virdon. He sounds to me quite a lad."

Zaria looked surprised.

"Is he young?" she said. "I had the idea he was old."

Doris laughed.

"Old, my foot! Don't you ever read the newspapers?"

She looked at Zaria again and said quickly:

"No, perhaps you don't—not that sort any way. Well, he was in the news last year when he unearthed a temple in Peru. I took a bit of interest at the time because Sir Mortimer Greaves, for whom I was working, knew Mr. Virdon and kept talking about him.

"After that, I sort of followed his movements. And, of course, when I heard I was going to be with him on this trip, I got quite excited."

Doris Brown gave a little laugh.

"But there you are! I was never cut out for archaeology. I just happened to tumble into the job when I was eighteen because Professor Johnson wanted an assistant secretary and my father was curator of a museum in Liverpool. I was almost brought up in the right atmosphere, you see."

"But didn't you find it interesting?" Zaria asked.

Doris Brown smiled.

"It got awfully monotonous," she said. "And now I'll tell you the truth. My Arabic is very limited. That's why, if I hadn't been going to tell you about

Ted, I should have been jolly nervous about coming along here."

She laughed, pulled on one glove and hurried towards the door.

"Cheerio!" she said. "You go and meet Cornelius Virdon instead of me. It'll do you good. You look as though you could do with a holiday . . ."

She stopped abruptly and put her fingers to her mouth.

"There, I oughtn't to have said that. I hope you won't take offence, but I always say the first thing that comes into my mind."

"No, no, I won't take offence," Zaria answered quietly.

The door shut behind Doris again and Zaria sank down in the chair. What was the girl talking about? How ridiculous! Of course she wasn't going to take Doris Brown's place as secretary to Cornelius Virdon!

And then the idea took hold of her, so that she could only stare blindly at the passport she held in her hand.

Why shouldn't she go? She really did know something about archaeology. She could speak Arabic— even if it was a little rusty.

It was such a stupendous idea that for a moment it seemed to her to come and go in her head like waves which she could not capture to hold still so that she could examine them. Then gradually everything cleared. It would be so easy.

All she had to do was to obey the instructions which had been given for Doris Brown.

The ticket was here in her lap; the money, the letter of introduction. No need to explain who she was. No need to say, "I am the owner of the yacht." Just go, while Doris Brown went north to Yorkshire to meet her future in-laws who were in the wool trade.

No, of course it was mad, crazy. She couldn't possibly do it. And yet, why not? And, when it came to that, what else was there for her to do?

Zaria looked round the hotel room. She already had not a dislike but a fear of it, because it was so impersonal, so luxurious, so unlike anything she had experienced before.

If she had not been so frightened, she would have turned away from the hotel the very moment the taxi stopped at the entrance.

A Commissionaire in his smart uniform had opened the door; she had been ushered up to the reception desk and before she knew where she was she was being escorted upstairs and into the small suite which the solicitors had engaged for her—sitting-room, bedroom, bath-room.

Nothing pretentious as far as they were concerned, but to Zaria they were the height, depth and breadth of unaccustomed luxury.

She had her luncheon sent upstairs because she was too frightened to go downstairs to the restaurant. She hadn't known what to order.

She had thought wildly of asking for bacon and eggs, but the waiter had persuaded her into having a small omelette followed by a lightly done steak. She had been too frightened of him to refuse, even though the prices on the menu had nearly made her faint with horror.

When the meal came, she had wanted to eat it so much that she had forced herself to walk up and down across the room and to count twenty before she sat down at the table. She tried to pause between each mouthful.

The omelette was gone in a flash and then, heart-breakingly, she had been unable to eat the steak. It

24

was no use, she felt as if it would choke her; she would be sick. So she had to send it away untouched.

'I must be sensible,' Zaria told herself. 'I know exactly what I am suffering from. I have got enough brains for that. Malnutrition! I need milk, food in small quantities with only short intervals in between. I can afford it. Oh, dear God, let me remember that I can afford it.'

And now she remembered that she could afford money for other things—clothes; a suit like the one Doris Brown was wearing, perhaps even better; high-heeled shoes; nylons!

Then she began to shake. It was no use, she couldn't do it. She didn't know how to begin, where to go, what to buy. She tried to remember when she had last bought a dress. Had it been in Inverness? If so, it had been many years ago. Mostly she tried to make her own things; knitting from wool she obtained by undoing an old pullover of her father's.

Once she had even managed to make herself a skirt out of an old tweed suit of his. He would not give her a penny to spend on herself. It was an obsession with him.

Once, a year ago, she had tried to run away, determined somehow to get a job, to escape from the miseries and privations of that horrible, dark little house on the moors.

He had caught her before she reached the main road, and dragging her back had thrashed her within an inch of her life.

"You'll stay here and work for me," he had shouted. "If you think you're going to go gadding about, you're very much mistaken. It's work I want from you, and work I'm going to get. Get on with those manuscripts."

She had never tried to get away again—not even when he had left home and she had been alone except for Sarah. She was an old woman who had worked for her father and mother when they were first married. She was very old, very deaf and surly because her arthritis hurt her, and she was always afraid the Professor would turn her out and she would have nowhere to go.

"Get on with it. You know it makes him angry if it isn't finished," she would say when Zaria paused for a moment, with aching head and smarting eyes from poring over the old papyri and trying to decipher writings on stones which had been in use thousands of years before Christ.

She felt at times that her head would burst, and yet she had gone on, too exhausted even to rebel, too undernourished even to turn away from the blows which her father aimed at her.

'What can I do?' Zaria asked herself now.

Somehow the decision was harder to make than any she had made in her life before.

She felt utterly lost, bewildered and frightened. London was so big, so impersonal. She wanted to ring up Mr. Patterson. He, at least, had been kind and spoken to her in a friendly fashion.

Then she remembered that he would be on the golf course. Besides, he didn't want her. Why should he? She had known from the look in his eyes he had thought her almost a joke.

She got up from the chair and went to stand at the mantelpiece, looking in the big mirror which, stood over it. She stared at her reflection—at the lank, untidy hair she cut herself; at the hideous national health spectacles with their steel frames, which her father had made her get when she said she couldn't see the faded writing in some of the manuscripts he had given her to decipher.

She pulled them off. Her eyes were red rimmed

and the lines beneath them almost black against the ash grey whiteness of her skin. Slowly the tears came into Zaria's eyes—slow, difficult tears because, despite all she had suffered, it was years since she had really cried.

'I am hideous,' she told herself—'hideous and friendless and utterly alone. Oh, I wish I were dead!'

She turned from the mirror and threw herself down on the sofa, hiding her face in the cushion. She was going to cry, but somehow the soft silk of the cushion made her think of other things—silk, satin, velvet, all the lovely things that a woman wanted to touch.

She thought again of Doris Brown, of the nylon stockings, the suede gloves she had been afraid to lose.

'I can have them! I can have them!' Zaria told herself.

She thought that, if she wished, she could go out of the hotel, she could go to a shop and buy anything she wanted. She could pay by cheque. And then she knew she was too afraid.

She couldn't do it. She couldn't face the expression in the eyes of the saleswomen.

"Who is this woman?" they would ask.

She had a wild impulse to run away, to go back to Scotland. Back to old Sarah, to the house with its damp walls and ugly Victorian furniture, with its tense atmosphere which always made her feel that her father was still there, was just coming into the room, was going to find fault, was going to curse her.

That at least was familiar; this was much more terrifying.

She gave a little moan and sat up. Something fell to the floor. She looked down. It was Doris Brown's passport. It had fallen open and she could see the photograph.

She could not help staring at it. It was indecisive,

just a face which might have been of any girl—two eyes, a nose and a mouth; nondescript hair which might, in real life, have been any colour, but which was curled over her ears and swept back in the latest fashion above the forehead.

"I could look like that," Zaria whispered.

She knew then that the die was cast. She would do it. She would take Doris Brown's place simply and solely because if she didn't there was nothing for her to do but to stay here in this frightening, unknown hotel and wait for something to happen.

And why should anything happen? She could go out and walk around the streets, fearful of the bustling, busy people, all intent on their own things and engrossed in their own lives.

She could come back and sit alone, day after day, night after night, with nothing to do and nothing to look forward to except, perhaps, the arrival of her money.

Then, if she wished she could change this hotel for another one, just as impersonal, just as terrifying. She could go to New York, to the South of France. Mr. Patterson had suggested that. But alone—all alone.

"Stop! Stop!"

Zaria screamed the words aloud and then trembled at the sound of her own voice.

She couldn't bear it. She couldn't bear the terror of being alone, of having nothing to do, of knowing that there were no manuscripts to read, no father to come and force her to work, no Sarah doddering outside in the kitchen, preparing the inevitable meal of oatmeal and tea.

"I will go! I will go!"

Zaria whispered the words to herself and then, with a resolution she was far from feeling, she rang the bell.

Even when she had done it, she sat trembling, her whole body tense and stiff as she waited.

At last a chamber-maid came—a rather smart, perky young woman. She looked as if she might resent being fetched in the middle of the afternoon.

"You rang, Madam?"

"Please," Zaria said, "I want you to help me."

"Yes, Madam. What can I do?"

"It's . . . it's this," Zaria said breathlessly. "I've got to go . . . abroad tonight. I've come down from Scotland without . . . any clothes. I've got to have a coat and skirt, a blouse, some stockings and some shoes. I can't . . . go without them. And, please I would like . . . my hair done too."

The chamber-maid looked at her contemptuously.

"Madam doesn't understand, it's Saturday," she said.

"Yes, yes, I know all the shops are shut. But couldn't I buy them from somebody else? Perhaps you have a suit you could sell me?"

The chamber-maid stared at her as if she had taken leave of her senses.

"Please," Zaria pleaded. "Please, it's desperately important to me."

It was woman calling to woman on the one subject which inevitably binds the female race, whatever their stratum of life, whatever their creed, colour or nationality—clothes.

"Well, Madam, I'll see what I can do," the chamber-maid said doubtfully.

Chapter Two

Zaria stood at the Hotel Britannia and watched the traffic move up and down the sunlit street below.

From there Marseilles looked like an ant-hill of industry and accentuated her loneliness and sense of isolation.

She had lain awake all night in the comfortable sleeper, wondering whether she was crazy to do what she was doing, wondering whether she would be wiser to return to London, wondering whether she should write to Mr. Patterson and tell him that she had taken Doris Brown's place.

And at the end she had come to no decision at all. She had done precisely nothing. She had just arrived in Marseilles and finding out that the hotel was not far from the station, had walked there carrying her suitcase in her hand.

The room was booked for her, as she had expected from Mr. Patterson's letter. She had been shown up to it with the sleek, polite efficiency of a well-run hotel, and then the door had closed behind her and she was alone again.

Now she turned from the window and, as she did so, saw her own reflection in the several mirrors which ornamented the room.

It was hard to believe it was herself. The suit that the chamber-maids had found for her had certainly not been cut by a master tailor, but it was infinitely smarter and more becoming than the terrible old tweed coat and skirt she had worn for years.

Zaria had crushed that into the wastepaper basket, being extravagant for the first time in her life in throwing away something which might have been used again.

It was very difficult to find something slim enough to fit her, but the chamber-maids—four of them—had entered into the spirit of the thing and had literally ransacked their wardrobes.

"You're just a bag of bones, that's what you are!" Elsie had exclaimed when one suit after another was discarded as being hopeless.

They had grown familiar by this time and dropped all pretence of calling her madam or treating her as an honoured guest at the hotel. She was just a girl like themselves, and somehow this was more warming than anything that had happened to Zaria for a long time.

"You must have been very ill to get as thin as that," one of the girls remarked. "Do you feel all right now?"

"Yes, quite all right, thank you," Zaria answered, and didn't bother to explain that it wasn't an actual illness that had made her look as she did, but years of malnutrition.

All the time at the back of her mind was the picture of Doris Brown, with her pointed little breasts, flouncy behind and jaunty air of well being.

'I've got to look like that, I've got to,' Zaria told herself.

But even when finally the chamber-maids had finished with her, the resemblance was not very obvious.

The suit she wore was a dark grey one. The blouse, of white *crêpe de chine,* was not unlike the one Doris had been wearing. But Zaria didn't manage to fill it out. It just hung from her shoulders.

"You've got to fatten up, that's what you've got to do," Elsie said.

The others sighed enviously.

"I wish you would say zat to me," said Helga, who came from Germany and was definitely on the plump side.

"If you'll stop guzzling cream cakes and chocolates, you'll lose pounds," Elsie replied unkindly.

They all laughed.

"I think this suit is very nice," Zaria said shyly, looking at herself in the mirror. "And now, please how much do I owe you?"

With the shoes, stockings, underclothes and a hat they provided for her she had to pay out eighteen pounds, and it was with the greatest difficulty that she prevented her fingers trembling as she drew the notes from her bag.

It seemed such a tremendous sum to spend on clothes. She almost expected to hear her father's voice roar at her, see his eyes—dark and yet at the same time fiery with anger, as they were when he lost his temper.

She had thought for a long time before his death that he was doping himself with some strange powder that he brought back from the East, or there might have been something in the cigarettes he smoked—they certainly smelt queer enough.

"And now your hair," Elsie was saying. "You can't go out with it looking like that."

"No, no, of course not," Zaria agreed. "I want it waved and turned at the ends."

Again she was thinking of Doris Brown with her smart up-to-date *coiffeur*.

"Well, there isn't a hairdresser open round here . . ." Elsie began.

And then she gave an exclamation.

"I know!" she cried. "Henri must do it."

"Henri!" the girls echoed. "Why Henri?"

"Well, didn't you know he was a hairdresser before he came here? He told me all about it. He just couldn't stand being cooped up in what he called 'the scented air,' so he became a waiter."

"And got savoury air instead," one of the girls remarked, and they all laughed.

"I'll go and tell him he's wanted," Elsie said. "He ought to have finished in the dining-room by now."

"You'll get into trouble if they catch you on the ground floor," someone warned her.

"They won't catch me," Elsie replied cheerfully.

She went from the room and in an amazingly short time came back with Henri. He was a thin young Frenchman and they all explained in chorus what was expected of him.

He stared at Zaria, then sent the girls in every direction—one to fetch some eggs from which he made a rinse; another for a shampoo, a third for towels.

But it was Elsie who by this time was producing Zaria as if she was being groomed for stardom, who remembered that one of the guests staying in the hotel had a hand-dryer.

"Her ladyship's away for the week-end," she said, "and she'll never know that we have used it."

By this time Zaria had ceased to wonder what would happen next. It was only when Henri had washed her hair and it was dry and he combed it out that she saw how different she looked.

It did not really resemble Doris Brown's fashionable head but there were soft waves against her cheeks, and the lank ends had all disappeared.

"Madam is pleased?" Henri asked with satisfaction.

Zaria didn't know how to pay him or how much she should give. Finally, because she was so shy and embarrassed she pulled a few notes out of her bag and slipped them into his hand.

It was only afterwards that she realised she had given him three pounds, and thought she must have been mad.

"Three pounds!" she whispered to herself in the train.

She and Sarah could have lived for weeks on that. In fact they often had to when her father was away or he was more than usually stingy with the house-keeping money.

And yet it was worth it, worth all the expense to feel that she was escaping from herself.

That was what she had known she was doing as she crossed the Channel, as she climbed onto the noisy French express waiting at Calais and felt herself being carried rapidly through the night.

She was getting away from the past. She was leaving behind the heart-break and the misery, the hunger and the cruelty which had been hers for so long.

And she knew it was only because she was so desperately anxious to escape from her memories and her fears that she had been brave enough to start out on this incredible adventure. It wasn't really courage which had got her to where she was now, it was fear—fear of the people, fear of London, fear of her new-found fortune, fear of everything that was un-familiar.

"You are Doris Brown," she said to her reflection in the mirror.

Then she laughed because she felt how insulted the real Miss Doris Brown would have been if she could have seen her.

When she laughed two little wrinkles showed on either side of her mouth. Yet somehow that didn't matter because her mouth was different too.

"I know what is wrong," Elsie had said suddenly when they were inspecting her newly arranged hair and looking at her in her white blouse and grey skirt.

"What's that?" Zaria asked.

"It's your face," Elsie said.

When the other chambermaids looked shocked, as if she had said aloud something they all thought but were too polite to mention, she added quickly, her colour rising:

"I don't mean that rudely. I'm trying to say that you're not made up. No-one has pale lips these days. It makes you look, well, sort of peculiar."

"Of course, that's it!" one of the other girls exclaimed. "Lipstick is what you want. I've got a new one somewhere and it's just the right colour. I paid seven-and-six for it only yesterday. You can have it."

"I've got some powder too," she went on, "but I'm afraid it will be too dark."

"Yes, of course it will," Elsie said scornfully. "Lydia uses the right shade. She's the only one of us who won't sunbathe."

So Zaria paid for a box of powder, a pot of foundation cream, which Elsie made her promise to rub in night and morning, and a new lipstick.

She had also taken off her glasses and thrown them away. She could really see perfectly well without them and she told herself that if the manuscripts which Mr. Virdon gave her were too difficult to read, she would buy some decent ones with tortoiseshell rims.

Somehow those ugly, steel framed ones would always remind her of her father and his bullying.

"Tired! You can't be tired! Come on, I want that transcription before tomorrow night. God knows why I'm cursed with a half-wit for a daughter. It's perfectly simple. It only requires a little concentration."

"But I'm tired, Father. I have been working late every night this week. I've got such a headache."

"You've always got something. Whine! Whine! Whine! That's all you're good for. Get down to it. You've had a nice lazy time while I have been away."

It was no use trying to explain to him that he had left her, during the three months of his absence, enough work to fill six. There was always a new treatise, a new book, a new catalogue to be done somehow.

Once she had been brave enough to suggest that she would like someone to help her, he had given her a box of her ear which had sent her flying across the room.

"You lazy little devil!" he stormed. "Help, indeed! What do you think you're for except to do what I tell you? You get that manuscript finished by the end of the week or I'll break every bone in your body."

His threats were never idle threats. He was a violent man and he invariably expressed himself by violent methods. Once or twice there had been ugly tales of his treatment of the natives who helped him in his excavations.

On one occasion sharp letters had passed between him and one of the District Commissioners.

"Soft, that's what people are becoming," he had ranted. "Soft and sloppy minded. No wonder the black man is getting supremacy all over the world. It wouldn't surprise me if they become our masters. We're asking for it and that's what we'll get. A black should be treated like a dog and then he will learn to obey orders."

Zaria had sometimes wondered if a dog would survive the treatment she herself had received. But there had been nothing she could do about it.

But when finally her father died she had still not

been able to get away. There was no money, there seemed to be no world outside that empty, desolate little house. What was more important, her will had gone. She was too frightened to escape.

Yet now she had done so.

Now she was free—at least for the moment. She was here in Marseilles and there was no-one to stop her going anywhere she wanted to go.

With a sudden impulse of revolt she opened her bag, took out her lipstick and slashed it vividly onto her lips. Red for defiance, red for energy, for animation and vitality and all the things she had never had the courage to possess.

Then, as she did so, the door suddenly opened. She had not heard anyone knock, and she turned in surprise, remembering almost guiltily that the key had been left outside the door.

With a sense of shock that was almost like a blow she saw a man come into the room.

He entered swiftly and almost silently so that he was there before she had time to realise what was happening. The door closed behind him and he stood with his back against it.

"What do you want?"

Zaria spoke in English, forgetting, in her astonishment, where she was. He answered her in the same language.

"You are Miss Doris Brown?"

"Y . . . yes," Zaria said hesitantly.

"Good! I thought I had come to the right room."

He spoke a little breathlessly as if he had been hurrying, and now she saw that he carried a suitcase in his hand and a mackintosh over his arm. He had very dark hair against a tanned skin and he wore sun glasses.

There was something about his accent, something which for the moment she could not place.

Zaria rose to her feet.

"I . . . I don't understand. What do you want?" she asked. "Why didn't you knock?"

"There wasn't time."

Again she had that impression that he was breathless. Perhaps he had run down the corridor or up the stairs. But why? She looked at him helplessly, not knowing how to cope with this situation.

Then, as if he sensed her uncertainty, he said in a quieter tone:

"Please don't be frightened. I heard you were here and I wanted to see you."

"Heard it! But who from?" Zaria asked.

"That doesn't matter," he replied. "What is important is that I need your help."

She realised now what was peculiar about his accent. He was an American. There was only a slight drawl but, nevertheless, an unmistakable one. He was a big man, broad-shouldered, and yet he could move quickly and with an agility which spoke of an athletic body.

"May I sit down?"

"Yes, I suppose so . . . I . . . I don't know. Ought you to come . . . bursting into my room like this?"

"Please, Miss Brown. I can explain everything if only you'll listen to me. Will you?"

"Yes . . . I'll . . . listen," Zaria faltered.

"Thank you."

He spoke quietly, then he turned swiftly. He opened the door, peeped into the corridor and shut the door again.

"I just want to make quite certain we are not overheard," he said.

"Why should we be? Why should anybody be interested?" Zaria asked. "I only arrived here a short time ago."

"Yes, I know," he said. "I saw you come in as it happens. I didn't think it was you. You didn't look like my idea of Miss Brown somehow."

Zaria felt guilty. There was somehow nothing she could say to this.

He crossed the room and sat down in an armchair by the window. As he lowered himself, she noticed that he winced slightly as if in pain, and now she saw that there was a piece of plaster on his ear and a strange, discoloured bruise over his left temple. He saw her glance and put his hands up to his forehead as if to hide the bruise.

"I had a motor accident," he said, "and I am a bit battered as a result."

"I see," Zaria said.

Because there seemed nothing else to do, she seated herself again on the stool in front of the dressing-table, turning so that she faced the stranger.

"Do you mind if I smoke?" he asked.

"No, no, of course not."

"You are quite sure? I hate smoke in bedrooms, but I don't think you will be sleeping here tonight. The yacht is in the harbour."

"Oh! They haven't let me know."

"It only arrived a short time ago. You will be hearing shortly and then you will go aboard."

"How do you know all this?" Zaria enquired.

"A friend of yours told me that you were coming," the American replied. "He asked me to look out for you."

Zaria digested this for a moment and then she said, because it seemed to be expected of her.

"Wh . . . what was his name?"

"I don't believe you'd remember him," the American replied. "But you met him in London, and he learned from some friends that you were going on this trip. He told me about it and that is why I am going to throw myself on your mercy."

"What do you want me to do?" Zaria enquired.

"Take me with you," was the answer.

For a moment she thought she couldn't have heard aright. She just stared at him—a strange man in dark glasses which somehow gave him an impersonality, made him seem completely unreal.

"I . . . I don't understand," she said at length.

"Listen, Miss Brown." He bent forward in his chair, clasping his hands together. "It is imperative, absolutely imperative for me to get to Algiers. My mother is ill. I have got to get there to see her."

"But there must be ships?"

"I haven't got any money."

"Oh!"

This, to Zaria, was a perfectly reasonable explanation, and yet, she thought quickly, he looked quite prosperous. His suit was well cut and he had drawn a cigarette case from his pocket, though, for all she knew, it might only have been worth a few shillings.

"I am sorry," she said gently. "I know what it is to be poor. But I don't see that I can do anything."

"But you can, you must," he replied. "You are a most important person on this voyage. My friend told me that. Mr. Virdon insisted on having a secretary who had a knowledge of archaeology and who could also speak Arabic. That's true, isn't it?"

"Yes, that is true."

"Well, then. All you have got to do is to say that you are bringing an assistant with you, that you realised that you couldn't cope alone with all the work which was likely to be the result of this expedition."

"What would Mr. Virdon say? He wouldn't believe me."

"He will believe you, I'm sure he will. He's got to believe you. You've got to be convincing about it."

"But why should I do this?" Zaria asked, almost piteously.

"Because I'm begging you to do it," the American replied. "I've got to get to Algiers. I've got to be with my mother. She's ill. My step-father is a brute and is treating her badly. I've got to get there, I tell you, before it's too late."

He spoke so earnestly that Zaria almost felt the tears rising in her eyes. Her impulse was to agree at once. Here was someone in trouble, here was someone appealing for her help with a sincerity which rang absolutely true.

Then she tried to clutch at her commonsense.

"Listen," she said. "I have never met Mr. Virdon. He is employing me through some solicitors in London. Supposing he says that he won't allow me an assistant? Supposing he is angry at my presuming to suggest such a thing?"

"I don't think he will be," the American said firmly. "Please do exactly what I say and I promise you it will be all right."

"But . . . but why . . . should I?" Zaria protested.

"Because I know you have got a kind heart, because this means more to me than I can ever tell you, because you, at any rate, have got nothing to lose by doing a generous action."

That was true enough, Zaria thought. She really had nothing to lose. If the worst came to the worst, she could just say it was her yacht. She knew she would be much too afraid to say anything of the sort,

41

but it was a comforting thought to realise that she could do so.

As if the American sensed her hesitation, he said:

"I have thought of a plan, if only you will agree to it. When you get the Captain's summons to say the ship is here, I want you to drive down to the docks with me. We will go aboard and I want you to introduce me as your fiancé."

"My fiancé!"

Zaria echoed the words with wide eyes.

"Yes, it's better that way. It will make it sound more reasonable why I am with you. I am not only your assistant in this very difficult work you are undertaking for Mr. Virdon, but we are also engaged. All the world loves a lover. I don't believe there will be many obstacles in our path.

"You can explain, of course, that we have only just got engaged and therefore you didn't want to leave me behind while you went off to Africa as Mr. Virdon's employee."

It did sound plausible as he put it, Zaria thought. And, after all, that was just what the real Doris Brown had done—got engaged—only she had chucked Mr. Virdon because of it.

"I . . . I don't know what to say," she said a little helplessly.

"Then just be a good girl and agree," the American pressed.

"But . . . I don't even know . . . your name."

"No, of course you don't. You must call me . . . Chuck. It's what my friends in college used to call me. My other name, by the way, is Tanner—Chuck Tanner. And incidentally, I do speak a little Arabic and I do know a little about archaeology."

"Well, that's something, at any rate," Zaria said.

But still she hesitated, and then, very shyly, the colour turning her cheeks suddenly crimson, she said:

"Would you . . . would you mind very much taking off your glasses?"

He did as she asked without comment and then, as a pair of deep grey eyes looked into hers, he asked:

"Why?"

"I . . . I just wanted to see what you looked like without them," Zaria answered, telling only half the truth because she was too embarrassed to say that she had always believed that a man or woman could be judged by their eyes.

His were honest eyes, steady and somehow—although she could not explain it to herself—absolutely trustworthy.

"Thank you," she said after a moment, and looked away because she was embarrassed.

He put his glasses on again.

"I have to wear these," he said. "I get blinding headaches if I don't, and I'm also a sufferer from hay fever."

The telephone by the bed shrilled suddenly making them both jump.

"That will be from the ship," Chuck Tanner said quickly. "Don't say anything about my call. Just say you will come down right away."

Zaria walked hesitantly towards the telephone. And then, even as she lifted the receiver, she suddenly found him beside her, his hand over hers to prevent her answering it.

"One moment," he said. "If it is anyone else, anyone at all, don't say I am here. You understand?"

"But . . . but why?" Zaria enquired.

"Just answer it," he commanded.

43

He released her hand and she picked up the receiver.

"Hallo!"

"M'mselle Brown?" a voice enquired.

"Oui."

"Attendez un moment, si'l vous plait."

There were various cracks and splutterings and then an English voice with a decided Cockney accent asked:

"Is that Miss Brown?"

"Yes, Miss Brown speaking."

"Oh, good afternoon, Miss. The Captain's compliments. *The Enchantress* is in dock and could you come aboard?"

"Tell the Captain I will come at once," Zaria answered.

"Very good, Miss. Number three dock, berth forty-seven."

"Thank you."

There was a crack at the other end of the line and Zaria put down the receiver. Only then did she realise that Chuck Tanner was standing close enough to her to have heard all the conversation. He smiled at the worry on her face.

"Everything is all right?" he asked soothingly.

"Who did you think it might have been if it hadn't been someone from the yacht?" Zaria asked.

"You never know," he said enigmatically. "There are a lot of unpleasant people about in the world, especially where millionaires are concerned."

"Oh, dear! I never thought of that." Zaria sat down suddenly on the bed. "You're not a confidence trickster? You're not trying to get on board so that you can rob Mr. Virdon, are you?"

Chuck Tanner laughed.

"I promise you that whatever else I do I won't do that," he said. "Nor am I a competitor for the

44

treasures that you and Mr. Virdon are going to find. No, as I have told you, I just want to get to Algiers, and there is no other way of doing it."

"Supposing . . . just supposing I could . . . lend you the money?"

She saw that her suggestion had taken him unawares, but after a second he had an answer for it.

"To begin with I don't believe you've got enough money," he said. "And, secondly, I have my faults, but I'm not in the habit of taking money from women."

"I . . . I'm not all happy about this idea, all the same," Zaria said. "Supposing the Captain says point blank that he won't allow you on board?"

"He won't," Chuck Tanner said confidently. "He will say that we will have to wait for Mr. Virdon's arrival—and that is where you have got to be very persuasive. I'm relying on you, Miss Brown. I'm trusting you. I promise you that this is not a whim, an escapade; it's a matter of life and death."

There was something in the way that Chuck Tanner said it that made Zaria shiver.

"And now I want you to do something else," he said. "Go downstairs and pay your bill. Then ask the commissionaire to get you a taxi. When you get in, tell the driver to take you to the docks.

"But as soon as you are out of hearing, rap on the window and tell him to stop at the chemist's shop in the Rue Garibaldi. Can you remember that? The chemist's shop in the Rue Garibaldi. I will be waiting for you there."

"Then . . . then you are not coming down with me?" Zaria asked.

He shook his head.

"No, I am going out through the back door. It is safer that way. I don't want anyone to see me."

"I . . . still don't understand," she said. "Are

you . . . escaping from the police? Have you done . . . anything wrong?"

"I have done a lot of wrong things in my life," he answered with a smile, "but nothing which at this moment concerns the French police. Please trust me. I know it all sounds crazy—a story out of the *Saturday Evening Post* or perhaps even a crime novel—but it's much more simple than that. It is just that I have got to get to Algiers and I don't want anyone to stop me.

"My step-father's relations—his sons as a matter of fact—don't want me to see my mother. They are afraid she may leave me her money. That's all."

"I see," Zaria said with a little sigh of relief. "I . . . will do as you ask."

She didn't know why, but somehow, despite the whole fantastic story, the American's odd manner, the way in which he had crept into her room, she was, in her innermost heart, glad that he was going aboard with her.

It wouldn't be so frightening to feel that he was there as it would be to face a whole crowd of unknown people—Mr. Virdon, the Captain, and the other members of the party.

"Well, now, we'd better go," the American was saying. "Don't forget, my name's Chuck; you're in love with me and I with you. I suppose I call you Doris."

"No, please don't do that," Zaria said almost involuntarily.

Then, as she saw him looking at her in what she fancied was surprise, she added hastily:

"It's my . . . my office name, you see. At home I'm called Zaria. I . . . I usually forget to answer to . . . Doris."

"Zaria!" he repeated the word softly. "That's a lovely name—an Arab name, by the way."

"Yes, my mother chose it because she thought it was so pretty."

"And it is," Chuck Tanner said. "Zaria! I shan't forget. We will keep Miss Doris Brown strictly for formal occasions."

Zaria had spoken impulsively. Now she almost regretted it. A host of questions seemed to be waiting to trip her up. Would her second name have been on her passport? Wouldn't it have been better to have let him call her Doris?

And yet she knew it was only one more thing to make her afraid. She might so easily not answer: she might forget. No, if they were to pretend to be on intimate terms, it was safer that he should address her in a way to which she would instinctively respond.

She picked up her suitcase.

"Is that all you have brought?" Chuck Tanner asked. "You are certainly travelling light."

"What about you?"

"I have got another case waiting for me at the chemist's shop."

"I . . . I shall have to buy some clothes when I get to Algiers," Zaria said hastily. "I came away in rather a hurry. The solicitors didn't tell me about this job until a day or so ago. They couldn't find anybody."

"Oh, I see! Well, *au revoir* for the moment, and thank you."

Chuck Tanner held out his hand. Zaria put her fingers into it. She had a sudden impression of strength, warmth and something protective. And then his hand was on the door.

"Just look down the corridor and see if anyone is about," he said.

47

Zaria obeyed him without comment. The softly lit, carpeted corridor was quite empty. Chuck pulled a soft hat low over his forehead.

"I will see you in about five minutes," he said almost beneath his breath.

Then he was hurrying away down the corridor, his footsteps quite noiseless on the soft carpet.

Zaria waited until he was out of sight, then she, too, walked down the corridor and rang the bell for the lift. It carried her down to the ground floor, where she paid her bill and walked towards the front entrance.

There were numerous people sitting around in the big open hall—men reading newspapers, women gossiping with each . other, families who had their children with them. Zaria wondered if any of these could be the men Chuck was frightened would prevent him from going to Algiers.

She could almost imagine the grasping step-sons trying to prevent the real son inheriting the money that was rightfully his.

'It is right that I should help him,' she said to herself, and stepping into the taxi she told the commissionaire to direct the driver to go to the docks.

Chuck was waiting just inside the chemist's door. As soon as the taxi stopped there, he came hurrying out, threw his small suitcase into the taxi and plonked a bigger one down beside the driver.

"Everything all right?" he asked as he got in beside Zaria.

"Yes, of course," she answered. "You didn't expect it not to be, did you?"

"I don't know what I expected," he said. "Perhaps I am being stupidly nervous, but one never knows. Now, you're quite certain you've got the story right? And by the way, we've travelled from London to-

48

gether. You will see that I've got London labels on my baggage."

"You are certainly thorough," she said. "But do you really think anyone will be likely to question our story?"

"You never know," he said enigmatically. "One of the first rules of telling a lie is to tell a really good one and be quite certain all the details are checked up. What's the matter?" he asked as Zaria turned her head away.

"I don't like telling lies," she said. "And I've always been a very bad liar. When you put it like that, I'm afraid."

"It will be all right, I promise you," he said soothingly. "Just don't be rushed into making a lot of statements which aren't true. Just keep to your story. We're engaged to be married and because of it, because, too, you need me for the work you intend to do for Mr. Virdon, it was quite impossible for you to leave me behind."

He put up his hand as he spoke and pulled his hat a little further down on the left hand side of his head.

"Did you get something for that bruise?" Zaria asked.

"As a matter of fact, I did," he said. "The chemist assured me it cures like magic, but I will believe it after I've tried it."

"Were you driving too fast?" Zaria enquired.

"Driving?" he queried.

"The motor accident."

"Oh! Yes, yes, of course. I'm afraid so. I'm always impatient. I can never wait to go slowly."

They sat in silence for the rest of the journey. They passed through the dock gates, were directed to berth

49

forty-seven, and there, tied up against the dock, Zaria saw *The Enchantress*.

She hadn't given much thought to what the yacht—her yacht—would be like. She had not expected it to be so white, so graceful, so altogether a luxury ship, with its gleaming brass, its red sun awnings, its low, comfortable chairs with red cushions, and its whole air of spotlessness.

"Mine! Mine!" She wanted to cry the words aloud.

Instead she waited while Chuck paid the taxi and turned to see two sailors come hurrying down the gangway to take their luggage.

The Enchantress was also much bigger than she had expected. The Captain, a middle-aged, bearded man, looking very smart with his gold buttoned uniform, came hurrying to meet them with outstretched hand.

"How do you do, Miss Brown?" he smiled. "I hope we haven't kept you waiting too long. I was rather afraid that owing to some minor repairs we shouldn't get here until tomorrow morning. But as you see, all is well."

"How do you do?" Zaria said nervously. "May I introduce Mr. Tanner, my . . . my fiancé?"

"Your fiancé! Well, that's a surprise, isn't it? I don't think we were expecting you to bring a gentleman with you."

"I am hoping . . . Mr. Virdon won't mind," Zaria said a little breathlessly. "You see, the solicitors were very insistent that I should come on this trip, and as I didn't wish to leave Mr. Tanner . . . behind, having just got engaged, they suggested that he should come as my . . . my . . . assistant. He is very experienced in this sort of work."

"Well, I expect it will be all right," the Captain said. "And there's plenty of room."

He turned to one of the sailors.

"Take this gentleman's luggage down to Cabin D."

"Aye, aye, Sir."

"Now, Miss Brown, I would like to show you your quarters," the Captain said. "And perhaps you and Mr. Tanner would like some tea? The steward is preparing a real English spread in the dining saloon."

"Oh, that will be very nice," Zaria said.

The Captain looked at his watch.

"I'm expecting Mr. Virdon about six o'clock," he said. "He came over on the *Cherbourg*, you know. She docked at Le Havre late last night and he's taking the day train here. They ought to be on board soon after six."

"I will be able to . . . speak to him then," Zaria said with a look at Chuck.

"That's right," the Captain agreed. "In the meantime, just make yourself at home."

He showed Zaria into a stateroom which seemed to her the height of luxury. Chuck was further down the passage.

"And now I will show you the cabin which Mr. Virdon asked should be set aside as a workroom," the Captain said.

He led the way down the passage into a large, very comfortably furnished cabin where there was a writing-table, a typewriter, a large number of files and what was obviously photographic and pottery cleaning equipment.

"We picked all this up at Cannes," the Captain explained. "Mr. Virdon had them stored there from a cruise he made last year."

"It all looks very businesslike," Zaria said, feeling something was expected of her.

"I haven't had the pleasure of meeting Mr. Virdon yet," the Captain smiled. "But I feel from his letters

51

and his instructions to me that is exactly what he is—a real business man, even if he is interested in the past."

"Yes . . . it seems like it . . . doesn't it?" Zaria stammered.

She walked slowly back to her stateroom. The Captain left her after telling her the way to the dining saloon, and she shut the door behind him. Then she put her hands up to her face.

Would a real business man ever accept this fantastic story of her fiancé she wondered? What was more, would he suspect by something she said or did that she was not who she pretended to be?—Miss Doris Brown.

She stood there, indecisive, then suddenly there came a knock at the door. Before she could answer it, the door opened and Chuck looked in. His lips were smiling and somehow, behind those concealing dark glasses, she felt that his eyes were twinkling.

"So far so good," he whispered. "The adventure begins! Are you excited or merely frightened?"

"Frightened! Terribly frightened!" Zaria answered.

"But, why?" he asked. "I'm here to look after you."

Chapter Three

Zaria stood on deck and watched the ship move slowly out of the great harbour.

It was very early in the morning; a mist still covered the horizon and the sea was translucent—so pale that it was hard to believe that later it would be the vivid blue of the Madonna's robe.

Everything seemed to have a fairy tale quality, as if the world itself was an illusion; and Zaria had the feeling that she, too, was living in a dream and was perhaps only a figment of some other person's imagination.

'This is really happening to me,' she insisted, and at the same time tried to credit the astounding fact that this yacht was hers—her own.

'I will never part with it,' she whispered to herself.

Then shrank from the idea that she must at some time acknowledge her identity.

How could she ever give orders to anyone so awe-inspiring as the Captain? It had been hard enough to make a choice between the many dishes that had been offered her the night before at dinner.

A frown of anxiety lined her face as she remembered the problems that lay ahead of her that day.

Mr. Virdon and his party had not arrived at six o'clock as expected. A telegram came to say they had been held up in Paris and would not be on board until nearly midnight.

"I suppose we must wait up for them," Zaria had

said to Chuck when the message was relayed to them by the steward.

"No reason," he answered. "It will be time enough in the morning to tell Mr. Virdon about us."

Zaria shook her head.

"I would rather get it over now and done with. I am terrified, anyway, of meeting him."

"Why?" Chuck asked, and then as she did not answer he said: "What a strange girl you are! You seem to be frightened of so many things. What is worrying you particularly? Apart from me."

Zaria looked away from him, glancing round the big, comfortable cabin which was not in the least like her idea of an office. For one wild moment she thought of telling him the truth, revealing who she was, explaining how she had come to be here on Doris Brown's passport.

Then she remembered that she knew nothing about Chuck; she had only met him a few hours ago. With an effort she tried to sound businesslike as she said:

"I think it would be more to the point if you told me something about yourself."

"Of course," he said disarmingly. "What do you want to know? I'm twenty-eight, an American with a French mother who has re-married a Frenchman. I know Europe fairly well. I smoke, drink and am fond of children. Is that the sort of thing you want to hear?"

"I suppose so," Zaria said doubtfully.

She had a feeling that he was deliberately hiding something even while he seemed so utterly at ease. And how different he was from herself.

She was tense and on edge, every nerve jangling when anyone spoke to her.

"And now let's go on talking about you," he said. "You've been ill, haven't you?"

Zaria was just about to deny it when she remembered how terrible she looked with her prominent cheekbones and dark lined eyes. He would never understand the truth, therefore she must lie if only for her self-respect.

"Yes, I have been ill," she said gently.

"I thought so," he answered. "And this is going to be a real rest cure for you—at any rate, as far as Algiers. I will do the work in exchange for my passage, and you put your feet up and rest."

"That's all very well," Zaria said with a faint smile. "But I don't believe you could do the work that Mr. Virdon will expect me to do. It's very technical, you know, especially when it comes to the translation of some of the ancient papyri."

"Oh, I'm not going to attempt to do that," Chuck answered. "What I will do is type with one finger while you dictate to me. I promise you it is with one finger—though actually I'm rather quick at it."

"What do you do for a living?" Zaria asked.

He hesitated before he answered and she knew she wasn't going to hear the truth.

"Oh, I've done quite a lot of things in my time," he answered evasively. "I've been a soldier, I can pilot an aeroplane, and I'm not such a bad plumber when the necessity arises."

'In other words you are not going to tell me,' Zaria thought to herself, but she was too shy to say it aloud.

The conversation between them seemed to lapse. She thought how gauche and awkward she was. It was because she had lived out of the world for so long, seeing so few people.

Often for months her only visitors were the shepherds and game keepers who passed the house on the way to the moors, while the only people she talked to were the tradespeople when she went into the village;

old Sarah whom she knew in her heart she had grown to hate; and her father when he was at home.

That was her circle of friends and acquaintances.

And yet she could look back and remember the days when her mother was alive, when their house in Edinburgh had been filled with interesting and amusing people. She could remember coming down in her party dress and being told to shake hands with Lord This and Sir Somebody That, with a famous professor and a celebrated conductor.

There had been laughter and witty conversation, for her mother seemed to stimulate and inspire everyone with whom she came in contact to give out the very best of themselves.

Then she had died. Zaria could remember those long wakeful nights when she had cried aloud in the darkness:

"Mummy, where are you? Come back to me, I want you."

She and her father had moved from Edinburgh. At first they travelled abroad, then when they returned to England they took rooms in London until finally Professor Mansford decided to settle in Scotland.

The house on the moors had never been meant to be anything but a shooting lodge, and Zaria could remember her mother saying how dull it was. Dull! She felt herself shudder now at the memory of those long winters when she and Sarah had been snowed up for days.

The loneliness, the emptiness and the aching misery in herself made her shiver as if an icy hand came from the grave to drag her back into it.

"It's lovely, isn't it?"

A voice speaking behind her unexpectedly made her jump and she turned to find Chuck had come up to her unawares.

"You are very early," he said.

"I thought Mr. Virdon might want me," Zaria explained.

"I think it's unlikely," he answered. "The steward tells me that they are all going to have breakfast in their cabins."

"All of them?" Zaria asked in surprise.

Chuck grinned at her.

"You don't understand the ways of the idle rich."

"Mr. Virdon isn't idle . . ." Zaria began, and then the words seemed to die away on her lips.

She was remembering how strange all three men had seemed last night when they arrived.

She supposed it was because she was embarrassed and frightened that they, too, had seemed ill at ease. She had the impression that two of them at least had been drinking.

It had been nearly midnight when they had come aboard. A big car had drawn up on the docks and they had walked up the gangway in silence, almost, Zaria thought, like naughty boys who were wondering what sort of reception they were going to get.

And then she knew that such an idea was ridiculous.

Mr. Virdon was dressed in conventional yachting kit—white trousers and gold-buttoned jacket and a yachting cap with a white top. He had shaken hands with the Captain and introduced his friends.

"Mr. Edie Morgan; Mr. Victor Jacobetti," and finally—surprisingly, because she had been last in coming out of the car—"Miss Kate Hanover."

"Hi, boys," a shrill voice called. "Wait for me. What's the hurry?"

She came hurrying after them, a swirl of honey coloured mink, jangling bracelets and flashing eyes. Her platinum silver hair hung to her shoulders, her red nails were an inch long. There was an almost overpowering fragrance of expensive perfume.

Zaria stared at her in sheer astonishment. She had never before in her life seen anyone quite like Miss Hanover, and she had never in her wildest dreams anticipated that such a girl was likely to be found on an archaeological expedition. But the Captain was introducing her.

"This is Miss Brown, Mr. Virdon, and she has something to tell you about another guest, Mr. Tanner."

"Mr. Tanner?" Mr. Virdon repeated, shaking Zaria perfunctorily by the hand.

"Here, what's this?" the short middle-aged man called Edie Morgan asked. "We weren't expecting a party aboard."

"One moment, Edie," Mr. Virdon interrupted. "Suppose we ask Miss Brown to explain."

Blushing and feeling herself tremble with embarrassment because they were all looking at her, Zaria began to stammer:

"I . . . I hope you won't mind. It's . . . it's just that . . . Mr. Tanner felt . . ."

"I am afraid my fiancée is rather shy," Chuck said in his deep voice. "I am hoping, Mr. Virdon, you will forgive me for barging in like this, but we didn't want to let you down at the last moment, knowing how insistent you had been that a secretary should be provided aboard the yacht.

"The truth of the matter is, Miss Brown and I have just become engaged and we didn't want to be parted. So we talked it over and decided it would be best if I came along. I can be of quite a lot of assistance, as it happens, because I can speak Arabic and also know a little about archaeology."

"Well, this is certainly a surprise!" Mr. Virdon said, and he looked at Edie Morgan as if for corroboration.

"Of course, if Miss Brown doesn't want to come . . ." Mr. Morgan began.

"There is a letter for you, Sir, from the solicitors," the Captain interposed. "Mr. Patterson wrote to me at the same time saying they had had the greatest difficulty in fulfilling your request for a secretary. I think that was why Miss Brown and her fiancé felt it would be very upsetting to let you down at the last moment."

"Yes, yes, of course, I understand," Mr. Virdon said hastily. "It is most kind of you to be so considerate. We are, of course, delighted to have Mr. er . . . Tanner with us."

"As he says, he can make himself useful," Mr. Jacobetti ejaculated.

He was a young man with a vacant face which was somehow belied by his sharp, shrewd little eyes. Pig's eyes, Zaria thought they were, as they had peered at her in a manner which told her instinctively that he was thinking of her as a very unattractive female.

"O.K.! That's settled," Edie Morgan said, as if it were he who was making the decision. "And now, what about a drink?"

"I felt that you might be wanting a meal, Sir," the Captain said, "and the steward has everything arranged in the dining saloon."

"I guess I can do with something a good deal stronger than food after that ghastly journey," Kate Hanover said in her shrill, nasal voice.

As if they all agreed, the three men followed Kate and the Captain down the companionway to the dining saloon. Zaria and Chuck were left on deck to look at each other in astonishment.

"Strange people," Chuck said softly.

"I didn't imagine Mr. Virdon would be like that," Zaria said.

59

"What did you think he would be like?" Chuck enquired.

"Clever-looking—perhaps with a beard. And not so smart. All the archaeologists I have met before looked as if they had gone to bed in their clothes."

"This is obviously the exception to the rule," Chuck said. "What about the dame?"

Zaria looked at him for a moment, wondering what he meant.

"Oh! Miss Hanover," she exclaimed. "What on earth will she do while they are excavating?"

"I shouldn't worry about that," Chuck answered. "If she gets any further than the main street of Algiers, I'll do a tummy dance."

Zaria couldn't help giggling. It was the first time she had giggled for years and it somehow made her feel more at ease with Chuck. She knew then that she was glad he was there, glad that she hadn't got to face all these strange people alone.

"Come on, let's go to bed," Chuck said. "You look all in. You may be quite certain they don't want to see either of us again tonight."

She obeyed him because she was desperately tired. She had not slept the night before for worrying.

She did not expect to spend a good night, but the moment her head touched the pillow she had slipped into a deep slumber which not even the hooting of the ships, the noise of the cranes or the rumble of the docks had been able to disturb.

Only as she heard the ship's engines start up had she opened her eyes, then hurriedly got up and dressed.

Now she looked at Chuck and realised that he, too, must have slept well. The strain that had been on his face the day before had gone, and though he wore his dark glasses, she felt his eyes were twinkling.

He no longer seemed to be looking over his shoulder, peeping round corners, frightened by those step-brothers of his who wished to stop him from going to Algiers.

She supposed it was because the ship had sailed that he seemed at ease and curiously at home.

He was dressed right for one thing. He wore an old blue, high-necked pullover like the fishermen wear and he had rubber-soled, white plimsolls on his feet.

"How's the bruise?" she asked.

"Can you still see it?" he enquired.

"No, now you speak of it it's hardly noticeable at all."

"That's because it's getting better," he said. "I want to forget it. Don't talk about it in front of the people here. They're sure to put a wrong conclusion on the fact that I had an accident at all."

"Do you think they will imagine you were drunk in charge of a car?" Zaria asked.

"I shouldn't be surprised," he replied. "It's what they would expect, being pretty hard drinkers themselves."

"Why do you say that?" Zaria asked.

"I'm only repeating gossip," he said. "The steward tells me they didn't go to bed until two o'clock. They were drinking all that time in the saloon."

"It doesn't sound as if we shall get much work done," Zaria exclaimed.

"Well, come and have breakfast, then we can be all ready in the office for any commands that might come our way," Chuck suggested.

The breakfast was delicious, as had been their dinner the night before.

Once again Zaria could only pick at her food, even though Chuck kept pressing her to bacon and eggs, sausages, cold ham, honey, *fraises du bois* and one of the huge hothouse peaches which stood with a mammoth bunch of grapes on the sideboard.

"I can't eat any more," she protested. "I am not used to so much food."

"That's obvious," he answered. "You look like one of those little fools who do a slimming diet, thinking it's going to make them more attractive, and then find their stomachs have shrunk."

"I shouldn't slim for preference," Zaria said, and was unaware of the sudden bitterness in her voice.

Chuck looked at her, but said nothing. She wished that he wouldn't wear his glasses indoors as well as out. There was something uncanny, she thought, in not being able to see his eyes clearly.

Of course, dark glasses were an American characteristic. Mr. Virdon was wearing them last night when he came aboard, and Kate Hanover had been carrying an enormous pair with pointed corners which she played with all the time she was talking.

'Perhaps I should look better with them, too,' Zaria thought to herself. 'They would at least hide the lines under my eyes.'

When breakfast was over, they went into the office. There was nothing to do and Chuck began taking some books out of the book shelves.

"Whoever bought these," he said, "was certainly no pedant. These are all the latest novels, the most recent biographies of well-known social personalities and, of course, inevitable for the British—*Debrett* and *Who's Who*."

Zaria had just been about to say, "My aunt was very social, I believe," and checked herself.

"I suppose they were chosen by the former owner of *The Enchantress*," she said primly. "She is dead, and one of her relatives has inherited the yacht."

"A nice legacy!" Chuck exclaimed. "I wonder what he or she is like?"

Zaria smiled to herself. She wondered what he would say if she told him the truth.

"Chuck!" she said suddenly. "Have you really got no money at all? What are you going to do when you get to Algiers?"

"Oh, I shall manage all right when I get there," he answered easily.

"Supposing your mother is too ill to give you any?"

"Then I shall have to get myself a job," he replied. "By the way, I was wondering if Mr. Virdon will consider paying me as well as you or whether you are expected to halve your salary?"

"I hadn't thought of that," Zaria said. "You can have half, of course."

"Don't be ridiculous! I was only joking," he smiled. "You know the trouble with you, Zaria, is that you are too serious. Don't you ever laugh like other girls? Since we have met, I believe you've only smiled once or twice and that was what I call a pretty poor effort."

"I think I must have got out of the way of smiling," Zaria said.

"Tell me why?"

Zaria shook her head.

"I want to forget it," she said. "And perhaps it is best for neither of us to be too confidential. We are only ships that pass in the night."

He put out his hand and covered hers.

"And you, if I may say so, are a very kind little mercy ship."

The cabin door opened and Edie Morgan came in. He looked distinctly unpleasant, Zaria thought. He was wearing a purple brocade dressing-gown with the legs of his orange striped pyjamas showing beneath it.

He had not yet shaved and his chin was dark blue. There was a puffiness under his eyes and a generally dissolute air about his face. He looked much older and even more repulsive than he had looked the night before.

"Oh, there you are, Miss Brown," he said, ignoring Chuck. "I want to get a cablegram off at once. We have a wireless operator, I suppose?"

"Yes . . . I think so . . ." Zaria said a little nervously.

"Then take this down. *Madame Bertin, Rue Clemenceau 15 Lyons III stop Will meet you Tarralisa tomorrow noon stop Bring Ahmed suggest he drives other car stop Reply stop Edie stop.* Have you got that?"

"Yes," Zaria replied.

"Then get it off at once. She should have reached Lyons by now."

He said the last words almost to himself and turned towards the door, but Chuck's voice arrested him.

"Are we going to Tarralisa, sir? I thought we were heading for Algiers."

For a moment it seemed as if Mr. Morgan was going to tell Chuck to mind his own business, and then the expression on his face, from being an almost aggressive one, changed.

"I suppose I should have explained, Miss Brown," he said. "We have arranged to pick up two of our guests at Tarralisa. One of them is Madame Bertin. I daresay you've heard of her. She is the famous *couturière,* a woman who is acknowledged to be one of the greatest dress designers in Paris.

"She's planning to open a shop in Algiers. That's why she's coming with us. You'll find her a real person."

With these words Mr. Morgan walked out of the cabin, shutting the door behind him.

"Then we are not going straight to Algiers," Zaria said. "Oh, I am sorry. I know how anxious you are to get there."

"It doesn't matter. A day won't make all that difference," Chuck answered.

"I will get this cablegram off." Zaria said, and hurried up to the Wireless Officer.

When she came back to the cabin, Chuck had got out a map and was looking up the distance from Marseilles to Tarralisa.

"I suppose we can get the yacht in there," he said. "It seems only a tiny place."

"The Captain will have said it's all right, I suppose," Zaria answered.

"I still think it's a funny place to pick up anyone."

"I should have thought it would be a long and difficult journey from Lyons in twenty-four hours," Zaria replied.

"You're right," he agreed. "A very difficult journey!"

"Why do you say it like that?" Zaria asked.

"Like what?" he replied with one of his quick smiles.

She couldn't explain. There had been something reflective in his tone as if he suspected some very sinister reason.

"Oh, nothing," she answered.

"Listen, there's nothing we can do here," Chuck said. "You come up on deck and get some sunshine. That's what you want. And by the way, I suppose you know you shouldn't walk about in those high-heeled shoes."

"I . . . I haven't got any others," Zaria confessed.

"Well, mine are certainly no use to you," he said. "I will go and have a talk with the steward."

He went away and in about five minutes came back with a pair of white plimsolls in his hand.

"Size four," he said. "Any use?"

"They are only half a size too big. They will be perfect," Zaria answered. "But whom do they belong to?"

"Well, I gather that a year ago they had a very small cabin boy on board. He only stayed a short time because he was such a nuisance, but as the owner of the yacht provided clothes for the crew—it was one of her eccentricities according to the steward—they got in a supply of clothes which haven't been worn since. I've told him to put a sweater and a pair of trousers in your cabin."

"For me?" Zaria asked.

"Well, why not?" he enquired. "You will be much more comfortable than you will be wearing that suit. And however many smart things you have, you won't be able to compete with Miss Hanover."

"I wasn't going to try," Zaria said.

She wondered if Chuck guessed that the coat, skirt and blouse she was wearing were actually the only clothes she had with her.

She thought now that she was mad not to have bought something in Marseilles. But she had been too frightened to do anything except what she had been told to do—go from the station to the hotel and wait there for instructions from the yacht.

"I . . . I'll try the things on," she said a little shyly.

The shoes were certainly more comfortable even if they were a little big. And the white woolen sweater with the yacht's name embroidered across the front was cosy and warm.

The trousers made her feel shy. Never in her life before had she thought of wearing trousers.

"At least," she told her reflection in the mirror, "I don't bulge in the wrong places or have a large behind like most women who wear shorts or slacks."

She was, in fact, so thin, that she looked exactly like a boy. But it was one thing to look at herself in the mirror; quite another to walk back to the cabin in search of Chuck.

It took all her resolution not to run away and hide when he turned to look at her.

"That's better," he said. "And now let's get up into the open air. That's my prescription for putting roses into your cheeks."

There was something about his breezy indifference which was infinitely reassuring. She followed him gratefully up the companion-way and into the sunshine.

The sea had more colour now. The sun was rising in the sky, the mists had gone; and looking back, they could see the hills behind Marseilles; and beyond them, far in the distance, were the snow topped peaks, very white against the blue of the sky.

Zaria felt the sun warm on her face and the wind in her hair, and then the tears came into her eyes. It was so lovely, so incredibly beautiful! In forty-eight hours her life had completely changed.

She remembered her terror as she had lain awake in the sleeper coming down from Scotland to London. She had been frightened of everything and everybody, and most of all of herself. She didn't know how to behave. She didn't know what to do.

Now already everything was different. She felt different. There was new life coming to her body and she wasn't alone. At least Chuck, strange, mysterious as he might be, was a friend.

She tried not to think what would happen when he went away. She tried not to admit, even to herself, how glad she was that they were going to Tarralisa instead of Algiers.

"I like the sea!" Chuck said suddenly. "Did I tell you that amongst other things I once went to Iceland on a whaling expedition? It was one of the most exciting things I've ever done in my life."

"Men are so lucky," Zaria sighed. "Whatever happens, there's always something exciting for them to do. Women are handicapped in every way, especially if they are not brave."

"They should be brave," he answered.

"And if they are not, if they are just silly . . . little . . . frightened fools?" Zaria asked with a little throb in her voice.

He smiled at that.

"If you are talking about yourself, you've got it all wrong. I think you have got a lot of courage. It took courage to bring me here, and I shall always be grateful to you. One day perhaps I shall be able to thank you for it."

She said nothing, but his words left a little glow of warmth round her heart. And then he went on:

"By the way, we mustn't talk like this again. It's dangerous. In a yacht even the walls have ears, and outside it is just the same. Words carry on the wind; a porthole may be open below decks. And remember another thing. Don't be quite so stiff with me. I'm your fiancé!"

"I will try," Zaria said obediently.

He put his arm through hers and walked slowly up and down the deck.

"We must appear to be talking about ourselves," he said in a low voice. "Actually, I am wondering

68

what particular excavations Mr. Virdon is going to start when he arrives in Algiers."

"I was wondering that," Zaria answered. "Last time I was there I went to Timgad with my father—but that was some years ago and I shouldn't think there's much left to uncover."

"So you have been there before?" Chuck said.

"Yes, but, as I say, it was some years ago," Zaria answered, feeling this was a dangerous subject.

"You must have been very young."

"I suppose I was," she admitted. "But my . . . father was taking part in the expedition."

"His name was Brown, I suppose?" Chuck asked.

"Yes, yes, of course," Zaria answered.

She freed herself from his arm and walked to the side of the ship.

"I wonder how fast we are travelling?" she said for something to say.

She guessed by the slow way in which he followed her, with a faint smile on his lips, that he knew she was deliberately avoiding his questions.

Then, before she could speak, before she could frantically think how she could answer anything that he asked of her, she saw Mr. Virdon, resplendent in his white trousers and yachting jacket, come up the companion-way.

He was wearing his dark glasses and he flopped down in one of the comfortable chairs under the sun awning.

Resolutely Zaria walked across to him.

"Good morning, Mr. Virdon! Is there anything you want me to do?"

She felt that his eyes were half closed behind his glasses as he peered up at her.

"Oh, good morning, Miss . . . er . . . Brown," he answered thickly. "No, I don't want anything. Yes, I do, by jove—a gin and tonic! Tell the steward to bring me a large one, will you?"

"Yes, of course," Zaria answered.

She went to find the steward and give him the order. When she came back, Mr. Virdon was still sitting where she had left him. Chuck, she noticed, had disappeared.

"The steward is bringing your drink right away, Mr. Virdon," Zaria said. "What I was wondering was whether you had any notes you would like me to type, or if there are any particular instructions you would like to give me for when we arrive at Algiers?"

"No, no, nothing," Mr. Virdon said. "You had better see Edie about all that."

"I will talk to Mr. Morgan then," Zaria said, and then added: "I was wondering where you were thinking of excavating. I am guessing that it might be Tipasa. I hear the excavations in nineteen-forty-nine uncovered the perron of a temple—but perhaps you have another place in mind?"

"Ask Edie about it," Mr. Virdon said. "For goodness sake ask Edie."

There was an irritability in his voice which Zaria could not possibly ignore. Realising that she was being a nuisance, she moved away, a flush on her face.

There was no need for Mr. Virdon to snap her head off, she thought. She was only trying to earn the money that he was paying her, to make herself useful as might be expected of a secretary, especially one who had been considered so indispensable to the trip.

She went to the bow of the ship. The trouble with a yacht, she thought, was that there was nowhere that one could get away alone. Even here she was conscious of the Captain on the bridge, of the crew moving about and the windows of the stateroom opening out on to the deck.

But either she must sit there, go below or encounter the disagreeableness of Mr. Virdon again. She chose the lesser of the evils and sat down with her back against a coil of rope, watching the sea shimmering in the rising sun. It had almost a hypnotic effect on her.

She felt herself relax, the warmth of the sun seep into her body.

She was half asleep when finally she was aware of someone coming towards her.

"Luncheon is nearly ready," Chuck announced.

"Then I'll go and wash," she said. "And, Chuck . . ."

"Yes?" he enquired.

"Wait for me in the office. I don't want to go in to the dining saloon alone."

"All right," he said. "But don't be long."

"I shan't be a minute," Zaria promised him.

She ran down the companion-way to her cabin. She washed her hands, ran a comb through her hair—the waves on either side of her face springing back nicely, just as Henri had set them.

She tried not to look at her trousers, they made her feel embarrassed, but the white sweater undoubtedly gave her a nautical air. Feeling suddenly rather gay, she hurried to open the door of the office.

"I'm ready," she smiled.

Chuck was standing at the other side of the writing-desk with a piece of paper in his hand. He looked up.

"There's something here that I want you to look at," he said. "It will amuse you."

Zaria walked across towards him and then, to her astonishment, as she reached him he put his arm round her shoulders. She looked up at him in surprise, stiffening instinctively at his touch.

"Darling," he said in a voice low and deep with apparent emotion, "I love you!"

71

Chapter Four

For a moment Zaria thought Chuck must have taken leave of his senses.

His arm round her shoulders, the closeness of his face threw her into what was almost a panic and she winced away from him, a cry of something like fear on her lips.

Then she realised that he was holding a piece of paper before her eyes and wordlessly commanding her to read it.

For a moment the words on the paper seemed to dance before her eyes. She was only conscious of Chuck, of the strength and bigness of him, and then they steadied and she saw that he had written:

"Someone is listening to every word we say. Play up."

"Actually I am rather angry with you," Chuck murmured, still holding her close.

"Angry!" Zaria managed to say.

The word seemed to stick on her tongue and to come almost thickly from her lips.

"Yes, angry because you haven't been with me all the morning. What have you been thinking about, you funny little thing, looking out to sea with that wistful look in your eyes? Aren't you happy? Listen, Zaria! We won't worry about my relations or anyone else. We'll get married soon—very soon."

Zaria managed to make some sort of sound in answer. She was trying to obey Chuck's instructions to play up, but somehow everything seemed to have gone out of her head.

"I . . . I think it is time for lunch," she managed to say at last.

"You are being maddening," he replied, still in that deep voice that sounded so unlike his usual tones. "Maddening, but I love you. Remind me to keep telling you that, my little sweetheart."

He stopped speaking and looked down at her. For one terrifying moment she thought he might be about to kiss her. Then with a laugh he released her.

"All right," he said. "I know you are hungry and I shall hope you will be nice to me after lunch. Come along. I could do with a drink, I don't know about you."

He took her hand almost as if she were a child, and led her from the cabin, shutting the door behind him. In the passage she turned to him quickly.

"What . . . what does it . . . ?" she began in a whisper.

But he put his fingers to his lips. In silence they walked along to the dining saloon.

Mr. Virdon was sitting there at the head of the table, a gin and tonic in his hand.

"What is happening to everybody?" he asked querulously as they entered.

"I'm sorry, sir, if we are late," Chuck said. "I was talking to Mr. Jacobetti and rather lost count of the time."

"What's Victor got to say?" Mr. Virdon asked.

"We were talking about aeroplanes," Chuck answered. It seemed to Zaria that Mr. Virdon almost looked relieved.

"Oh, Victor's quite a boy in the air," he remarked.

73

The door opened to admit first Kate and then Edie Morgan. Kate was really very pretty, Zaria thought in astonishment. Last night she had merely thought her fantastic, but in daylight there was no doubt about her good looks.

Her skin, tanned golden—doubtless by artificial sunshine—was a vivid contrast to the soft silver blonde of her hair. Her eyelashes were made up like little exclamation marks, but they fringed very large blue eyes, and her mouth was a perfect cupid's bow.

She was wearing jeans and a sweater—useful in theory, but its real purpose was obviously to reveal the enticing, seductive curves of her body. Round her neck she wore four rows of huge pearls and her wrists were once again a jangle of gold bracelets of every sort and description.

She walked across the cabin and dropped a kiss on Mr. Virdon's forehead.

"Hi'ya, honey. Feeling better this morning?"

"I've still got the hell of a headache," Mr. Virdon answered.

"I told you not to mix them," Kate said briskly.

She looked across the table at Zaria and Chuck and gave them a smile that radiated out almost like a beam from a lighthouse.

" 'morning, folks," she said, and then was obviously suddenly arrested by the letters on Zaria's sweater.

"s.s. The Enchantress," she read aloud, with a little drop of poison in her tone. "Well, you certainly believe in advertising."

Zaria had nothing to say. She merely felt the colour rising in her cheeks. But Chuck was quite equal to the occasion.

"She always enchants me," he said.

"Oh, well, that's all that matters, isn't it?" Kate asked.

74

With a little shrug of her shoulders as she seated herself on Mr. Virdon's right and patted the chair next to her with an inviting look at Edie Morgan.

He had shaved and was wearing linen slacks and a round-necked sweater. But he looked even worse, if that were possible, Zaria decided, than he had in his dressing-gown.

"Where would you like us to sit?" Chuck asked, his hand on Zaria's arm.

"Anywhere you fancy," Edie Morgan answered. And then, as if he remembered that he was not the host, added: "What do you say, Corny?"

It was the first time that Zaria had heard Mr. Virdon addressed by his christian name and she thought that only someone as unpleasant as Edie Morgan could have shortened the rather attractive name of Cornelius into anything so nauseating as Corny.

"Whatever suits the others," Mr. Virdon answered, holding his glass out to the steward in a silent command for him to refill it.

Drinks were being served all round before Victor Jacobetti appeared. He seated himself on Mr. Virdon's left which was the only seat left, and said:

"I've just been telling the Captain that this ship moves too slowly for my liking. If we're going to be in Tarralisa by noon tomorrow we'll have to put on a bit of speed."

"Don't worry, we'll do it easily," Chuck exclaimed.

They all turned to look at him as if he had said something sensational.

"What do you know about it?" Edie Morgan enquired, and there was an ominous note in his voice.

"I merely looked it up on the map," Chuck answered almost apologetically, "and then worked out how long it would take us at the speed the engineer told me we were doing at the moment."

"Smart guy, eh?" Edie Morgan asked. "What else do you know?"

Chuck's eyebrows went up above his dark glasses. "About what exactly?"

"Anything. I haven't quite tumbled as to why you're on this trip."

"I thought we explained that last night," Chuck answered. "Mr. Virdon made it very clear that the one thing he must have was a secretary who could speak Arabic and knew an appreciable amount about archaeology. Miss Brown was the only person who was available. It is not easy to find people proficient in both these subjects."

Deliberately he paused and took a sip from his glass before he continued:

"When we got engaged, I wanted my fiancée to chuck up the whole trip but she didn't feel she could possibly break her contract at the last moment. After all, when you get to Algiers, you'll find it very difficult to do without her. And so, rather than disappoint Mr. Virdon, I came along to give what help I could."

"Jolly good of you!" Victor Jacobetti remarked, but with a slight sneer in his voice as if he meant it sarcastically.

"So that's the set up, is it?" Edie Morgan said.

"I hope none of you gentlemen think I am gate-crashing," Chuck smiled. "If you do, of course, both Miss Brown and I could leave you when we get to Algiers."

"No, I think that would be a mistake," Edie Morgan said firmly. "We certainly need someone who can speak Arabic, don't we, Corny?"

"We do," Mr. Virdon agreed briefly.

"Oh, heck! Do we have to keep talking business?" Kate asked. "I think it's very nice to have Mister . . . er . . . what's your name?"

"Tanner—Chuck Tanner," Chuck supplied.

"I think it's very nice to have Chuck aboard," she said with a smile. "The more the merrier where men are concerned. And if you're not busy, Miss Brown, perhaps you'd give me a hand with my unpacking. If there's one thing I loathe it's trying to put things away in drawers."

"I should be glad to help you," Zaria answered.

"O.K.! O.K.! Well, let's be a bit more cheerful," Kate demanded. "What we all want is a proper drink. Here, steward! Bring up some of that champagne you were offering us last night."

"Yes, Miss."

The steward looked as he spoke at Mr. Virdon.

"Do what Miss Hanover said," Edie Morgan ejaculated. "Champagne—several bottles of it, and quickly."

"Very good, Sir."

The steward went from the saloon. The party helped themselves to the excellent *hors d'oeuvres* which had been laid on the table. There were small langoustines, moules done in the French way, herring smoked in Scandinavian fashion and a dozen other tempting dishes.

"You must try and eat," Chuck said to Zaria in an affectionate, solicitous manner which made her remember that she must play up to him as he had requested.

"I'll try," she said humbly.

"That's right," Victor Jacobetti said. "Feed her up. No man should marry a thin woman; they're always disagreeable."

"So that's your experience, is it?" Kate ejaculated.

"Well, let me tell you, Victor, that I've known some pretty mean women in my time who bulged in all the wrong places."

"Maybe, but on the whole the fat ones are more cheerful and more generous," Victor remarked. "It's the ones who are slimming, like you, Kate, who'd take the last dime out of a blind man's tin."

"Thanks for the compliment," she replied. "Actually I'm not slimming at the moment."

"Well, you don't eat much," Victor retorted. "Get all your calories in booze I suppose."

"You're just being disagreeable," she pouted.

She put her elbows on the table and stared across at Chuck.

"You haven't told us your opinion," she said in a soft, seductive voice.

"I belong to the school of fat and happy," he answered.

"Women are only happy when men take the trouble to make them so," Kate answered, looking at him from under her long black eyelashes.

"Then Zaria's going to be a very happy girl," he answered.

"Zaria! What a strange name," Kate exclaimed.

"It's Arabic," Zaria explained, feeling she must say something.

"When we get to Algiers, I think perhaps I'll go native," Kate said. "What do you say, to seeing me in a yashmak and doing a tummy dance?"

"That ought to draw in the crowds," Victor Jacobetti said, "if nothing else does."

There was a little twist on his lips as if there was a double meaning to his words. It seemed to Zaria that Edie gave him a warning glance.

"When we get to Algiers, we shall all be busy," he said sharply.

"Chuck and I won't be," Kate answered. "Will you take me to see the Dance of the Ouled Naïl? Isn't that what they call it?"

"That's right," Chuck replied. "And you'll find plenty of shows of that sort put on for tourists."

"Oh, I don't want to go to the tourist places," Kate said petulantly. "I want to see the real thing. I'm told that some of the women are absolutely beautiful and that every cent of what they earn is expended on gold necklaces and gold bracelets until they are weighed down with them."

"You'll feel quite at home, won't you?" Victor said nastily.

She gave him a withering glance.

"I'm not asking you to take me," she said. "Or Edie, or Corny. I'm asking Chuck. I've a feeling he knows a bit about entertainments of that kind. A man of the world, eh, Chuck?"

"When I was last in Algiers, it wasn't safe for a white women to mess about in that sort of place," Chuck answered.

"Aw, shucks! That's what people always say," Kate cried. "I'd feel quite safe with you."

There was no mistaking that she was going out of her way to be deliberately flirtatious with Chuck. Zaria suddenly felt as if she would choke if she ate another mouthful of food.

But the men at the table seemed to take no notice of Kate's behaviour. They merely ate solidly and kept calling for their glasses to be refilled.

Zaria had shaken her head when the steward came to pour her out a glass of champagne, but somehow he had not noticed and she realised now that her glass was full. She took a sip.

She remembered the last time she had tasted champagne. She had come down to dinner as a treat, and when her father had filled up the glasses, her mother had said:

"Give the child a teaspoonful in which to drink our health. It won't do her any harm."

They had drunk to her father's new book.

"And to us all, every one of us." That had been her mother's toast.

The taste of the champagne brought it all back. The small dining-room with its red curtains and polished mahogany furniture. Her mother's eyes sparkling with excitement, a smile on her lips.

Even then she had been in pain, though no-one had realised it—a pain which had increased week by week and day by day until finally the doctors had said there was nothing they could do for her except keep her under morphia.

Zaria felt the tears sting her eyes and quickly put down her glass. She dared not be sentimental. She had cried helplessly and so often for her mother until she had learned not to arouse the nostalgia which would bring the tears so easily to her eyes.

"Drink it up!" Chuck was smiling at her.

Somehow she felt a sudden impulse of gratitude towards him; almost a desire to thank him because he was thinking of her and speaking to her instead of to the attractive, seductive woman staring at him from the other side of the table.

Kate suddenly lay back in her chair.

"What are you gay cavaliers going to do this afternoon?" she asked.

"Personally, I'm going to get a bit of shut-eye," Edie Morgan replied. "I've got a lot to catch up with. What about you, Corny?"

"Perhaps Mr. Virdon would like to do some work," Chuck suggested.

"Work!" Mr. Virdon repeated as if it was a word

with which he was not familiar. "What can we do at the moment?"

No-one seemed to have an answer to that, and he rose to his feet carrying his glass in his hand.

"I'm going to sit on deck," he said. "Might as well enjoy the sunshine while we're here."

He moved from the cabin—tall, broad-shouldered, yet walking with a heaviness which somehow proclaimed that already, although the day was young, he had had quite enough to drink and it was making him lethargic.

Kate got up and stretched, the action showing to the full the somewhat exaggerated charms of her figure.

"Well, I must say you're a lousy lot," she said. "Come along, Miss Brown, we'd better get that unpacking done. Then I think I, too, will take a nap."

Zaria rose and then, a little hastily, looked at Chuck. As if he understood what she was trying to ask him without being able to say it in words, he said:

"I shall be sitting in the stern of the ship if anyone wants me. Good-bye for the present."

He put out his hand in an affectionate gesture and squeezed Zaria's fingers. She made an effort and smiled at him, then followed Kate out of the saloon and across the companion-way into a big cabin opposite.

"He's certainly very attractive, that boy of yours," Kate said. "Where did you find him?"

"In . . . in London," Zaria answered, thinking to herself that she must warn Chuck of everything she said so that they would not contradict themselves on another occasion.

"He's got something! Actually he reminds me of someone but I can't think who it is. How did you meet him?"

"We . . . we were . . . introduced," Zaria answered.

"Well you certainly have been clever to get him tied up," Kate said.

She ran her eye over Zaria as she spoke and the English girl was miserably conscious of what she was thinking—the contempt in those blue eyes was quite apparent.

"Well, what about my unpacking?" Kate said. "You can see what a mess the place is in."

It certainly was in a mess.

There were trunks scattered all over the floor—some full, some half full, some with their contents spilled on to chairs and others with garments bulging over the edge of the trunk as if Kate had pulled out a piece of clothing from the very bottom and not worried how she disarranged what had been on top of it.

Fortunately the cabin had plenty of cupboards. They were built into the walls and there were cunningly arranged bars for shoes, and drawers wherever it was possible to contrive that a drawer should be fitted.

Zaria started to put the things away, trying not to gaze too enviously at the wonderful underclothes and nightgowns in every colour and shape, at plastic bags full of nylons, at the suits, dresses, slacks and evening gowns which all seemed to be scented with the same exotic perfume which Zaria had noticed as soon as Kate came on deck.

"Do you think they are honest on this yacht?" Kate asked her as she rustled the tissue paper back into one of the boxes she had completely emptied.

"I am sure they are," Zaria answered.

"I brought my jewels with me, but I wouldn't want them swiped," Kate said. "I suppose, really, I should have left them in the bank."

"I should have thought that would have been safer," Zaria said, but then Kate went on:

"We might not go back to New York—not for some time, at any rate. One never knows with Edie."

Zaria looked at her curiously.

"Are you Mr. Morgan's . . . er . . . guest?" she asked.

Kate, who was lying on her back, lifted one slim leg towards the ceiling.

"Sure," she said. "I've been Edie's girl for two years now. He's a knock-out, I can tell you that."

"What is his business?" Zaria asked.

Kate's leg came down again on the bed and she sat up. Zaria had the impression that she had made a *faux pas* in some way or the other.

"Say, you've been mighty quick with that unpacking," Kate said. "If you think you've finished, I guess I'll hit the hay. Sea travel always makes me sleepy."

"Yes, of course," Zaria answered. "As a matter of fact, there's only one more box. If you like, I'll leave that for the moment and do it when you wake."

"That's not a bad idea," Kate said. "And thanks a million for what you've done already."

"That's all right," Zaria answered.

She was only too glad to get away. She shut the cabin door behind her and almost ran up the companion-way on to the deck.

She had to get to Chuck; she had to find out what everything meant—that extraordinary scene in the cabin, the message he had written on a piece of paper, which he had thrust deep into his trouser pocket, she remembered now, meaning, she was sure, to destroy it later.

She came up on deck. Mr. Virdon was lying comfortably in one of the red-cushioned chairs under the awning. Edie Morgan was sitting beside him, talking

83

intently. In another chair Victor Jacobetti was quite obviously asleep.

Zaria slipped by, hoping that they wouldn't notice her. Chuck was where she expected to find him—in a deck chair well away from the superstructure, isolated, as it were, so it would be very hard to overhear anything that was said.

He made to rise when she reached him. But she sank down beside his chair curling her legs under her.

"Tell me," she said breathlessly.

"Give me your hand and look as if you're pleased to see me. You've no idea who's watching."

She did as she was told and he folded both his large hands over her thin, cold little fingers.

"It's almost like holding a captured bird," he said gently. "I can feel your fingers fluttering. Don't be so afraid."

"But I am," she answered. "I don't understand what it's all about."

"Nor do I," he answered. "But they are obviously suspicious."

"How do you know?"

"I found a microphone—one of the very latest type that have only recently been invented—fixed on to the desk. I had a feeling that Jacobetti was keeping me in my cabin talking for some particular reason. He went out of his way to make conversation. Morgan must have been in the office fixing it."

"But why? Why?" Zaria asked.

"Just to make sure, I suppose."

"Make sure of what?"

"That we are what we appear to be."

"Why should it matter?"

He hesitated for a moment as if he were about to say something, and then, a little indifferently, remarked:

"Perhaps Virdon thinks he is on to something big. There's fierce competition amongst these archaeologists, you know. They wouldn't want any leakage before he'd established his claims so to speak. I might be a spy from a rival expedition."

"Yes, of course."

Zaria couldn't explain it, but she somehow felt disappointed. It was not what she had expected him to say. She had somehow thought there was a secret behind it, something that he would tell her. Maybe that was ridiculous because there was nothing to tell.

"They seem strange people," she said at length.

"What do you think of Virdon?" Chuck asked.

"I . . . I don't know. He's not like any archaeologist I've ever seen before—but, then, the ones I've known have mostly been old."

"Did you expect him to be old?"

"No, because someone told me that he was young and that he had made some brilliant discoveries in Mexico. But . . . well, I didn't think he'd be quite the way he is. But, then, it's only a side line with him."

"Did this friend tell you that?" Chuck asked.

Zaria hesitated.

"The solicitor said he had inherited a great deal of money and made a lot more, then when he got bored with playing the markets he went in for archaeology. And now he'd 'got bitten with it,' I think that was Mr. Patterson's expression."

"Very descriptive," Chuck said drily.

"I suppose we shall get down to work when we get there," Zaria said. "There certainly doesn't seem much to do at the moment."

"Did you unpack for the vivacious blonde?" Chuck enquired.

"Yes! Why do you call her that?"

85

"It describes her, doesn't it?"

"I suppose it does," Zaria said. "She's very pretty."

"Do you think so?"

"Lovely," Zaria said, thinking of those large eyes, the red, pouting mouth.

Chuck smiled, but he said nothing. Zaria's fingers moved beneath his.

"May I take my hand away now?" she asked.

"Do you want to?" he enquired.

He turned to look at her. She dropped her eyes before his.

"I . . . I just felt it might be a nuisance for you."

"And for you," he said. "O.K! Let's relax. But we will have to be careful."

"What would they do if they found out?" Zaria asked a little breathlessly.

"Well, I suppose they could always put me off at Tarralisa," Chuck said.

"Oh, that mustn't happen," Zaria said with what was almost a little cry of horror.

She suddenly realised how frightened she would be if Chuck were not there. It was ridiculous, of course. She had only to explain her position—her real position as owner of the yacht—and everything could be changed, as it were, in the twinkling of an eye.

But every nerve in her body shrank even from the thought of doing such a thing.

It made such a difference having Chuck with her. And then she remembered that, if the rest of the party were strange and mysterious, he was even more so. She knew nothing about him save that he had come to her room to ask for her help.

At the same time, he wasn't a complete stranger. He had a friend who knew the real Doris Brown.

86

"What are you thinking about?" Chuck asked suddenly.

"I was thinking about you," Zaria answered.

"Still afraid of me?" he asked.

"Afraid!"

"As you were at first," he answered. "I don't blame you. It must have been very frightening, my bursting into your room like that. But there was nothing else I could do. You were very good about it. I will try and make it up to you."

"But, you have," Zaria said. "I was just thinking that I was glad you are here. These people frighten me. Chuck, they frighten me!"

"Why?" he asked.

"I don't know. It's silly I suppose. But Edie Morgan and the man Jacobetti; they don't seem like people one would expect to meet in a yacht like this with a man like Mr. Virdon."

"They do look like something out of a bad movie, if it comes to that," Chuck agreed. "But don't worry your head about them. The great thing is for us to keep calm, to do what we are told. That is, after all, what you are paid for, isn't it?"

She had a feeling that he was deliberately playing down the situation, making it appear more simple than it was. Because she was frightened, she was prepared to snap at any straw of comfort.

"Perhaps when we get to Algiers Mr. Morgan and Miss Hanover will leave us," she said hopefully.

"I wonder?" Chuck said. "I just wonder?"

He looked out to sea as he spoke and from where Zaria was sitting below him his profile was sharply edged against the blue of the sky. There was something strong and determined about him, she thought.

She had a feeling that he would always get his

own way, however many obstacles there were against him.

She had a sudden remembrance of Kate leaning across the table towards him, her dark eyelashes dropping a little seductively over her blue eyes.

"Kate is Edie Morgan's girl," she said aloud.

"Who told you that?" Chuck enquired, an almost amused note in his voice.

"She did. She said they had been together for two years."

"Quite a time, I should imagine, both for her and for him," Chuck answered.

"What do you mean?"

"Merely that Kate Hanover is not the lingering type—here today and gone tomorrow. Edie Morgan must be worth more than I imagined."

"I can't understand how people like that can interest Mr. Virdon," Zaria said, puzzled.

"Are all the archaeologists you've known so respectable?" Chuck asked.

Zaria thought of her father and turned her head away.

"Not where women are concerned," she said. "But their men friends nearly all seem to talk the same language."

"But then -you forget, Virdon is an American tycoon. Big business! I'm sure Edie Morgan can talk that with him."

"Yes, I suppose so," Zaria said.

She was feeling her fears and hesitations begin to be ironed out by Chuck's smooth, easy acceptance of everything which had seemed to her strange and unreal.

"Listen," he said suddenly. "You ought to be lying down. Shall I go and get you another chair or are you going to have a rest on your bed like the others?"

"I'm all right," Zaria said quickly.

"But, you're not," he said. "You're not resting sitting in that position. I'm trying to take care of you. Can't you see that?"

"Yes, of course," she said, remembering it was part of the act. "And I would rather have a chair here, please."

He got to his feet and went to fetch one. When he brought it she saw that he had also brought with it a cushion and a rug.

"You'll feel the cold even though you think you won't," he said. "People as thin as you have to be specially protected, by wool, hot-water bottles and expensive furs."

She laughed at that, but sat down in the chair, put up her feet and felt him cover her with the rug. She had not been in the least cold, but now she thought how warm and snug it was to have her legs covered.

"By the time we get to Algiers you're going to be as fat as an Arab housewife. At the moment no Mohammedan would look at you; he would feel he wasn't getting his money's worth."

Chuck spoke lightly as if trying to force her into smiling. But Zaria thought miserably that no man was likely to look at her anyway.

She had been bitterly conscious of the difference between herself and Kate as she had unpacked the lovely things the blonde had in her trunks.

Once or twice she had caught a glimpse of herself in the mirrors round the cabin and had seen the sharpness of her jaw, the pointedness of her nose, the prominent cheekbones, and she had felt repulsed.

Why couldn't she have a round, unlined face like

Kate? Why couldn't her hand be warm and plump and soft like other women's, instead of hard and bony and dry?

"You're looking miserable again," Chuck said suddenly. "Stop thinking of whatever you are thinking. It's doing you no good."

She glanced round at him in surprise. Somehow she had never thought that anyone could be so perceptive as he appeared to be.

"I was thinking of Kate," she said.

"And comparing yourself with her, I'll be bound," he said.

"Yes, I was," Zaria admitted.

"Wishing you were like her?"

Zaria nodded.

"I suppose all women are the same," he said. "Never content with what they are. Kate is the success story, the girl who's made good and flaunts it in your face so that you can't miss it."

He paused a moment, turned to look at Zaria and then, to her surprise, took off his glasses. His grey eyes were very kindly.

"You're just like a little, unfledged bird," he said, "that hasn't got any feathers and has fallen out of its nest. The moment I saw you I felt you were lost and bewildered. I don't suppose you were, really, but that's what I felt about you. I had a dog once that looked rather like you.

"He had been badly treated and the people to whom he belonged went off for a holiday and just turned him loose.

"I happened to pick him up—or, rather, he picked me up one night when I was walking home from a party. He was skin and bone, hadn't eaten for days. At first he was so frightened that every time I moved he jumped a yard in case I kicked him. But after a time he grew used to me and for seven years he was the greatest friend I had."

"What happened to him then?" Zaria asked.

"He got knocked over by an automobile. He was killed instantaneously and he didn't suffer, but I think if ever a man was near to being murdered it was the driver of that car."

Zaria saw by the expression in Chuck's face just how much it had mattered and that he had lost an old friend.

"I'm sorry," she said simply.

"Sometimes I think I am an expert at picking up strays," Chuck said. "There was a small boy whom I found in Rome. He was left on my doorstep one night. He was two years old and no-one would claim him. He's eight now, and doing rather nicely with a foster mother I found for him."

"Did you adopt him?" Zaria asked.

"Sort of," he answered.

"But how could you afford it?" she asked suddenly.

There was a moment's silence while she had the impression Chuck was thinking quickly.

"Well, as a matter of fact," he said, "I had a bit of money at that time and I invested a lump sum which brings in a certain amount each week. It doesn't cost much to keep a kid in Italy."

"Oh, I see!"

Curiously enough, while she noticed his hesitation, she felt this was the truth. And again, as if he knew what she was thinking, he said:

"You're wondering why I'm so hard up at this moment that I can't afford my fare to Algiers, and yet I could provide for that small boy. Isn't that what you're asking?"

"I haven't said so," Zaria replied.

"You're as transparent as a five cent piece at the

bottom of a glass of water," he said. "Come on, tell the truth. You're curious about me."

"Of course I am," she answered briefly.

"When we get to Algiers, I'll tell you everything that you want to know," he answered. "In the meantime, I'm going to ask you to trust me, to try and believe what I tell you, because it will make things easier if you do. And to do what I tell you, too, because I promise you one thing—nothing I shall do in any way will hurt you. Do you believe me?"

"Yes, yes, I believe you," Zaria said, and wondered why her voice sounded a little breathless.

Perhaps it was because his grey eyes were looking down into hers, because their chairs were very close together. She could feel the strength and vitality of him reaching out towards her. He was so strong, she thought suddenly, and she was content, utterly content, to rely on him.

It was not exactly a sound behind them, but some sixth sense that made Zaria turn her head swiftly. Standing only a few feet away was Edie Morgan. He must have come up to them almost noiselessly in his rubber-soled shoes; and as she turned her head he drew nearer, standing over them as they sat in the low deck-chairs.

"You two love-birds look real cosy," he said in his nasal drawl. And then, as Chuck made to rise, he put his hand on his shoulder and said: "No, don't move. I've only come to speak to Miss Brown."

"Does Mr. Virdon want me?" Zaria asked quickly.

Edie shook his head.

"No, Mr. Virdon's having a rest," he said. "So I told him that I'd come and talk with you."

"What about?" Zaria asked a little apprehensively.

She was well aware that Edie Morgan had not sought her out without a reason and she saw that in his hand he carried a slip of printed paper such as the wireless operator used on which to write messages. At her glance he slipped it into his pocket.

"Well, see, Miss Brown, it's like this," Edie began. "Mr. Virdon and I have been having a talk and we think it's hard on you young folks, seeing that you're going to get spliced, to take you out into the desert and keep you employed on our concerns when you'd so much rather be together."

"But . . ." Zaria began, only to be silenced by an imperious upward movement of Edie Morgan's hand.

"Wait, now," he said. "We've been doing some hard thinking. We don't want to be unfair to anyone, but Mr. Virdon's decided that it would be best, Miss Brown, for you to terminate your employment with him when we arrive at Algiers."

Chapter Five

"But, why?" Zaria asked. "Mr. Patterson told me that Mr. Virdon was most insistent on having a secretary."

"Yes, I know," Edie Morgan replied. "But circumstances have altered a little. As a matter of fact Madame Bertin is bringing someone with her who can talk the language."

His fingers played with the piece of paper in his pocket.

"I . . . I see," Zaria said.

"As I have said, Mr. Virdon's a fair man," Edie Morgan went on. "And he wants to do the best for you, Miss Brown, and he's very grateful for your coming as far as you have on this trip.

"So he's going to arrange a nice passage for you and your young man on one of those small pleasure cruisers which go back to Marseilles via the Balearic Islands. You'll enjoy that, the two of you. All expenses paid and a month's salary as well."

"A slow boat to China!" Chuck exclaimed suddenly before Zaria could answer.

Edie Morgan's eyes narrowed and his voice was sharp as he asked:

"What do you mean by that? We're doing the best for Miss Brown, aren't we?"

"Yes, of course," Chuck answered. "But I was only thinking perhaps it would be best for her to go ashore tomorrow when we arrived at Tarralisa."

"Now, see here, big boy!" Edie Morgan said. "We didn't ask you to come on this trip, you invited yourself. You keep out of this. Mr. Virdon's decided what's best for Miss Brown and if she's a sensible girl, which I'm sure she is, she'll take the offer as it stands."

"Yes, of course," Zaria said quickly.

She was afraid both of the note of Edie Morgan's voice and the look on Chuck's face.

"I quite understand if Mr. Virdon doesn't want me, and it's very kind of him to think of paying me a month's salary and sending me back to London."

"Then that's settled," Edie Morgan said, and turning to Chuck he added: "And no more wisecracks from you, young man: Is that understood?"

"But, of course," Chuck said easily and with a smile that was distinctly provocative.

"And don't forget it," Edie Morgan said sharply, and walked away, his feet making no sound on the deck.

But even when he was gone it seemed for a moment as if his presence still hung over them—distasteful, unpleasant and somehow infinitely menacing.

"I don't understand," Zaria said at last in a whisper.

"Don't worry about it," Chuck said. "We aren't at Algiers yet."

"It's so uncomfortable to stay here when he doesn't want me, when there's nothing for me to do. Why can't we get off tomorrow? I'm sure that's the best solution."

"Morgan didn't seem to think so, and what Edie says goes!"

"But why? Mr. Virdon's the boss, isn't he?"

"I wonder!" Chuck said ruminatively.

"What do you mean by that?" Zaria asked.

"Nothing," he said quickly. "Rich men usually have some sort of factotum who does all the dirty work. Virdon wouldn't want to be embarrassed himself by giving you notice and so he got his bodyguard to do it. But, nevertheless, he means every word of it, you can be sure of that."

"Mr. Morgan terrifies me," Zaria said. "I wish I hadn't come."

"Do you really wish that?" Chuck enquired. "If you hadn't been there, I shouldn't have been able to appeal to you; I shouldn't have known how kind and generous you were in helping me to get to Algiers."

"No, of course not," Zaria said. "It was lucky for you, wasn't it? Even if it was unlucky for me."

She gave a little shiver as she spoke and Chuck said:

"Look, it's getting cold here. You go below and have a lie down on your bed. The wind is rising and the climate at this time of the year can be very treacherous, especially if you are not well. You go and have a sleep and when you wake, ask the steward to bring you some tea. There's no need for you to come to the saloon for it."

"I think I'll do as you say," Zaria answered.

She was reluctant to leave Chuck, feeling that she must cling to him as a drowning man clings to a straw. And yet there was no doubt that it was colder and she had no thick coat with which to cover her jersey.

The sea was getting rough and the boat was pitching as it met the white crested waves. Chuck rose to his feet and helped her out of her chair.

She thought as he did so how nice it was to have a man to be attentive, to take the rug off her knees, to put a steadying hand on her arm as she raised herself from the low chair.

"Now, sleep! Don't forget," Chuck admonished. "It will do you good."

Zaria hesitated.

"If, by any chance, Mr. Virdon should want me, you would come and call me?" she asked.

"Of course I would," he said. "But I shouldn't mind betting half-a-dollar to a five cent piece that he isn't going to want you this afternoon—or tomorrow afternoon!"

"Why do you say that so positively?" Zaria asked.

"I just think Mr. Virdon is taking a holiday from work," Chuck answered.

She had a feeling he was not telling her the truth, but he was smiling at her and she didn't feel like arguing. Instead, she walked across the deck a little unsteadily, owing to the movement of the ship, and went down to her cabin.

It felt very warm after the sharpness of the breeze above and she was glad of the softness of the mattress and the feather-filled pillows as, having taken off her clothes and put on her nightgown, she snuggled into them.

She had wanted to think, wanted to remember all the things Chuck had said to her, to try and let the significance of having received the sack percolate into her mind.

She wanted to make plans for her homeward journey. But, somehow, nothing seemed concrete, nothing seemed clear-cut, and almost before she knew it she had drifted away into a dream in which she was warm, comfortable and incredibly happy.

"I love you," Chuck was saying. "I love you." And his arms were holding her close . . .

She awoke with a start to hear someone tapping on the door.

"Come in," she called, and when the door opened she saw it was the steward with a tray.

"I've brought you some tea, Miss," he said. "When

you didn't come to the saloon, I guessed you must be resting."

"Is it tea-time already?" Zaria asked drowsily.

"It's after half-past five," he replied. "But I felt that, being English, you wouldn't want to miss your cup of tea."

Zaria sat up in bed, pulling the sheets and blankets high up her chest. She wasn't used to having a man wait on her.

"It's very kind of you," she said as the steward set down the tray beside her.

She looked and saw that he had brought her sandwiches, scones, butter and honey, and quite an assortment of different cakes.

"I won't be able to eat all that," she said with a little laugh.

"You ought to try, Miss," the steward answered. "And the chef has suggested that he makes you a little special broth. Something very different from ordinary soup—it's what our late owner, Mrs. Cardew, had after her last operation. She was ill, very ill, when she came on board. I swear it was partly the broth that put her on her feet."

"It sounds quite magical," Zaria said. "And will you thank chef for thinking of it?"

"Well, you know, Miss, I was telling the chef about how you wanted feeding up and how little you eat. It was his idea; he said, 'What about what Mrs. Cardew always had? That put the weight on her again, didn't it, Jim?' "

"But I haven't been ill," Zaria said.

"No, Miss?" the steward asked with an incredulous note in his voice that told her he did not believe her. "Well, if you haven't been ill, then you must have been dieting too hard."

"Perhaps that's it," Zaria smiled. "But, anyway, I'd love to have the broth if it's no trouble."

"It's no trouble at all," the steward assured her. "And there's something else I was thinking about, Miss."

He put his hand in his pocket and brought out a box.

"What's that?" Zaria enquired.

"They are some vitamin pills, Miss. Mrs. Cardew always took them. She kept several boxes of them here in the yacht. Many a time she said to me:

'Take some vitamin pills, Jim. They'll keep you young and keep you enjoying your work.'

"I used to take one or two to oblige her. I'm not saying they didn't do me good, but as long as I'm at sea I never have an ache or pain in my body anyway."

"And now you're thinking they will do me good," Zaria said.

"I want you to try them, Miss," the steward said earnestly. "With a vitamin pill three times a day and the broth the chef is making you we shall have you a different person before you can say 'knife.'"

"We shall have to hurry then," Zaria said. "I am leaving the ship at Algiers."

"Leaving it!" the steward ejaculated. "And, why, Miss? If I may be so bold as to ask."

"Mr. Virdon has dispensed with my services," Zaria said. "There's someone arriving with Madame Bertin tomorrow who speaks Arabic, and he doesn't require a secretary after all."

"Well, that surprises me," the steward said, scratching his head. "Mr. Patterson wrote to the Captain about all the trouble they were having to get a secretary to fill Mr. Virdon's requirements. There were all sorts of instructions to be carried out—how we were to pick you up at Marseilles, and so on. It's queer that now you're here he doesn't want you."

"I think Mr. Virdon must be allowed to choose who he wants to work for him," Zaria said. "But I am sorry, because I should like to have gone into the desert again."

"I'm sorry too, Miss," the steward said. "And, if you'll excuse me saying so, we like having English people aboard. Nearly all Mrs. Cardew's guests were English, and, to be honest, I just don't understand these Yankees."

"Nevertheless they have paid a big sum to charter the yacht," Zaria said.

"Oh, yes, I know that," the steward answered. "But we've always been a very quiet ship. Most of us, with the exception of two of the younger men, have been aboard *The Enchantress* of over ten years. Mrs. Cardew used to be proud of the years of service we'd put in.

" 'It's like a family business, Jim,' she'd say to me many a time."

The steward gave a sigh.

"Ah, well! I suppose we've got into a groove, stuck in our ways, and don't like to be disturbed. That's what it really comes down to. But these Americans hardly seem human somehow. You don't know what to do for them.

"They don't care for food, they don't seem to want valeting, and they are certainly not interested in the ship itself. I suppose that's natural seeing they're not a sea-going nation, but I heard Mr. Morgan today saying he was fed up with being cooped up in a chicken-house."

The steward drew himself up and seemed to bristle with rage.

"Those were his very words, Miss—with a few rude invectives thrown in."

Zaria wanted to laugh, but she knew it would offend Jim's pride in the yacht, which he looked on as his home.

"Perhaps the next charter will be different," she said.

"I hope so, indeed," Jim said gruffly. Then added: "I shall be sorry to see you go, Miss, I shall indeed. And Mr. Tanner. He's a very nice gentleman, if you'll excuse my presumption in saying so, and I hope you'll be very happy with him."

"Thank you," Zaria said a little shyly, feeling somehow it was wrong to deceive this nice, genuinely sympathetic little man.

"And now you eat your tea, Miss—as much as you can," Jim said. "And I'll be bringing you some of that broth when you're dressing for dinner. That was the time Mrs. Cardew always had a cupful. Better than any cocktail she called it."

He went from the cabin, shutting the door quietly behind him, and Zaria poured herself out a cup of tea.

But when the time came when she should have been dressing for dinner, Jim knocked on her door and told her that the sea had grown so rough that everyone was having dinner in their cabins.

"Don't you move, Miss," he said. "I'll bring you something to eat."

"But isn't that an awful trouble?" Zaria asked.

"Lord bless you no," Jim answered. "I'm used to the rough weather. It never troubles me. And there won't be so very many dinners to take round tonight, I can promise you that."

He gave an almost impish grin as if the idea delighted him.

101

"Mr. Virdon says he wants nothing, and Mr. Morgan only asked for another bottle of whisky."

"What about Miss Hanover?"

"Oh, she took a sleeping draught about four o'clock and said no-one was to disturb her until tomorrow morning. She hates the sea. Told me she was allergic to it."

"Well, if you really think I needn't get up," Zaria said, feeling a curious reluctance to leave the comfort of her bed.

"You stay exactly where you are," Jim admonished her. "It's a great mistake for landlubbers to go walking about in a sea like this. It's not so much that they're sick, but that they are likely to break a leg or get thrown over and bruised. You stay right where you are."

He was just going when Zaria's voice arrested him.

"And . . . and Mr. Tanner?" she asked.

"Oh, Mr. Tanner's all right. He's up with the Cap'n. They're on the bridge exchanging yarns. The place is that thick with smoke you'd hardly be able to see a lighthouse at fifty yards."

Jim chuckled and added:

"It's only my little joke, Miss. Oh, Mr. Tanner's all right. You needn't worry about him."

"I won't then," Zaria answered.

After a delicious dinner of which, to Jim's consternation and reproach, she could only eat very little, she took one of the vitamin pills to please him and then went to sleep again.

She wanted to dream about Chuck. She wanted to hear his voice telling her he loved her, to feel his arm around her shoulders. To pretend it was not pretence that a man—any man—found her attractive.

But whether it was the sea air, the food she had eaten or the fact of being so warm and comfortable, she slept as she hadn't slept for years—a deep, dreamless sleep which seemed to ease all the tension from her bones and leave her warm and happy when she awoke in the morning.

She had asked Jim to bring her a cup of tea an hour before she need dress for breakfast, but instead he called her at nine o'clock with her breakfast on a tray.

"Nobody's down except Mr. Tanner," he said with satisfaction. "And they're all telling me what a terrible night they've had."

"Was it rough?"

"Just a Mediterranean squall," Jim said. "The old ship pitched a bit. That's what always upsets them that's not used to it—the pitching. They can stand a roll, but pitching always finishes them off."

He was obviously delighted at the thought that Mr. Virdon and Edie Morgan had succumbed so easily.

"The Cap'n says we shall be in to the harbour at noon," he added. "So don't you hurry, Miss. The sea is subsiding and when we've had time to get under the lee of the land you won't feel it more than a baby feels someone rocking his cradle."

Zaria laughed and started to eat her breakfast with a better appetite than she had had the previous day. She could quite understand why her aunt had loved the ship and why she had spent the last years of her life cruising.

Poor Aunt Margaret! Zaria wished she could remember her more clearly, but it was easier to recall her father cursing all his relatives, his sister included.

"Vipers and serpents who prey on one's feelings!" he had shouted once. "All this sentimentalising because someone happens by chance to be born of the same parents as one had oneself. Tell my sister to

103

go to hell—and the quicker the better as far as I'm concerned."

He had flung a letter at Zaria and gone out of the room, slamming the door. She was used to answering all his letters and she picked it up wondering why, after they had not spoken for two years, her aunt had written at all.

It was only a letter about some family securities which had to be transferred from one bank to another, but at the end she had said:

"I wonder if you've ever thought of looking at Father's and Mother's grave? I wish you would do so. I hate to think that perhaps it is being neglected."

It was that which had put her father in a rage, Zaria thought, merely because he was afraid that it might cost him money. His meanness had, by that time, become a mania. He was a miser not only because he had to be, but because he enjoyed his miserliness.

Resolutely, now, she shook her head to dispel the memory of him. He should no longer haunt her now he could no longer torment her. Already she was beginning to think how weak and stupid she had been after he died not to have made an effort to go away, not to have contacted her aunt immediately in the hope that she might have forgiven the past and let her join her wherever she might be.

And she knew that, although she said she had not been ill, her inertia, coming from over-work, undernourishment and mental bullying had sapped her health so that she was far more ill than many people who had doctors and nurses constantly in attendance.

'I must get better, I must,' she told herself now.

Then with a sinking of her heart realised that perhaps in forty-eight hours' time she would be alone again; this voyage would come to an end. She would not have Jim to talk to and Chuck would have gone.

She faced the fact in that flash of a second just what it would mean to her to lose Chuck, to lose that feeling of dependence upon him—and then tried to laugh because it was all so ridiculous.

He was a man she didn't know, a man she had met for the first time such a short time ago that she was ashamed to calculate how short it was.

And yet, she told herself wonderingly, it was as if she had known him all her life. There was something so kind about him, something that made her instinctively rely on him even while, in a way, he was relying on her.

'I want to see him,' she thought, and hurrying over her breakfast got up.

She had nothing to wear but the seaman's trousers and thick woollen jumper that she had worn the day before.

She took extra pains with her hair, peering in the mirror to see if it had a little more strength and vitality in it, wondering as she brushed it if it would ever be thick and curly as it used to be when her mother was alive. She could hear her mother's voice, now, saying:

"You've got lovely hair, darling! You must always remember to brush it. A shining head is one of the most attractive things a woman can have."

It had been so thick then. Her mother had often laughed and said:

"With what we have to cut off we could fill a mattress."

Zaria felt herself smiling over the memory, and then, with something that was almost a little sob, she remembered how her mother had put her arms round her one night after she had brushed her hair and kissed her.

105

"You're going to be very pretty one day, my little Zaria," she said. "But however many men love you, try to remember that you have a mother who loves you too."

"Oh, Mummy, as if I would ever forget," Zaria had said.

"Darling, you will grow up like everyone else," her mother answered. "And I hope you will find a wonderful man to love. But remember one thing—that love is a very exacting taskmaster. When one loves, one has to give everything of oneself."

"I will remember, Mummy," Zaria had answered.

She had not really understood what her mother meant and the memory of her words had often puzzled her. "You have got to give everything of yourself."

She thought of it now and wondered what she would be feeling if she was really engaged to someone, if she and Chuck loved each other.

Quite unaccountably the thought brought a flush to her cheeks and she stared at her reflection in the mirror, seeing only the deep lines beneath her eyes and the sharpness of her jawbones.

'Who would ever want to love me now?' she thought bitterly, and turned away to go up on deck.

Chuck was leaning over the rail, watching the coast of Spain—the high cliffs and behind them undulating ground rising in the far distance to mountains which were topped with snow.

"Oh, it's beautiful!" Zaria exclaimed involuntarily as she reached his side.

"Good morning! Do you feel better?" he asked. "Yes, I can see you do."

"How can you see that?" she asked.

"Haven't you looked at yourself this morning?" he parried. "Jim tells me he's feeding you up. I think it's beginning to work."

"Jim is an incorrigible gossip," Zaria exclaimed. "But he has been very kind."

"Why not?" Chuck asked. "Isn't everyone kind to you?"

He was not prepared for the way her face darkened and her eyes fell before his.

"Not always," she murmured, as if his words had brought recollections from the past which over-shadowed her happiness in the beauty of the morning.

"Then forget it," he said seriously.

"Forget what?" she asked.

"Whatever you are thinking about at this moment," he said. "Never remember the past unless what you are remembering is happy or constructive. The rest has gone, it is finished with. Put it behind you, because it is tomorrow that counts—never, never yesterday."

"Is that your philosophy?" Zaria asked.

"Of course," he answered. "Live today fully, look forward to tomorrow. There's every chance that it will be far better than today. If it isn't—well, there's always the day after that."

Zaria found herself laughing.

"No wonder you look happy," she said.

"I am happy," he answered.

The smile faded from her lips.

"You haven't forgotten . . ." she began, and then remembered that the fact that she had to leave the ship at Algiers would not affect him in any way.

He had always been going to leave when they arrived there. Mr. Virdon and Edie Morgan would think that they were sending two people back to London, but actually they were only sending one. She would go alone and everyone else would be left behind.

"Listen, Zaria . . ." Chuck began with a sudden seriousness in his voice.

Then before he could say more, they heard Edie's

voice coming up the companion-way and stood in silence while he came up on deck.

"What a goddam awful night!" he exclaimed as he saw Chuck. "If anything would keep me from going to sea again, it would be this sort of experience. And we came across the Atlantic without a ripple."

"The Mediterranean can be very treacherous," Chuck said quietly.

"You're telling me," Edie answered savagely, leaning over the rail beside them and chucking a half-smoked cigar into the water. "Well, it's calming down now. I suppose one must be thankful for that."

"It will be smooth by luncheon time," Chuck assured him. "Everyone else all right?"

"Victor says he's got a headache," Edie Morgan answered. "But if you ask me that came out of a bottle."

He seemed to ignore Zaria deliberately; and though she thought him rude, she was thankful for his lack of interest in her.

The ship moved on. They were now under the shelter of the land and she was running extremely steadily. Nevertheless, it was some time later before Victor Jacobetti came up on deck.

"Why do you choose such a hellish place to get to?" Zaria heard Victor say to Edie Morgan.

"If you know of a better hole, you find one!"

The answer was snapped back with all the force of a pistol shot.

"It must have been hard for Lulu to get there."

"She got cars, hasn't she?" Edie snapped. "Plenty of the tourist trade starts at this time of the year. What's the matter? Getting breezy?"

"No, of course not," Victor answered. "You know your own business best."

"Nice if some of you could manage to think so," Edie Morgan replied.

It was not so much what he said as the rude way in which he said it which caused Victor to walk away to the end of the ship, his hands deep in his trouser pockets.

'What a funny crowd they are,' Zaria thought to herself. 'They none of them seem to like each other.'

Kate came up the companion-way looking extremely pretty, but yawning.

"Aren't we there, yet?" she asked. "I could have stayed in bed a bit longer."

"I should have thought you'd stayed there long enough," Victor retorted.

She gave him a glance which seemed to Zaria to express nothing but contempt.

"That comes well from you," she said. "I hear you weren't so strong on your legs last night. In fact, the steward tells me that Mr. Tanner was the only survivor of the storm."

She smiled at Chuck and slipped her arm through his.

"Tell me, big boy, how do you do it?" she asked. "Is it pills or natural competence?"

"I think it's just a little thing called having one's sea legs," Chuck answered easily.

"Aren't you clever?" she said with an exaggerated intonation, smiling up at him provocatively, her long, mascara'd eyelashes flickering against the pink and white of her complexion.

Zaria looked away from them, feeling suddenly miserable.

'Why can't I talk to him like that?' she thought. 'Why can't I be gay? Laughing, joking, making jests, instead of feeling frightened and tongue-tied. What's wrong with me that I can't be like other women?'

She knew the answer to all her questions, but that didn't make it any better. She wanted to be more like Kate—lovely, with the voluptuous curves of her high breasts showing beneath the pale knitted sweater she wore, which was tucked into linen slacks of the same colour.

There was a turquoise blue handkerchief round her neck and her fair hair, bleached and dyed though it was, seemed somehow to echo the sunshine.

"Do you think there are any shops in Tarralisa?" Kate asked. "We might all go ashore looking for souvenirs."

"You'll do nothing of the sort," Edie Morgan said sharply. "We're going to stop for just a few minutes to pick up Lulu and Ahmed, and then the Captain's instructions are to get the hell out of it."

"Oh, Ahmed's meeting us here, is he?" Kate asked.

"Yes—it was obvious, I should have thought, that we would need him, and I told Lulu that he could drive the second car."

Kate giggled.

"Can't you see Ahmed in a chauffeur's cap? What a lark!"

"Your sense of humour was always mistimed," Edie answered sourly.

The conversation got more and more mysterious, Zaria thought, and yet there seemed to be a connecting thread which should have made it all clear to her if only she had some sense.

"So they won't let us go ashore," Kate said pouting up at Chuck. "I was going to buy you a lovely Spanish tie with a matador on it. It would have suited your complexion and your hair. Isn't that sad?"

"Never mind, you can buy me one in Algiers," Chuck said. "And I will buy you a drink at the best bar in the Rue d'Acosa. Is that a bargain?"

110

"Of course! I can't wait," Kate answered flirtatiously.

Zaria saw a look pass between Edie Morgan and Victor Jacobetti, and although they said nothing, Zaria was quite convinced that they told each other that Chuck would be got out of Algiers as soon after they arrived as possible.

Was Edie Morgan jealous? she wondered. That was understandable because, after all, Kate was supposed to be his girl. But why was Victor Jacobetti involved?

The ship was rounding into the bay and the small harbour of Tarralisa was in sight. It was nothing more or less than a fishing village—a few white cottages sloping down to a long quay. There was the pointed spire of a church and behind it several buildings which were not very interesting, archaeologically or otherwise.

Behind the town there were vineyards sloping up, step by step to the far summit of the low hills which gave protection to the harbour. Beyond that, very little, only a general air of poverty.

"There's Lulu!" Kate screamed suddenly.

They saw, standing on the quay, a small, squat figure and behind her a great pile of baggage—cabin trunks, boxes, suitcases. All looking in their smart colourings very out of place on the dirty quayside.

"What an enormous collection of luggage!" Zaria remarked.

"But, of course," Kate replied. "Didn't you know Madame Bertin is starting a shop in Algiers? She'll want a lot of clothes and they must all come from Paris. Suits, day dresses, evening gowns. Just think what you would have to order to fill a shop with every size and every type of dress a woman could want."

"That's right," Edie Morgan said. "A shop needs a

111

lot of planning unless it's to fail—and we can't afford failure on this one, eh, boys?"

"Certainly not," Victor agreed.

"And what about you, Corny?" Edie Morgan enquired of Mr. Virdon, who was standing silent, his arms resting squarely on the rail of the ship. "What do you think?"

Mr. Virdon was wearing his inevitable white flannels with the brass-buttoned blazer and white-topped yachting cap in which he had come aboard. Now he raised his head and asked, with what seemed to Zaria almost heavy sarcasm:

"Are you really interested in my opinion?"

"Sure," Edie Morgan answered. "We certainly are. Isn't it your money that we're spending in this enterprise?"

There was a deliberate accent on the pronoun. Mr. Virdon replied:

"Of course! So naturally I hope it will be a success."

"Your enthusiasm overwhelms us," Edie Morgan said. Then in an aside to Victor Jacobetti he added: "Where the hell's Ahmed?"

"In a bar I expect."

"Very funny," Edie Morgan ejaculated.

The ship drew near, coming in slowly to tie up against the end of the long jetty. Kate was waving and so was Madame Bertin. Zaria could see now she was a middle-aged woman, heavily made up with deep blue eye shadow and lips so thickly painted that they seemed almost as if they were lacquered.

She was ugly, with dark hair, thick lips, a heavy jowl and a thick-set body. And yet she had the almost indescribable chic which every Frenchwoman seems to acquire by nature.

There was something in the way in which her hat was set on her head, in the huge rope of artificial

112

pearls round her neck, in the big ear-rings and the rings which were the only ornamentation to the severe and expensive cut of her clothes, which made one look at her and look again.

Although she was ugly, she was attractive, dumpy yet chic, middle-aged, yet in her own way seductive.

"Hi'ya Lulu!" Edie Morgan was shouting, and she shouted back:

"*Soyez le bien venu!* It's good to see you. Ah, *mes amis* I am glad you have arrived."

The tide was in and the bay was deep, so they managed to tie up at the extreme end of the jetty. A Customs official came aboard and immediately behind him Madame Bertin.

"I must introduce this gentleman," she said with an expressive glance at the Customs officer which made him twirl the ends of his moustache. "He has been so very kind to me, so charming. Would you believe it, his assistant wanted to unpack all my beautiful gowns! I said to him:

" '*Le liable vous emporte!* If you put your dirty fingers on these clothes what will they be worth? Nothing! And there are thousands—no millions of *francs* in these very precious cases.'

"But he did not understand. Ah! He is an imbecile that one. *Monsieur* is different. *Monsieur* is an artist. He likes pretty women—whether they wear pretty clothes or whether they wear nothing."

There was a shriek of laughter at this. Edie Morgan was shaking the officer by the hand and introducing him to Mr. Virdon. Then they disappeared into the saloon and there were the sounds of Edie Morgan shouting for the steward and the clink of glasses.

"How are you, Lulu?" Kate asked, pressing her cheek affectionately against that of the older woman.

"You are prettier than ever, Kate," she replied. "But

your hair is too bleached. *Je vous dit* a darker colour would suit you better."

"Gentlemen prefer blondes," Kate answered.

"So, you know some?" Madame Bertin asked in affected surprise, and then patted Kate on the arm. "*De grâce.* But we must not fight so early. It is always the same when you and I meet, the sparks fly. But you are a pretty girl and you will show off my beautiful gowns to the very best advantage."

She turned to look at Chuck and Zaria who were standing a little back from the others, just watching.

"And who is this?" she asked.

"Oh, this is Miss Brown," Kate said, "and her fiancé, Mr. Tanner. They are getting off at Algiers. By the way, where's Ahmed?"

"I was just going to ask the same thing." Victor Jacobetti said.

He had not gone into the saloon, but had been giving some instructions to the sailors about getting Madame Bertin's great pile of luggage aboard.

"Oh, Ahmed! He is not with me," Madame Bertin replied.

"Not with you!" Victor Jacobetti ejaculated. "But I understood that he was driving one of the cars."

"*Oui, mais . . . quelle catastrophe,*" Madame Bertin seemed to hesitate for words. "At the Spanish frontier his papers were not in order. They . . . they sent him back."

"Oh, I see!"

Victor Jacobetti was watching her instantly, almost as if he was reading some message from her eyes rather than from her lips.

"Everything else all right?" he asked.

"*Comme ci, comme ça,*" Madame Bertin answered. "But do not let us linger here too long."

"No, no, of course not."

He went across the deck and put his head round the door of the saloon.

"Shall we start bringing the luggage aboard?" he asked.

The answer was obviously in the affirmative and he shouted to the sailors.

"Hurry up with that luggage, and handle it carefully. It's all got to go below in the hold."

"Pas tout!" Madame Bertin screamed. "There are three or four for my cabin—they have labels marked 'cabin' on them. Do not muddle them with the others."

Victor Jacobetti was about to repeat the order when suddenly she put her hand on his arm.

"Non! J'ai une idèe," she said in a low voice. "Put them all in the cabins. It is safer. The holds are always inspected first."

"Yes, yes, of course," he answered. "Choose what you want and put some in Kate's cabin as well."

Madam Bertin hurried down the gangway and started giving orders—first in English to the sailors and then in Spanish to the local men who were helping them.

The noise was almost deafening as everyone seemed to be talking at once with Madame Bertin's voice drowning everybody else's.

The luggage was beginning to come aboard and as it did so, the saloon door opened and the Customs officer came out wiping his lips with the back of his hand—a hand which Zaria noticed immediately was holding a good wad of dollar bills.

He slipped them into his pocket, saluted smartly and went down the gangway to give orders ashore.

Zaria thought she would go below. She didn't want the Spaniards to make a mistake and put the baggage in her cabin instead of Kate's. But there was so much

115

it seemed likely that every cabin would be filled with trunks and cases.

She might be able to help, she thought. Self effacingly she moved away from the little group of people watching and reached the top of the companion-way. As she did so, she saw Victor Jacobetti take Edie Morgan by the arm and pull him to one side.

"Wait a minute, Edie!" he said. He spoke in a low voice, but Zaria could hear him quite clearly. "Have you heard the news? That damned fool Ahmed has been copped!"

Chapter Six

Zaria slipped quickly down the companion-way. The passage below was cool and dim and as she reached the bottom step, steadying herself for fear she should fall, she heard Edie Morgan say:

"The goddam fool! I said it was a mistake in the beginning to try and bring him."

He spoke in a low, almost hissing whisper, yet every word was clear, and instinctively, without consciously realising that she was eavesdropping, Zaria paused for Victor Jacobetti's reply.

"It's all right or she wouldn't be here. She will have said he was only her chauffeur."

"What a risk!" Edie exploded, still with his voice so low as to make every word sound sinister and yet overcharged with emphasis.

"I know. But apparently she's got clear."

"Then let's get the hell out of here."

"O.K!"

Zaria was just about to go on towards her cabin when she heard Edie add, almost as if it was an after-thought:

"And what are we going to do without Ahmed when we get to Algiers?"

"Of course, I'd forgotten that," Victor answered. "Well, there's always the girl."

"It's taking a chance," Edie said sharply.

"Oh she's all right," Victor answered. "It's the man I'm worried about."

"We'll have to deal with him, that's all," Edie said.

"Now tell the Captain to put to sea and be prompt about it."

They walked away from the top of the companion-way and Zaria, gripping the hand-rail, realised that she was trembling.

For a moment she felt incapable of moving, and then suddenly, galvanising her strength, she ran to her own cabin and shut the door behind her, pressing her slim body against it as if in a sudden terror that someone might try to come in.

What did that strange, whispered conversation mean? She pressed her fingers to her forehead trying to make the words into sense, trying, at the same time, to refuse to believe what her mind told her was the truth.

These people were crooks! She was sure of it. And yet what had she got to go on? Only a few words whispered in low undertones to which she had eaves-dropped and which she might easily have misunder-stood.

And yet one had only to look at Edie Morgan, one had only to listen to him, to know there was something wrong. But what about Mr. Virdon? Did he know? Was he part of this extraordinary set-up? And, if so why?

Zaria locked her door and then walked across to sit down on the low, comfortable armchair beneath the porthole. The sunshine was streaming in, making a little golden pool on the floor.

Above she could hear footsteps, the chatter of for-eign and English tongues, a sudden laugh, the sound of luggage being moved across the deck and down into the hold.

Other footsteps were coming down the companion-way and into the passage outside. She could hear doors opening, Jim's voice with its Cockney accent giving instructions.

She put her hands up to her face, was she mad that she should think such things? This was an ordinary party—of course it was. Just friends of Mr. Virdon going out to Algiers with him. If she found anything peculiar about them, it was simply because she was out of touch with the world.

"There's the girl." She could hear Victor's voice saying it and they were referring to her.

It could only mean one thing, however much she might pretend. Now that Ahmed was not coming, they would use her to speak the language.

She felt herself began to tremble. There was a menace that she could sense yet could not put into words. What did they want of her? What were they planning to do?

And Chuck! Edie had said they would "deal with him". There was something ominous and distinctly sinister in the way he had said it.

Zaria sprang to her feet. She must get hold of Chuck at once and warn him. She must rely on him to deal with this. It was too big for her, beyond her comprehension.

Perhaps he would laugh at her fears and tell her how stupid she was. There was no reason for Mr. Virdon, the rich American tycoon, to be mixed up with anything shady.

And what could interest people like Edie, Victor and Kate except money?

She felt sure that Chuck would tell her that. At the same time, he would have to explain what Edie had meant by saying that they would deal with him.

'I've got to be sensible. I've got to keep calm over this,' Zaria thought, and knew that her heart was fluttering beneath her breast.

She glanced in the mirror and saw that her face was paler than usual between the heavy waves of her hair.

Almost angrily she tried to rub some colour into her cheeks.

'They will suspect something if I go up looking like this,' she thought to herself, and then with a little wry smile remembered how little notice anyone seemed to take of her.

She was of no consequence—or hadn't been until Ahmed had been "copped" at the frontier.

She unlocked the door and went down the passage. The door into Kate's cabin was open and she could see Jim instructing one of the sailors to put one of Madame Bertin's trunks into a corner where it would not be in the way.

She had a sudden wild urgency to be beside Chuck, to hear his voice, to feel the strength and bigness of him reaching out to protect her.

'He will understand what to do,' she told herself, trying to calm her fluttering, frightened heart beat.

She reached the deck just as the gang-way was being pulled in to the shore. The Spaniards who had helped with the luggage and the Customs official were standing on the quay bidding them Godspeed.

"*Adios, señores! Adios!*" It was obvious from their smiles that they had been well paid for their work in bringing the luggage aboard.

The yacht began to draw away. The Customs official raised his hand in salute. Madame Bertin was waving to him.

"Such a charming man," Zaria heard her say to Mr. Virdon.

"You certainly used your fascinations on him," Mr. Virdon responded.

Madame Bertin gave him a look from under her heavily mascara'd eyelashes.

"I . . . how do you say? . . . hypnotised him," she said with an expressive movement of her hands, then burst out laughing.

Zaria looked round for Chuck. There was no sign of him and she felt her breath almost stop in sudden terror lest something should have happened to him already.

He was certainly not beneath the red awning where Victor was now sitting, the inevitable drink in his hand.

Hastily she walked for'ard and then, as she passed the superstructure on deck and came in full sight of the bow, she saw Chuck. He was standing on the prow beside Kate and her arm was linked in his as they watched the ship nose its way out of the harbour into the open sea.

Kate was looking up at him, speaking earnestly, her attractive profile with its little tip-tilted nose and full mouth silhouetted against the blue of the sky. And Chuck was looking down at her.

There was something in the closeness of them and their obvious oblivion to everything and everybody except their own conversation, which made Zaria feel as if she had been turned to stone.

She couldn't move; she could only stand and stare, and after a moment lean weakly against the bridge. She couldn't hear what they were saying and yet she knew that it was intimate and personal.

It was difficult to see the expression on Chuck's face in the sunlight, and yet she was sure that he was smiling.

The fragrance of Kate's exotic and expensive perfume would be in his nostrils as he looked down into that alive, vivacious and pretty face.

Zaria must have stood there for almost half a minute before she turned and very slowly retraced her steps.

She walked slowly, almost as if she had suddenly become an old woman or as if something young and tender had gone from her leaving her utterly defeated.

Wildly, a hundred thoughts rushed through her head. What did she know about Chuck? Nothing! Who was he? Where had he come from?

How could she explain even to herself why she had trusted him when he had burst into her room, throwing himself on her mercy and begging her help? Was it surprising, now that he had got what he wanted, that he had little use for her?

And it had been obvious, even last night, that Kate found him attractive and was determined to get hold of him.

'Why should I mind? What is it to me?' Zaria asked herself.

She knew that she could never explain in words what Chuck did mean to her, except that he was the one secure, one understandable thing in a world that was almost too bewildering to be tolerated.

She had reached the companion-way and would have gone below if she had not felt a touch on her arm and found Edie Morgan standing beside her. Without meaning to she shrank away from him, but he caught hold of her and in a friendly, familiar way slipped his hand under her elbow and drew her to where the others were sitting under the red awning.

"Come along, Miss Brown," he said. "We've been wanting to see you."

He paused and smiled down at her small, shrinking figure.

"And why the heck do we call you 'Miss Brown' all the time?" he asked. "Zaria's a real pretty name, and that's what your young man calls you, isn't it?

Well, Zaria, Mr. Virdon wants to have a word with you."

'I know what's coming,' Zaria thought wildly.

There was nothing she could say or do but let Edie Morgan lead her across the deck and settle her comfortably in one of the red-cushioned armchairs beside Mr. Virdon.

She was very conscious as she did so of Victor's pebble-like eyes staring at her and of Madame Bertin's quite undisguised curiosity.

"Lulu," Edie said, turning to the latter. "You haven't met Zaria have you? She's Corny's secretary and a pretty good one you can be sure of that, although Corny hasn't got down to much work so far this trip."

"*Enchantée*," Madame Bertin said. "I am delighted to meet you, Mademoiselle!"

Zaria wanted to rise from the chair and shake hands, but Edie pressed her back, not understanding that his very touch made her shiver.

"No formality," he said firmly. "We're all friends here, just good friends, eh, Corny?"

"I hope so," Mr. Virdon said a little stiffly, and as if he had said something extremely witty, and the others all roared with laughter.

"Now see here, Zaria," Edie said, seating himself beside her. "When I told you yesterday that Corny was going to send you and your young man back home because he thought it was unfair to keep you at work when you wanted to be together, he was just being unselfish.

"That's the trouble with Corny. He's always impulsive, always thinking of other people. Isn't that right, Corny boy?"

"I hope it's right," Mr. Virdon said. "I certainly

try to do so. Too many rich men in my position forget that others are less fortunate than themselves."

He spoke with great solemnity, his face quite impassive behind his dark glasses. Somehow Zaria felt the words didn't ring quite true. She couldn't believe that he had been thinking of her, but only of the fact that she was of no use to him because Ahmed had been expected.

"Well, that's Corny all over," Edie Morgan went on. "But now, just through being warm-hearted, he's put himself in a spot. A friend of ours who was to have turned up with Madame Bertin has been . . . er . . . unavoidably delayed. As a matter of fact he's ill and it's very unlikely he will be able to join us on this trip.

"And so, Zaria, we're going to ask you to be a real sport and forget the little suggestion we made yesterday. Instead of going back to England with your young man, you stay with us! That's what we're asking you to do, isn't it, Corny?"

"We shall be very grateful if Miss Brown will stick to her original arrangement," Mr. Virdon said.

"What about Mr. Tanner?"

Zaria didn't mean to ask the question, it slipped out, and she saw the glance that passed between Edie and Victor before the former said:

"Where you go, Mr. Tanner goes! That's the arrangement, isn't it? We're not quarrelling with that. Glad to have him. He seems a nice boy, eh, Corny?"

"Of course, we're delighted to include Mr. Tanner in our party for as long as he wishes to stay," Mr. Virdon replied.

"Then that's settled," Edie Morgan said with satisfaction. "Thank you, Zaria. You're a real sport. And now we must have a drink to celebrate the new understanding between us all. What do you say, Lulu?"

"I could certainly do with another one," Madame Bertin replied, looking at her empty glass.

"Steward!" Edie Morgan shouted. "Where the heck's that steward? What we want on this goddam boat is a cocktail bar where we can help ourselves. I hate these English servants snooping about behind one and bringing a drink when they think they will—and not enough at that."

"One must get used to the European way of life," Mr. Virdon said. "Over here they don't care for our rough American ways."

Edie gave him what seemed to Zaria almost an angry glance, but his words were smooth enough.

"You're right, Corny, as you always are. Attaboy! We'll behave with immense circumspection. Steward!"

Jim appeared at that moment with a bottle of whisky on a silver tray and several glasses.

"I felt this was what you would be wanting, Sir," he said.

"Clairvoyant, that's what you are becoming," Edie answered. "Stick it down on the table. Anyone want anything different? What about you, Zaria?"

"I have got some soup for Miss Brown," Jim said before Zaria could answer. "Cook is just preparing it. I'll bring it in one moment, Miss."

"Soup! What sort of drink is that?" Victor said. "You want something stronger to make your eyes sparkle and your lips smile."

"I think he is trying to fatten me up," Zaria explained in her shy, deprecating voice.

"*Non, non.* He must do nothing of the sort," Madame Bertin cried. "You are so lucky to be thin. I have been dieting since January and look at me—only about three pounds lighter."

"You'll never be any lighter than that, Lulu," Edie

said. "You drink too much and you're much too fond of your food."

"Trust an American to tell one the truth," Madame Bertin replied disgustedly. "A Frenchman would have said that I am perfect as I am."

"You never can believe a word these Frogs tell you," Edie said rudely, pouring out a liberal measure of whisky and passing it towards her.

Madame Bertin replied with a witticism which made them all laugh, but Zaria wasn't listening. She was trying not to look over her shoulder to see if anyone was approaching them from the prow of the ship.

Were Chuck and Kate still talking there she wondered? What could they be saying to each other? What could Kate be telling him?

She felt within her breast a sudden hard lump that had been growing from the moment that she watched them and now was so large that it constricted her very breathing. Kate was so pretty; Kate knew how to handle a man—to wheedle him, to provoke him, to be seductive as the women Zaria had read about in books.

With her tight, coloured sweaters, chunky jewellery, long red fingernails and blue-shadowed eyes, Kate was a magazine picture come true.

There was something tremendously vital about her. Something alive that made Zaria understand exactly how she could hold a man's attention even while what she was saying to him was the utmost triviality.

Why wasn't Edie Morgan jealous? she wondered, and turned to look at him as he sat talking to Madame Bertin. He was an ugly man, repulsive and, in some obscure way, cruel. Zaria was certain of that, and Kate was his girl.

Yet he didn't seem to care that she was flirting with another man at the other end of the yacht.

There were footsteps behind her; but when Zaria

turned her head eagerly, it was only Jim with her soup.

"Chef's compliments, Miss, and drink it as hot as you can. He says it tastes better that way."

"Thank you," Zaria smiled. "Please thank chef and tell him I find it delicious."

"He'll be glad of that, Miss," Jim said.

"Quite the pampered baby, aren't you?" Edie Morgan teased. "Nobody offered me any soup. What about you, Vic?"

"You wouldn't know what to do with it," Victor answered rudely. "The only liquid you use, besides Scotch, is tooth-water. And I believe even that gets a shot to make it palatable."

"Luncheon is served, Sir," Jim announced.

Edie was spared an answer to Victor's badinage and said instead:

"Come on. I expect Lulu's hungry. Where's the rest of the party?"

"I've already informed Miss Hanover and Mr. Tanner," Jim said.

Even as he spoke Kate and Chuck appeared.

"Haven't you kept a drink for me?" Kate demanded.

"No, and you can't have one because you're late," Mr. Virdon answered. "Grub's up—let's eat. It may get rough later and I don't want to miss any more meals."

"No, indeed!" Kate exclaimed. "Lulu, you've no idea how rough it was. We all felt absolutely ghastly."

She slipped her arm into Madame Bertin's and they walked down to the dining saloon chattering gaily. Zaria found herself looking up at Chuck. He smiled at her, but she fancied there was something lacking in his smile, some warmth, something that had been there before.

I am imagining things,' she told herself, but she was still too miserable to do anything but turn blindly away and follow the others.

Luncheon was delicious, but as far as Zaria was concerned she might just as well have been eating sawdust. From a long way away it seemed to her there was the noise of voices and laughter. Somehow she couldn't understand what they were saying.

All she could think of was Chuck and wonder what he was thinking as he sat beside Kate on the other side of the table from her.

"You come here," Kate had said with her inviting smile, and he had obeyed her without any protest, leaving Zaria to sit in a vacant place on Victor's right.

Madame Bertin was between Mr. Virdon and Edie Morgan and was regaling them with a very amusing account of her struggles to get all her boxes on to two cars.

"Always there are two left over," she said.

" 'You will send these, by train, Madame?' the porters asked.

" 'No, no,' I said. *Faites donc.* Where I go my dresses go! They are too precious, too expensive to be left behind. I do not trust you, any of you, not to steal them.'

"They laughed at that and finally we got them all on and set off—*à toute vitesse.*"

"What sort of dresses have you brought, Lulu?" Kate asked.

She had been whispering something to Chuck, something which Zaria could not overhear, and now her attention seemed to have been caught by the idea of clothes.

"*Toutes les choses,*" Madame Bertin replied. "And at every price. I go to all the big houses and I look

128

at what they have, and then I go home and design my own collection. Exquisite! Unique! Divine! And all for Algiers. It is no use taking to Algiers the gowns that would be correct in London, in New York or Rome.

"I make clothes which the women of Algiers will want. And, remember, they are French; they have taste!"

"Meaning," Kate said with a little grimace and pointing to herself, "that we brash Americans haven't got any."

"I am not saying that, *chérie*," Madame Bertin replied. "But you know as well as I do that French women are far more particular about what they buy than any other women in the world."

"And after all that fuss I don't think they look as hot as all that," Kate said spitefully.

Madame Bertin's eyes flashed.

"You do not understand what you are saying, you stupid child. It is easy for Americans and the English to look pretty because they have fair skins, fair hair and blue eyes—attractive dolls with frills, laces, ribbons and jewellery. Bits and pieces become them and they get away with it."

"But a Frenchwoman is different. She has not the complexion, the hair or the figure of an American girl, but because of the care she takes, because of her good taste, she makes herself the best dressed, the most *chic* woman in the whole world."

"I must say I think Lulu's right," Victor said. "The French girls have certainly got something, you can take it from me."

"But that's not because of their clothes," Kate answered. "That's because they are women and you're a man. They would attract you just the same if they were dressed in a piece of sacking."

"En voila une idée!" Madame Bertin shrieked. "It is clothes that makes the woman! It is what she wears and how she wears it which makes her outstanding. It is easy for you to talk, Kate, you are a very attractive girl. But the average French *jeune fille* has not so many advantages.

"She may have a sallow skin, greasy hair, her figure may not be so well proportioned. And yet, when I have dressed the French girl, the men will look at her and not at you."

"It's a lie!" Kate exclaimed. "It's a lie, isn't it, Chuck? You tell them."

"Give me a girl, any girl," Madame Bertin said, "and by teaching her how to make the best of herself and by dressing her with genius—yes, genius is the right word—I will make her outstanding even though you are competing with her, my pretty, flamboyant Kate."

"Well, I don't believe you," Kate said petulantly. "It's all very well to talk like that, but I'll bet my bottom dollar it's what a girl leaves off that attracts a man, not what she puts on."

"One day I will prove it to you," Madame Bertin said. "I will show you just how easily France can succeed where America fails. You young people think you know everything there is about the arts of seduction. Pouf! French women have ruled the world in the right way—through their men—since the beginning of time."

"Well, I think if it comes to a competition I'll put my money on Kate," Edie said.

"Darling, we'll have one," Kate laughed, "and it'll cost Lulu a pretty penny."

"But I'm not certain I don't back Lulu," Victor remarked. "She's got something, you know, just as

I tell you those French girls have. It isn't their looks and it isn't their figures, it's something else."

"It is their clothes," Madame Bertin reiterated, her voice rising almost to a shout.

"Well, I would certainly like to see this competition," Chuck said. "Although I shouldn't care to be the judge."

"But you shall be," Kate said suddenly, a little glint in her eyes. "You shall be judge, Chuck, and so shall Corny and Edie and Victor. We'll make Victor eat his words as well."

"What do you mean?" Victor asked curiously.

"We will have the competition here and now," Kate said. "I'll put on my best for tonight, I'll show you what I look like when I'm got up to kill. And Lulu! There's your model. Make what you can of her."

To Zaria's astonishment and consternation Kate pointed across the table to her, her finger outstretched, her blue eyes alight with mischief as she said again:

"There she is. Now, Lulu, prove your words and turn Miss Brown into a beauty."

"No!" Zaria said quickly. "No, I do not want to take part in this."

"Now, don't you get het up," Victor said. "It's only a bit of fun and we've got to pass the time somehow. Let Lulu do her best—or her worst. That is if she agrees. What do you say, Lulu?"

Zaria felt Madame Bertin's dark eyes flickering over her, taking in every detail. It almost seemed to Zaria as if she undressed her and her pitifully thin, bony body was exposed to the ridicule of those watching.

Then to her complete astonishment Madame Bertin said:

"*Bien!* I accept. What I have said I have said. What are the stakes?"

131

"A hundred dollars?" Edie said. "Two hundred?"

"Five hundred dollars," Madame Bertin replied. "That is what the challenge is worth to me; and what is more, I want a secret ballot. No-one will know who has voted for which girl. Is that understood?"

"Agreed," Edie said briefly. "And no cheating, Kate. I'm not having you take the hell out of me for the next six months if I vote against you."

"You vote against me and I'll kill you," Kate said. "And that goes for you, too, Chuck," she said, turning her face up in a seductive gesture which no-one could misunderstand.

"I shall be as impartial as I think Mr. Morgan will be," Chuck answered.

"But, please! I don't want to do it," Zaria said, her voice so low as to be almost indistinct.

"Go on, be a sport," Kate admonished. "It's only fun. I want an excuse for dressing up. And it will do Lulu good to open those boxes of hers—there is certainly enough of them."

"We shall need them," Madame Bertin said.

She was watching Zaria with her eyes narrowed and Zaria felt as uncomfortable as if she was lying under a microscope.

"I would rather not," she said almost despairingly, looking across the table at Chuck, appealing to him desperately, her eyes beseeching his co-operation.

But he only smiled at her.

"Madame Bertin is very famous," he said. "Most girls would jump at the opportunity."

They were all against her. It was part of their enjoyment and nothing she could say or do, Zaria realised, was going to prevent them using her for their entertainment.

She gave a little despairing sigh as Victor raised his glass.

"To the judgment of Paris," he said. "Wasn't he the guy who gave an apple to the girl he liked best? I always thought it was a pretty mean reward!"

"It was a golden apple as a matter of fact," Chuck answered.

"That's different," Victor replied. "All the same, I bet she complained that it wasn't set in sparklers."

"How clever of you," Kate said. "Diamonds are my favourite present at any time or at any season."

Zaria felt as if she wanted to cry. She was alone and deserted. Only this morning she had felt safe because Chuck was there.

She had gone to sleep last night thinking of how he said he would look after her, remembering the warmth of his hand, the look in his grey eyes which had told her, indisputably it seemed at the time, that she could trust him.

And now she had lost him. Kate had captivated him and there was no-one to whom she could turn for advice or help.

Madame Bertin pushed back her chair.

"*Helas!* I am going below," she said, "to plan my campaign. Tonight you are all going to have a great surprise, and you are going to say to me afterwards: 'Lulu, you are a very clever, very wise woman. And Kate, *pauvre* Kate, she is just a doll!' "

Kate gave a little shriek of laughter.

"We'll see what we will see," she said, "I can promise you one thing, Lulu Bertin—I'm not afraid."

She turned to Chuck and narrowed her eyes.

"Do you think I need be?" she asked softly.

Zaria pushed back her chair with a little bang. She felt as if she could bear no more. She wanted to cry out to Chuck, to say aloud what she had heard this morning—the threat that had been in Edie's voice. And then she knew with a sudden sickening feeling of impotence that it was more than likely he would not believe her.

Things had changed, things had altered since yesterday. He might only think she was jealous. He might just laugh at her for being imaginative.

"Zaria, *venez avec moi,*" Madame Bertin commanded. "We have a lot to do, you and I. We are going to show these imbeciles that while they may know a lot about some things in the world, they know just nothing about women. Come!"

She walked from the dining saloon, and because Zaria felt there was nothing else she could do, she followed her blindly. She didn't even look back at Chuck. She had made her appeal and it had failed, and somehow nothing else seemed to matter.

They went down to Madame Bertin's cabin.

It was the largest one in the yacht—a double one with two beds, a bathroom opening out of it and a number of fitted mirrors which seemed to reflect and re-reflect the pitiable object she appeared as she followed the Frenchwoman into the cabin.

"Sit down, *ma petite,* and let me look at you," Madame Bertin said as she shut the door.

"Oh, please, *Madame,* this joke has gone far enough," Zaria said. "Let me go to my cabin and say I am ill. They will excuse me for tonight and prevent you from having to bother with me. I shall only disgrace you. You haven't got a chance of winning the wager."

"Why should you say that?" Lulu Bertin asked. "Do you not believe that clothes can alter and change a woman?"

"I am sure they can when a woman has got anything to start with," Zaria said. "But you can see

134

what I am like." She spoke humbly and almost despairingly.

Madame Bertin merely smiled and taking out an onyx and diamond cigarette holder fitted a cigarette into it.

"I see what you have made yourself," she said. "I see, too, you have been ill. That does not matter. Your figure is good, very good. A little too thin, but that cannot be helped for the moment. Now, let us consider your type, point by point."

Zaria clasped her thin fingers together.

"Please listen to me," she pleaded. "You are going to make me a laughing stock, a joke! However wonderful your dresses—and I am quite sure they are wonderful—I shall only look a scarecrow in them. I do not know how to wear clothes; and I do not know how to make myself look nice.

"All I know is that I am ashamed of my looks. I have been ill, if that is what you like to call it, but at any rate one cannot pretend for a moment that I shall look anything but a mess whatever you do to me."

Madame Bertin gave a little cry of exasperation, her hands going up, her shoulders rising.

"Sacré nom d'un chien," she said. "Could any woman talk in a more ridiculous fashion? *Quelle folie!* What foolishness! You are young, you have life—what else matters? Must you look like a chocolate-box? Must you copy Kate—that overpainted, stupid, *petite chatte?*

"Do you not know that you breathe? You have eyes, you have hair, you have a figure. And what is more, you can smile. Forget everything else; just remember that above all you have a heart.

"It is the heart that matters. It is the heart that must show in the face and on the lips."

"I do not think I understand," Zaria said, but for the first time there was an answering sparkle in her eyes as she looked at Madame Bertin.

"I have been watching you," Madame Bertin said. "Shall I tell you something which helps us more than anything else?"

"Oh, yes! What is it?" Zaria asked.

"That you are in love, *ma petite!*" Madame Bertin smiled.

Chapter Seven

For a moment it seemed to Zaria as if everything stood still. She just stared at Madame Bertin, and then something clicked in her brain and she remembered.

Of course, she and Chuck were engaged! She had said so, everyone aboard the yacht knew it. With an effort the world began to move and spin back into perspective.

"Of course," she said in a low voice. "Mr. Virdon has been kind enough to allow my fiancé to come on this trip."

Madame Bertin laughed.

"That is not what I meant, *chérie,*" she said. "Women talk about 'my *fiancé,*' 'my husband,' and what does it mean? Something legal, something which, in my country, has often been arranged—*un mariage de convenance*. But love, that is a very different thing! It is when a woman is in love that it alters her face. You, *mon enfant*, are in love!"

Quite suddenly Zaria realised the truth. It came to her like a blinding flash, as if a streak of lightning suddenly illuminated the cabin or she shot on a falling star across the dark firmament into an unknown universe.

She was in love! It was the truth, even though she could not believe it, could not grasp what her senses and her heart told her. In love with Chuck!

A man of whom she knew nothing, whom she had only just met, who had come into her life in the strangest and most suspicious circumstances.

It was so incredible, incomprehensible, ridiculous—
and yet she loved him! She knew now why she felt
secure when he was beside her, felt her fingers flutter
beneath his touch, ached for him when he was not
there. And why she had felt despair and misery when
she had seen him smiling down at Kate.

It couldn't be true! It couldn't! And yet it was!

"Eh, bien," Madame Bertin said with a little smile
as if she could almost read Zaria's thoughts. "You
are beginning to understand. Every woman can be
beautiful. It is her heart that matters, not those ridiculous things people call features. They are inci-
dental because we are born with them, cannot alter
them very much, and we must accept them for what
they are. But beauty . . . ah, that is something we
can create for ourselves."

With a tremendous effort Zaria tried not to think
of the new awakening knowledge within herself and
the strange emotions rushing through her body which
made her legs feel weak and her hands tremble.

Striving to be matter of fact she said:

"You are very kind, *Madame,* but I feel you have
undertaken the impossible. I am distressed that you
should lose your money."

"But I must not lose it," Madame Bertin said.
"I need five hundred dollars—need them very badly.
Come, we will see how we can win them."

Zaria gave a little laugh that was almost a sob.

"With me, *Madame!* You must be blind. How can
I compare with Kate, with her wonderful figure,
her pretty face and exquisite clothes?"

Madame Bertin suddenly stamped her foot.

"Pourquoi? You doubt my word?" she demanded
almost angrily. "I, Lulu Bertin, am acknowledged
one of the most brilliant *couturières* in all Paris. I
have made hundreds of models famous overnight.

I have brought in new fashions and changed those that were already in existence simply because of my disapproval. When I say I succeed, I will succeed. *Voilà!* You have but to believe in me."

'I wish I could,' Zaria thought to herself, almost hypnotised by the power and passion in Madame Bertin's voice. 'If I could be beautiful, perhaps Chuck would look at me, perhaps he would love me.'

Then she almost laughed aloud at such a non-sensical idea. What had she got to offer Chuck Tanner? He might be poor, he might be even a crook— as the other people were on this yacht—but he was a man and good looking. He had his health and strength and a quick, alert brain.

What more could anyone want so long as they were free and unhampered, with all the adventure and excitement of the world in front of them?

"You have got to believe in me!" Madame Bertin was saying. "You have got to put yourself in my hands and trust me. *Enfin!* Then I can make you what I will."

'She is hypnotic,' Zaria thought, but aloud she said:

"I want to believe you. You cannot think that anyone could look like me and be happy about it. But I . . . I have had rather a . . . difficult time."

"Je vois bien," Madame Bertin answered. "But do not be ashamed of it; do not be afraid it will spoil you. Hardships, and even unhappiness, leave their marks on a woman's face. But they are not always ugly marks; they can give a spiritual look as if one is tempered steel, as if one has come through the fire of experience and emerged triumphant."

She spoke in a low, deep voice, almost as if she were moved by some power beyond herself. And yet all the time her shrewd, dark eyes were watching Zaria, taking in every detail of her appearance—

the thin, almost angular face, the heavy, lifeless hair falling to her shoulders, the too-slender lines of her young body, the sensitive nervousness of her hands.

Suddenly she gave a cry.

"Sacré nom!"

Her voice was loud and her shout so unexpected that Zaria jumped as if in alarm.

"Faites donc. I have the answer!" Madame Bertin cried triumphantly. "I have been thinking, concentrating on you, seeing through you, finding out what you were inside. And now I know how you must look. *Vite! Vite!* Take off your clothes—that terrible sweater, those horrible trousers."

"They are not mine," Zaria explained with a little smile. "They belonged to the cabin boy. I have only borrowed them because I had nothing else but a suit, and that somehow didn't seem very suitable for yachting."

"Put on this *robe de chambre,*" Madame Bertin said, throwing a pretty dressing-gown across the bed as she rapidly unpacked a suitcase that she had opened on the floor.

A pair of slippers followed—one thrown in one direction and the other in another.

"What size do you take?" Madame Bertin asked over her shoulder.

"Three-and-a-half . . . I think," Zaria replied.

"Good! That is my size," Madame Bertin said. "We are lucky."

Zaria looked down at Madame Bertin's feet in surprise. She had expected her to take a far bigger size, but it was true. Under her heavy body her feet were small—in fact they almost had the effect of table legs—such small supports for such a large expanse above them.

"Mon Dieu! But this case is not what I want.

140

It is my other baggage that I must have. They will have put it in Kate's room, I daresay."

Madame Bertin pulled open the cabin door and ran into the passage shouting, "Steward! Steward!" at the top of her voice.

Zaria could hear Jim come running and heard them both go into Kate's cabin next door. There was the murmur of their voices, the banging of heavy objects as if they heaved boxes about in the effort to find what was wanted.

Slowly Zaria sat down on the stool in front of the dressing-table, staring at herself in the mirror, searching her face for what *Madame* could see there.

She was in love! How did it show? To herself she looked very much the same. A little better, a little less tired perhaps. The lines under her eyes were not so deep, the eyes themselves seemed larger. Already food and rest were producing the obvious results.

But she was still ugly. She was not so stupid as to deceive herself. She was ugly and therefore Chuck would not find the beauty he was seeking in her, but in Kate.

For the moment Zaria felt she could not even resent this. Love was something so new, so overpowering.

She was almost content to know that she loved him and to ask nothing more. It was a happiness beyond belief to imagine that she was feeling again the comforting pressure of his hands, seeing that steady, sympathetic look in his grey eyes.

'Why didn't I realise that I loved him yesterday when we were sitting on deck?' she asked herself.

And knew that although she had not put it into words the feeling had been there—the joy and contentment because he was beside her and talking to her, the sense of protection that had been shattered only when Edie Morgan appeared and told her that she was to leave the ship at Algiers.

With a start Zaria realised that she had not had a chance to tell Chuck what she had overheard. Somehow she must find him alone, somehow she must get the opportunity of telling him what these people were really like.

She had half risen to her feet, anxious to go to him then and there, when the door was flung open and Jim appeared carrying a heavy trunk, with Madame Bertin behind him lugging a small suitcase.

"This is what I want," she cried happily. "Fortunately I had the good sense to label the boxes with the sizes of the models I had packed in them. *Regardez,* on this label you will see, '*Très Petite.*' That is you, *ma chère,* and even then I think some of my clothes will be too big.

"*Merci!* Thank you, Steward," she said to Jim, who went from the cabin after smiling at Zaria in an understanding way as if he found the Frenchwoman not only incomprehensible, but also a little mad.

Madame Bertin flung back the trunk lid and looked inside.

"*Bien!* They are all here," she said. "Now then, there is a lot to do before we come to the clothes."

"Wh . . . what?" Zaria asked nervously.

In answer Madame Bertin walked across the room and picking up a comb, ran it through Zaria's hair.

"So ugly!" she exclaimed, "and so English!"

"But it was set by a Frenchman," Zaria protested. "It looked much worse before he did it."

"Bah! A Frenchman living in England loses his touch," Madame Bertin related scornfully. "It is only in Paris that they really study a woman before they play about with her hair. Hair should always be a frame to the face, not an ornament on its own."

"I thought it looked much better," Zaria said a little wistfully.

"Then before it must have looked very bad," Madame Bertin replied. "These heavy waves, they are not right for your little face. Can you not see? All those downward lines make your face more pointed, more thin, more—how do you say in English?—more peaky."

"Perhaps you are right," Zaria agreed humbly.

"Perhaps!" *Madame* said flinging her arms wide. "Listen to me, *ma petite*. Do you know what I did before I came on this voyage?"

She paused and Zaria asked what was expected of her.

"No, what did you do?"

"I will tell you," Madame Bertin said. "I, Lulu Bertin, the great *couturière*, the great designer, went back to school! I went as a pupil—an ordinary, humble pupil—to Antoine. Do you know who he is?"

Zaria shook her head.

"Bah! What ignorance!" Madame Bertin exclaimed. "Antoine, *ma chèrie,* is the king of hairdressers, the man who stands supreme—an artiste, a genius! So I went to him and I begged him to teach me the secrets of his craft. At first he laughed at me, and then he saw I was serious."

"You learned to set hair?" Zaria asked.

"I learnt to style hair," Madame Bertin corrected. "Styles which suited the individual, styles which showed the personality of the wearer."

"But, why?" Zaria asked.

"I hoped you would ask me that question," Madame Bertin answered with satisfaction. "I will tell you. I go to Algiers; I start up a new business; I plan

143

to make a big splash. How can I do so if the women who wear my clothes are not chic? They do not go to Paris, they live in Algiers! If their hair is frizzed or cut all wrong in the old-fashioned, stupid way that is now so out of date, what can I do about it?"

She paused for breath and Zaria said:

"I . . . I suppose it is important—the hair, I mean."

"Important!" Madame Bertin screamed. "It is everything. It is almost the first thing you notice about a woman. What did some poet call it?—'Her crowning glory.' He was absolutely right!"

"So you learnt hairdressing," Zaria said.

"Me, I am not proud, I am not ashamed to say I do not know," Madame Bertin replied. "So, I sit at the feet of Antoine, he shows me the clever things he do; he show me how to cut, how to create. At the end he say to me:

'*Madame*, if ever you want a job, my *salon* is yours.' "

"How clever of you," Zaria breathed.

"Clever! You do not realise, I am unique! I am Lulu Bertin! That is why I tell you I can make you beautiful, far more beautiful than that chocolate box Kate! Bah! Women like her are to be found in their thousands in every big capital. Now come! This is no time for talking."

"What are you going to do?" Zaria asked nervously.

"I am going to cut your hair as it should be cut," Madame Bertin answered.

She took some scissors from a drawer and holding the comb ran it through Zaria's hair, then, holding it high, began to cut. Zaria gave a little cry of horror.

"You are cutting it off!" she said.

144

"Oui," *Madame* answered. "I am cutting it off. It is going to turn up, not down; it is going to curl, not wave. Do you know what I am doing? Do you know what style I am giving you?"

"No," Zaria answered a little nervously.

She began to think that perhaps Madame Bertin was mad as she saw large pieces of her hair falling one by one on to the floor.

"I will tell you," Madame Bertin said, snipping away. "Two hairdressers—big men, men with large salons—were visiting Italy on their holiday. They were walking in the mountains and they saw two shepherd boys watching their sheep and while they watched, one was cutting the other's hair.

"Because it amused them they stopped to watch and they saw that the boy employed a very different method from any they had known before. First he wetted the hair and then he cut it—cut it in little tiers or steps, one above the other, so that in the end his friend looked like the god Pan. His hair was curling naturally and all he wanted to complete the picture was a pipe of reeds."

Madame Bertin paused for breath and stood back to look at her handiwork, and then she went on:

"The two hairdressers were very excited. They came back to Paris full of what they had seen. Soon *tout le monde* was trying the new cut—the cut which did away with permanent waves, with crimped, tight curls, with that artificial look which is death to true beauty. 'The Shepherd's-Boy' cut became *la mode—le dernier cri!"*

"Is that what you are giving me?" Zaria asked.

"Naturellement! But keep still," Madame Bertin said. "You can look afterwards. Now you must *reste tranquille.* I must not cut too much or too little. It

is the line that counts. Remember *toujours* that beauty depends on line."

'I am sure I ought not to let her do this,' Zaria thought to herself. 'I shall look worse than ever—a scarecrow.'

But she knew it was impossible to argue, impossible to assert her own mind or wishes against *Madame's*. And perhaps, she thought as she heard the snip, snip round the back of her head, Madame Bertin did know what she was talking about.

She could not get over how, despite her age and unattractive features, the Frenchwoman managed to give an impression of smartness and elegance. There was an air of mystery and even of allure in her heavily shadowed eyes and on her deep red, protruding lips.

Zaria gave a little sigh, and then, almost before she knew it, she had forgotten Madame Bertin and the snipping of the scissors.

She was thinking only of Chuck, wondering what he was doing, knowing, with a stab of her heart, that Kate would be looking up at him with those liquid blue eyes, her slim, white arm linked in his.

How could any man resist her? Zaria thought miserably. And how could she expect Kate to resist Chuck?

She began to go over in her mind all the little things he had said to her since the very first moment they had met. He was so kind. That, she felt, was more characteristic of him than anything else.

Never for one moment had he made her feel ugly, unattractive or out of place.

She felt a lump in her throat as she remembered his little attentions which had touched her from the start of their acquaintance.

The way he had helped her in and out of the

taxi; his hand beneath her arm as she had stepped on to the gang-way of the yacht; the manner in which he drew out her chair as she sat down for meals; and how he had wrapped the rug about her legs yesterday afternoon, telling her she must keep warm.

All these and so many other things. Because he had thought of getting her the right sort of clothes for the yacht. Because he had promised that she could trust him and he would look after her.

'Oh, God, don't let Kate have him.'

Zaria almost said the words aloud; and then, as she checked them, she looked into the mirror and saw Madame Bertin's eyes watching her.

"You are suffering, *ma petite*," she said. "What is it? Are you afraid your *fiancé* will succumb to the attractions of Kate? Do not be afraid. He will soon find that she has nothing in her—a little birdlike brain, a body which might well be full of sawdust because when *Le Bon Dieu* made her He forgot to give her a heart."

"Do you know her well?" Zaria asked.

Madame Bertin laughed. It was not a pleasant sound.

"Well enough," she said.

"I thought they were all . . . great friends of yours," Zaria said a little hesitantly, afraid of sounding critical.

Madame Bertin laughed again.

"They say that you are born with your relatives and that you choose your friends," she said. "*Ma foi!* It is not always true. Sometimes your friends are— how shall we say?—thrust upon you!"

Zaria said nothing, but she was thinking quickly. Edie Morgan and Victor somehow got Madame Bertin entangled in their intrigues? She was sure of it and yet she knew she must be careful, she must say nothing which might make even Madame Bertin suspicious that she had heard too much or was curious.

As if her mind had gone off on other things, Madame Bertin said:

"*L'amour!* That is the real point of existence. All women need it, all women seek it. Even at my age I am still chasing the will o' the wisp! It is wonderful! Magnificent! Thrilling! *Fantastique! N'es-ce pas?*"

"I haven't had . . . very much experience of it yet," Zaria answered hesitantly.

"You have not been betrothed for long?" Madame Bertin enquired and, without waiting for Zaria's answer, continued: "*Bien!* Then all the adventure of getting to know each other lies in front of you. And let me give you a piece of good advice, *ma petite*. You must always surprise him. Never let him be sure of your love.

"Never let him know exactly what you are going to say or what you are going to look like. Surprise, mystery, that is what keeps the chase alive, what compels a man to go on hunting."

She gave a last snip with the scissors, flung them down on the dressing-table and combed Zaria's hair upwards until it stood out all round her head like a little halo.

"*Voilà!*" Madame Bertin said, and Zaria looked at her reflection in amazement.

It was astonishing what a difference it did make. Instead of the heavy waves falling on either side of her face there was now a mass of soft, natural curls turning upwards from her neck to her temples.

They stood out like little tongues of fire and framed her face so softly, so delicately that one forgot to notice the too sharp lines of cheekbones and chin.

"It is . . . extraordinary!" Zaria exclaimed. "I look much . . . better."

"*Mais oui,*" Madame Bertin smiled. "Of course it is better. Lift the hand-mirror and look at yourself sideways. *C'est ravissant.* See how beautiful the line is! Now one can see the shape of your head and the length of your neck. *Charmante! Délicieuse!* You might be a pretty choir boy or a busy little angel!"

"I look different—quite different," Zaria said incredulously.

"But I have not yet finished," Madame Bertin said. "*J'ai beaucoup des choses à faire.* Lie down on the bed, the wrong way round, your feet where one should put one's head, your head where one should put one's feet."

Without argument Zaria obeyed her; and then, having covered her with the silk eiderdown and put towels over her hair and neck, Madame Bertin set to work. For the first time in her life Zaria had a face massage. She could feel the strength of Madame Bertin's fingers as they patted and smoothed soft, scented creams into her taut and dry skin.

And after a time she began to grow sleepy. It was all so soothing. Her eyes were shut and all she could hear was the soft pat of Madame Bertin's hands, the hum of the engines and the lap of the water outside.

She began to dream. Not those frightened, terror-stricken dreams she had dreamt in Scotland when her father had been particularly angry with her and when she had been too hungry and too utterly worn out to sleep anything but fitfully.

This was a dream in which she drifted along in utter contentment. Chuck was beside her. She could feel his arm around her shoulders, hear his voice talking to her . . .

149

How long she slept she did not know. She awoke with a start and knew by the stillness that she was alone. She tried to open her eyes and found there were pieces of cotton wool on them. Her face was covered with cream.

She wondered whether Madame Bertin had finished with her and whether she should get up or stay where she was. She was still lying there indecisive when she heard the door open.

"The child's asleep," she heard Madame Bertin say in a very low voice. It sounded as if she was standing in the doorway.

"What about this damn-fool bet?"

It was Edie Morgan's voice, but he, too, was hardly speaking above a whisper.

"*S'amuse,*" Madame Bertin replied. "We have to occupy ourselves until we get there. You are all so—how do you say—jittery."

"What do you mean, jittery?"

"What I say. *Prenez garde* of the steward. I would not be surprised if it was because Ahmed talked too much that he was stopped at the frontier."

"I thought you said they suspected that his papers were forged."

"*Mais oui,*" Madame Bertin agreed. "But who tipped off the officials so that they looked more closely into them? They were good enough if he had been passed through in the ordinary, routine way."

"You're quite sure you weren't followed?"

There was a note of real anxiety in Edie Morgan's voice; and though she was lying with eyes closed, Zaria somehow knew he had laid his hand insistently on Madame Bertin's arm. She knew, too, that Madame Bertin shrugged her shoulders in a characteristic manner.

"If so, would I be here?" she asked.

"I suppose not."

There was a note of relief now in Edie's voice.

"Lay off the drinks and think about something else," Madame Bertin's voice had risen a little and Edie said quickly:

"Shut up!"

He must have pushed her into the cabin and come in after her.

"Do you want the whole damned boat to know what we're talking about?" he asked angrily. "How do you know that girl's asleep?"

"Because my massage always makes them sleep," Madame Bertin answered. "She was tired, *très fatiguée.*"

"It's a damn nuisance having her here," Edie Morgan said. "But we'll have to use her. Not one of us can speak the accursed language."

"I did my best," Madame Bertin replied deferentially. "It is not my fault that Ahmed was arrested."

"It was that motor job last year I expect," Edie repeated. "I said it was a mistake to use him on something so small and insignificant. 'Keep him for the big game,' I said, but nobody listened."

"Hush! Do not talk so much," Madame Bertin said.

She walked across the cabin and stood beside the bed. Zaria knew she was listening. For the first time since the door had opened she began to feel afraid.

If they thought she wasn't asleep, if they thought she had overheard what they were saying, what would they do to her?

Her mouth felt suddenly dry, there was a constriction in her throat. With a desperate sense of self-perservation she forced herself to breathe naturally, to breathe deeply as someone does who is really asleep.

151

She had an insane desire to open her eyes. She could feel Madame Bertin there, feel her presence, feel her personality and her will power.

She was watching, she was waiting, she was listening. Behind her was Edie—Edie who Zaria was sure could be utterly ruthless if anyone crossed him, if anything threatened his plans.

"She's asleep?"

Edie's voice hissed from the background.

"Dead asleep," Madame Bertin answered. "But get out *toute de suite!*"

He obeyed her without another word. Zaria heard the cabin door shut and Madame Bertin still stood there saying nothing. Then at length, very softly, she asked:

"Are you awake?"

Zaria didn't answer and she repeated in a louder tone:

"Zaria, are you awake?"

Slowly, as if she came back from a great depth, acting with an ability she had no idea she possessed, Zaria stirred and moved. She turned her head from side to side as if she did not wish to waken, she stifled a little yawn and then seemed to drop into heavy slumber again.

She knew without seeing Madame Bertin, without looking at her, that she relaxed and the tension died out of her. The Frenchwoman was satisfied.

Zaria snuggled against the pillow until in a very different tone Madame Bertin said:

"Come, *ma petite,* it is time to wake up!"

It was two hours later when Madame Bertin flung open the door of the saloon where the rest of the party were waiting for dinner. They were drinking, as they had been the whole evening.

The men had the inevitable Scotch at their elbows, Kate had a glass of champagne in her hand. She raised it now with a little grimace to Chuck who was sitting on the arm of her chair.

"Now we shall see what we shall see," she said with a little giggle. "May the best girl win."

It was obvious that she had no doubts as to the outcome of the contest. It was hard for anyone looking at her to think that she could be eclipsed.

She wore a long skin-tight gown of silver sequins which made her look like a voluptuous mermaid. Every line and curve of her body was revealed and the dress was cut down to the waist at the back and was so low in the front that one could see the narrow valley between Kate's pointed breasts.

Round her neck she wore diamonds and the same tones flashed in her ears. Her fair, silvery hair fell in a big burnished wave on to her naked shoulders and her red pouting mouth matched her long finger nails and the elegantly painted toenails which showed through her transparent nylons.

She was lovely, sophisticated, a complete product of the modern age when every artifice is used to make a woman not only beautiful but a synthetic product of beauty.

"You are all here?" Madame Bertin asked from the doorway unnecessarily.

"You can see we are," Kate replied.

"Come on, bring her in. We're all waiting," Victor said unsteadily.

Already he had drunk too much and his dark, lustful eyes seemed to leer unpleasantly as Zaria came through the doorway.

"*Allons y!*" Madame Bertin cried. "*Voilà la beauté de Bertin.*"

Zaria stood for a moment quite still, as Madame

had instructed her to do. Though she was shy and frightened, she could not help hearing the sudden gasp, the indrawing of breath which to any woman means more than applause.

"Good God!"

It was Edie who spoke first. Zaria hardly heard him. She was looking across the room at Chuck, watching him rise slowly and almost incredulously to his feet, seeing the expression on his face.

Suddenly she felt wildly, ecstatically happy.

"I wouldn't have believed it! I wouldn't have believed it!" Edie exclaimed, while it was left to Mr. Virdon to say in his quiet, rather serious way:

"You're a genius, Lulu. If I was never sure of it before, I am now."

"Give me a drink, I deserve it," Madame Bertin said.

She held out her hand to Chuck, but he did not see her. He was handing a glass of champagne to Zaria. She took it from him almost blindly and felt the colour coming into her cheeks.

"Your skin is white, a beauty in itself," Madame Bertin had said before they left the cabin. "But you must have colour otherwise you will look like a ghost, and men are afraid of ghosts."

Her words came back to Zaria now.

'I am not a ghost,' she thought to herself. 'I am alive.'

She felt a tingling excitement go through her, a sudden knowledge that she was young and attractive and that Chuck was looking at her.

"I think there is no need to drink your health," he said softly. "Instead I shall drink to your future."

"That is a surprisingly pretty speech," Madame Bertin interrupted before Zaria could answer:

"Come along all of you, drink to Zaria's future— the future to which I have shown her the right way."

The men raised their glasses, everyone conscious that there was no need for a secret ballot, no need to ask who was the winner of the contest. Wordlessly, with his back to Kate, Edie passed a roll of green backed dollars over to Madame Bertin.

Kate poured herself out another glass of champagne, her lips turned down sourly. Then she said aggressively:

"I, too, hope Zaria's future is what she expects. Fate has a way of producing some very nasty surprises when one least expects them."

Mr. Virdon laughed, but Zaria hardly heard the words. She was tingling with this new consciousness of herself. She knew that the dress that Madame Bertin had chosen for her made her look lovely, with a beauty she had never known she possessed.

Made of soft pink brocade shot with silver, it billowed out in an enormous bouffant skirt from a tiny waist. The bodice was embroidered with pearls and there was a cloud of pink tulle draped round her shoulders to hide the thinness of her arms. Three rows of pearls encircled her neck, the soft, pinky sheen of them somehow throwing into prominence the white, magnolia texture of her skin.

She looked like a girl from a dream, young, innocent and untouched as the apple blossom in May.

At the same time there was something spiritual and elusive in her beauty—as though it was not obvious but had to be sought for, if it was to be found and appreciated.

She had not believed it was herself when she looked in the mirror and saw how large her eyes were when they were shadowed with green and her eyelashes were brushed upwards with a little eyeblack.

There were strange lights in her hair that she had never seen before; there was a fullness on her red lips.

But it was not only the artistry which made Zaria so different. It was the confidence Madame Bertin had instilled into her.

It was the words of wisdom and advice that she had given her which made Zaria carry her head high, made her conscious that she could, in these soft, silken, wonderful clothes, look like a woman and feel like a woman.

"Forget the past, forget what you have suffered," Madame Bertin admonished. "I do not want you to tell me what you have been through—or to tell anyone. Forget it. It is gone. Yesterday is behind you; it is today that matters. Do not even trouble your head about tomorrow.

"To every woman it is the present that she should consider, the moment which she can never have again."

It was those words, perhaps more than anything else, that made Zaria walk into the saloon with her head up, a little smile on her lips.

For one moment she had felt afraid, and then she had remembered that Chuck was there—Chuck, whom she loved, Chuck who was with her for this moment whatever might happen tomorrow or the day after.

She had heard the swish of silk as she moved, smelt the exotic fragrance of the perfume which Madame Bertin had sprayed over her. And then she had known, as an actress knows as she stands before the footlights, that her audience was with her.

She took a sip of the champagne she held in her hand, and then, as they toasted her, said quietly:

"Thank you. I hope my future will be happy, but I am happy now—terribly happy."

She did not know quite why she said the words,

she only knew that she was telling Chuck something, asking something of him, hoping that in some inexpressible way he would understand.

And then with a little deflated feeling she thought perhaps she had failed, he didn't know what she meant. He was just standing there; she couldn't see his expression because of his dark glasses.

And then suddenly Victor struggled out of the chair in which he had been sitting.

He had difficulty in doing it for he was drunk enough to be unsteady on his feet and in reaching out a hand to assist himself he knocked over a bottle of whisky. It crashed to the floor, but he took no notice of it.

"I don't believe it," he said thickly, slurring his words. "It's a trick, there's something wrong. How could Lulu make her look like that? She's a spy! She's been sent here to spy on us! That's what she is, I tell you—a spy!"

Chapter Eight

Five pairs of eyes were staring at Zaria and instinctively she knew that the speculative expression in them meant danger, not only for herself but for Chuck.

For a moment she felt paralysed. Then, because of her love for him, because it seemed to her she had known all the time that he was in an infinitely more precarious position than she was, she rallied all her strength to save him.

She knew she must refute the drunken accusation of Victor, which seemed to hang over the whole assembly like a drawn dagger.

And because her fear was not for herself but for Chuck, because in that moment she knew that whatever his feelings might be towards her, she loved him with every fibre in her body, some hidden strength within her came to the rescue.

"A spy!"

She heard her own voice, high, a little unsteady but full of laughter, repeat the words.

"You flatter me, Mr. Jacobetti. I wish I was clever enough to act the spy for one of the big model houses in England or New York. I know, of course, they do try to get in on the newest collection before it is seen. I know that they send people to take particulars and make sketches.

"But I'm afraid I am not clever enough. Madame Bertin can trust me with her secrets, however important they may be. I shouldn't be able to betray them even if I wanted to."

As she talked, rambling on like an excitable young

girl, she could feel the tension relaxing, she could see the menacing glitter dispersing and she could feel Edie's reaction even before he took charge of the situation.

"Shut up, you fool!" he said almost beneath his breath to Victor. And then aloud:

"You're drunk, old boy. This is only Zaria Brown, the girl who's been with us the whole trip, the girl we're trusting with all our secrets. In fact, we couldn't have one from her even if we wanted to. A good secretary knows everything, doesn't she?"

"Yes, yes, of course," Zaria answered.

Chuck came to her assistance.

"I can assure you that we are both as trustworthy as the Bank of England," he said, and now Zaria felt his arm go round her waist and he gave her a little squeeze as if to say: "Well done!"

"I'm wrong, so I'll apologise," Victor said, slurring his speech a little and swaying as he stood facing them. "I've made a mistake. Stupid of me. Might have guessed that Edie would see there were no spies on this boat."

Once again Edie Morgan muttered at him, giving his arm a sharp blow as he went towards the table to pick up a glass.

"Isn't dinner ready?" he asked impatiently. "I think everybody has had enough booze, if you ask me."

But Victor hadn't finished yet.

"I apologise," he replied. "I can't say more! No hard feelings, eh, Zaria?"

He lurched towards her and instinctively she backed away from him.

"No, of course not," she said quickly.

"Then kiss and make up," he suggested. "Got to show you're not angry with me. Can't bear people being angry with me. Give me a kiss to show we're friends."

159

"No!" Zaria said sharply.

Victor seized hold of her hand and started pulling her towards him.

"No! No!" she cried again in a sudden panic, and turning towards Chuck she held on to him.

"Stop him! Please stop him!" she begged, her head thrown back in the desperation of her appeal.

"We've all got to be friends," Victor slobbered.

"I quite agree with you," Chuck said in his quiet, steady voice. "But I cannot allow you to kiss my fiancée. Only I can do that, you know."

"Is that so?"

Victor relinquished Zaria's hand and stood staring at Chuck a little aggressively.

"Who made such a silly rule?" he asked of the company in general. "Who said I can't kiss Zaria and say I'm sorry for thinking that she was a spy?"

"Keep your mouth closed, Victor," Edie ejaculated, but Victor took no notice of him.

"I say there's no harm in it," he went on, his voice growing increasingly plaintive. "I say it's only right I should apologise. If I apologise, then I expect Zaria to accept my apology. Only a cruel, hard woman would say no when a man apologises, and Zaria isn't like that—or is she?"

"I accept your apology, of course I do," Zaria said in a small voice.

But her head was turned away from him. She was still holding on with one hand to Chuck.

"Then there's no harm in a little kiss," Victor continued. "No harm at all."

"Forget it, there's a good chap." Chuck said. "Just forget it, and let's have another drink."

"Why should I forget it?" Victor asked with the persistent obstinacy of someone who is very drunk.

"Because I tell you too," Chuck replied patiently.

"Zaria belongs to me. She's my girl. You get that into your head."

"I don't think I believe you," Victor said. "I've seen you messing about with Kate all the afternoon. I don't think Zaria belongs to anyone, if you ask me."

"Well, I assure you that she is engaged to me," Chuck said, "and that's all there is to it."

He spoke sharply as if his patience was wearing thin.

"Then what about a kiss for the bride?" Victor asked.

"If there's any kissing to be done, I'll do it myself," Chuck replied, and this time there was no mistaking the irritation in his tone.

"Very well then, kiss her," Victor said. "Kiss her for me. Kiss her and let's see if you're as fond of her as you pretend."

There was something uncanny, Zaria thought, in his drunken perception that something was wrong. He wasn't certain what, but he was gnawing at the matter in a manner which made her tremble.

It made her more certain than ever that she and Chuck were in danger.

She looked up at him now, wondering what he would do, wondering where the scene would end, and terrified that the undercurrents in the conversation would eventually land them into some indiscretion which the others would be certain to recognise.

Her lips trembled a little as she whispered, almost without realising she did so:

"Chuck! Chuck!"

It was as if his name was a magic talisman to which all her faith was directed in the hope that he could save them from this strange and unexpected danger.

She felt his arms go round her shoulders. There

161

was something infinitely comforting in the strength of him. And then he looked at Victor and smiled.

"But, of course I'll kiss Zaria if that's what you want," he said. "Why not? It's something I very much enjoy doing."

He bent his head. Zaria would have turned her face away from his lips, but she was taken by surprise. She did not expect any such response from Chuck, any such reply; and while she hesitated, while she merely stared at him with her eyes wide, she felt his lips.

For a moment she was too astonished to do anything but remain passive. And then, as she felt his arms tighten still closer about her, his mouth took complete possession of hers.

She knew, with a sudden stab of intensity, that she was being kissed for the first time in her life. A man was kissing her. Chuck was kissing her. And somehow it was quite different from what she had ever expected.

She felt the warm strength of his lips, and suddenly something within herself responded without her conscious volition, without her even thinking of it. She felt a strange thrill run through her, she felt as if her whole being was lit as if from a fire.

Then she was tingling and quivering with wonder and glory such as she never believed the world contained.

And yet it was all over in a split second.

Almost, it seemed to her, as he possessed her, he freed her. And yet in that moment she knew eternity.

She felt the colour rush to her face, she felt suddenly as if her knees were too weak to hold her. And then she heard Chuck give a little laugh. It seemed to her there was a note of triumph in it.

"Is that what you wanted?" he asked Victor. "Now can you understand why nobody shall kiss Zaria but me?"

"I can't think why nobody wants to kiss me," Kate wailed. "It doesn't seem fair that Zaria's getting all the attention. In fact, I won't stand for it!"

She got up from her chair and slinked across the room towards Edie.

"I'm being left out in the cold," she complained.

"That's a new experience for you, honey," he answered.

He kissed her cheek and she threw her arms round his neck and hugged him, looking over his shoulders as she did so at Chuck, her eyes half closed, her mouth pouting provocatively.

"Some people need lessons in kissing," she announced to the world in general.

"Eh bien, and I am sure that you are quite prepared to give them—at a price," Madame Bertin snapped.

Zaria had the impression that Madame Bertin was uneasy. During the little scene that had just passed she had almost been holding her breath, as if she was fearing a sudden explosion might result from it. Now she drank a glass of champagne very quickly and asked for another.

"Dinner is served, Sir."

It was Jim's quiet English voice from the doorway which seemed to restore them all to sanity.

'This can't really be happening,' Zaria thought to herself.

Yet she knew the feeling of Chuck's lips on hers was very real, the tingling thrill within her body was still there.

'I shall never be the same again,' she thought to herself as she walked into the dining saloon behind Madame Bertin and Kate.

Chuck was beside her and as he sat down he pressed her hand gently as if in reassurance. At his touch she felt herself tingle again. But when she looked at him, he was looking across the table at Kate and answering something she had said to him.

'It is all a pretence for him,' Zaria thought, and felt some of the glow and radiance die out of her.

She knew then that she had got to hold on to her common sense. Chuck didn't care for her. Why should he? He was only using her as a means to an end. She must be grateful for the sense of protection that he had afforded her so far. He certainly owed her nothing.

She was in debt to him, for without him she knew that her terror would have been far more intense, her fears would have been almost unbearable had she been alone.

Because everybody had had quite a lot to drink by now, dinner was a most uproarious meal. There was badinage and arguments and quite a battle of wits between Madame Bertin and Kate while the others applauded.

Only Zaria was silent. She could think of nothing but Chuck.

He had kissed her! She could not help wondering if it was the only kiss that she would have to remember for the whole of her life.

It was quite obvious that Kate was determined to get Chuck into her toils. If Victor had been convinced by the display of affection that he had shown towards Zaria, it had merely acted as a spur as far as Kate was concerned. She was determined to flirt with Chuck whether he wished it or not. She made what Zaria thought was a dead set at him.

Unhappily it seemed to amuse and even interest him.

"After dinner we will dance," Kate said looking across the table at Chuck.

"I can't do any of the newfangled dances," he answered.

"I'll teach you," she told him.

"*Toujours* you wish to teach," Madame Bertin snapped. "What about *un morceau* of learning for you?"

"On what subject?" Kate drawled, looking at her with scarcely veiled hostility.

"Why not try good manners—*la politesse?*" Madame Bertin enquired.

Kate made a rude face at her.

"You used to be amusing, Lulu," she said, "but now you have become just a big bore."

"*La, La!* I suit myself to the company I am in!" Madame Bertin replied. "Come, let us go into the other cabin!"

She rose and led the way, the others following— although Zaria noticed that Victor and Mr. Virdon stayed behind to pour themselves another liqueur before they left the dining saloon.

"I think perhaps I had better go to bed," Zaria said to Chuck in a whisper.

He shook his head.

"Not yet," he answered.

"I must speak . . ." she began, and then realised that Kate was listening.

"Put the radiogram on," she ordered Chuck.

"I warn you, I'm out of date," he replied, but he followed her across the saloon to the radiogram, leaving Zaria standing alone.

She stood for a moment, uncertainly, and then moved towards a chair and as she did so she saw herself in one of the mirrors. It was hard to believe it was her own reflection. She had never known before that she had a good figure, she had no idea that her eyes were so big or her neck so long.

"You look like a rather nice choir-boy or a very busy small angel," Madame Bertin had said.

At the thought of her words Zaria found herself smiling at her own reflection.

It was incredible what a difference Madame Bertin had made to her. The lovely, wide skirt billowing out from her tiny waist, the soft tulle round her shoulders, gave her an almost ethereal look, and for the first time she realised that perhaps, in contrast to the obvious voluptuousness of Kate, she might, in some very different way, seem attractive.

But not to Chuck! He was dancing now with Kate, swinging her round on the tiny patch of parquet floor from which they had rolled back the rugs.

The lights in the saloon were low, but not low enough to stop Zaria seeing that Kate's hand was pressed against the back of Chuck's neck and that she was nestling close against him, her cheek touching his.

Zaria felt suddenly that she could not bear to look, could not bear to stay in the same room.

She turned sharply and would have gone below to her own cabin if Madame Bertin had not put out her hand and beckoned her from the sofa on which she was sitting, a drink in her hand.

"Come and talk to me, *ma petite protégée*," she invited. "I was very proud of you tonight. You stunned them, as I knew you would."

"I was just thinking what a difference clothes can make," Zaria said.

"*Connu!* They are everything to a woman. They give her confidence and that is very important. *Ecoutez*, when a woman has faith in herself, she has won the first part of the battle."

Zaria looked across the room again at Chuck, and suddenly for a moment the dull pain in her heart seemed to lessen. Why should she give in so easily? she asked herself. Why should she let Kate have him?

He had kissed her—had that meant anything to him?

She felt herself quiver again at the thought, and something new seemed to be buoying her up. It was a courage that she had not known she possessed, a courage which she had thought had died many years ago beneath her father's blows.

'I will fight,' she thought. 'I will fight for him.' Impulsively she turned towards Madame Bertin. "*Madame,* I want to ask you something."

"*Qu'y a-t-il pour votre service, ma chérie?*" Madame Bertin enquired.

She had had quite a lot to drink and while she was not the least drunk like Victor, she was, Zaria saw, mellow and pleasant; the world seemed a rosy place and she was comfortably aware of the effects of a good dinner.

"I want you to let me be your first customer," Zaria said.

The words seemed to burst from her lips, not as if she were afraid to say them, but as if something within her forced them out.

"My first customer!" Madame Bertin repeated, raising her eyebrows.

"Yes." Zaria answered. "I want to buy a lot of your lovely clothes."

She saw Madame Bertin's eyebrows go up and went on talking:

"I can pay, I can promise you that. The only difficulty is that all I have with me at the moment is a cheque that Miss Mansford, the owner of this yacht, gave me before I left London. I think you will find that any bank will cash it, as she is . . . er . . . very rich. It is made out to me and. . . and, of course, I only have to endorse it."

The words came tumbling out and even as she

167

said them they sounded, to Zaria, rather strange. Madame Bertin seemed to take them quite seriously.

"*Tiens!* So you know the owner of *The Enchantress!*" she said. "*Je comprends* that is how you obtained the job."

"Yes, yes, that's it," Zaria agreed. "And she owed me for some previous work I had done for her. It's . . . it's quite a lot of money, as it happens—two hundred . . . pounds. She gave me the cheque and as I came away in a hurry I didn't have time to cash it. Will that be all right if I . . . give it to you?"

She said the sum in trepidation, feeling as she said it that she almost committed a crime. And yet Madame Bertin took it quite simply.

"Two hundred pounds," she said, "*C'est bon!* I can give you some very charming clothes for that—enough to fit you up for a few months at any rate. The cheque is on a good bank?"

"On a very good bank," Zaria said. "There is certain to be a branch of it in Algiers."

"That is excellent," Madame Bertin approved, then added quickly in a low voice: "Do not speak of this to the others, *vous comprenez?* Say nothing. I do not wish them to know that I take money from you."

"No, no, of course not," Zaria answered.

"I will choose some gowns for you tonight," Madame Bertin promised, "*et les autres* tomorrow morning. We arrive at Algiers about eleven o'clock."

"As early as that," Zaria answered. "I hadn't heard."

"That is what Edie was saying this evening. *Dites donc,* you will bring me the cheque tonight?"

"Yes, as soon as we go to bed," Zaria answered.

"*A votre aise.* Do not let the others see."

"No, no, I won't," Zaria promised.

She was about to say something else when Chuck came across the saloon towards her.

168

"Aren't you going to dance with me?" he asked.

She was so surprised that for a moment she could only look up at him in astonishment.

"I am afraid I . . . don't dance as . . . well as Kate," she managed to stammer at last.

"Does that matter?" he enquired. "Come and try to this tune; it's one of my favourites."

Half reluctantly Zaria let him lead her towards the small dance floor by the radiogram. Kate, she saw, had turned her back on them and she was sitting on the arm of Edie's chair pouring him out a drink. Victor was talking to Mr. Virdon.

She and Chuck seemed to be alone for the moment—unnoticed, forgotten. Because of it she ceased to act and became only herself.

"I don't dance well enough," she whispered. "Please, Chuck you needn't be polite."

"Do you think that's what I'm being?" he asked.

He pulled her into his arms as he spoke and started to dance. For a moment she stumbled, and then she relaxed.

There was something in the closeness in which he held her and in the clasp of his hand which told her what he was going to do without her having any knowledge of the steps, or indeed, of the music.

She only knew that the closeness of him made her feel a part of him. Because his arm was round her, she was in a heaven which swept away all the questions and the problems and the difficulties. Nothing else mattered.

She was close to him. She almost felt that she could hear his heart beating—or was it her own?

'If only I could die at this moment,' she thought suddenly, 'I should be happy.'

She had a sudden terror that tomorrow would come

169

too quickly. It would take him away from her and she would never see him again.

Algiers at eleven o'clock! At least she had until then; as least he was beside her and, for the moment, she was in his arms.

"Frightened?" he asked softly.

"Not at this moment," she answered.

"You look wonderful!"

She wanted to cry because she knew that his voice was quite sincere. They moved round and round again in silence, and then he said:

"Madame Bertin is a genius! I was always quite certain you could look like that, but I didn't quite know how it could be done."

"You are laughing at me," Zaria said.

He did laugh gently then.

"Just like all the British, you are afraid of compliments," he said. "I'm speaking the truth."

"There is something I must tell you," Zaria whispered.

"Be careful," he said, so softly that she hardly heard the words.

"I am, but how?"

"I don't know," he answered. "I will try to find a way."

The gramophone record came to an end and as Chuck went to put on another, Kate came shimmering across the room.

"Victor wants to dance with you, Zaria," she said.

"No, I am going to bed," Zaria said quickly.

"Une bonne idée," Madame Bertin remarked from the sofa. "I am going too. Better come to my cabin, Zaria, and let me help you off with that gown. It mustn't be spoilt, it's one of my best models."

"Good night, Chuck!"

Zaria turned towards him and as she did so realised that he had not wanted her to go. There was a little frown on his forehead as he answered:

"Good night, Zaria. Sleep well."

"Which is more than we shall do," Kate said. "Come on, Chuck. Let's make a night of it."

Zaria turned away suddenly sick at heart.

'What's the use of fighting?' she thought.

Kate was so much cleverer than she was. She realised now that it was absurd for her to leave Chuck and Kate together, to get out of the way, to go below where there was no chance of proving her rivalry.

The men by this time were talking at the far end of the saloon. They never even raised their heads as she slipped past them with Madame Bertin following her. When they had descended the companion-way, Madame Bertin said in what seemed to Zaria almost a stage whisper:

"The cheque, get it now!"

Zaria went to her own cabin and took out her cheque book. Very carefully she wrote out a cheque for two hundred pounds to 'Miss Zaria Brown' and signed it with her own name.

Two hundred pounds! She felt almost faint at the enormity of the sum. All that money to be spent on clothes! And yet she knew that having tasted the success of being attractive and having seen the difference that clothes made to her, she could never go back to wearing what she had worn before.

She had seemed different to Chuck, too, and that was what really mattered. Or did it? When they reached Algiers he would disappear to find his mother.

She felt suddenly as if she was travelling on an express train which was going quicker and quicker, and she couldn't stop it. Time was passing, the hours were going, and then Chuck would be gone.

She endorsed the cheque, folded it and crumpled it

a little as if it had been in her bag. Then she opened the door of her cabin and went along to Madame Bertin's.

"Here is the cheque," she said.

"Hush, *mon enfant!* Do not talk so loudly," Madame Bertin answered. "I have told you, I do not wish anyone to know that you have given it to me. I shall say you are going to pay me for the clothes out of your salary, a little bit every week. Is that understood?"

She looked at the cheque, reading the name of the bank and its address carefully.

"Zaria Mansford!" she said. "She has the same name as you."

"I . . . I was called after her," Zaria said.

Madame Bertin accepted the explanation without question. She put the cheque into her bag quickly and with what seemed to Zaria an almost greedy movement.

"That will pay for some charming gowns," she said. "Not the most expensive models, of course, but the copies and some of the simple dresses that I have brought for the hot weather. They will be a good buy."

Madame Bertin talked on, quite obviously absorbed in her favourite topic. Zaria was hardly listening to her. As she slipped the soft cloud of tulle from her shoulders and took off the rustling silk gown, she was wondering what was happening upstairs. Was Kate nestling against Chuck? Was he enjoying having her in his arms? Did he wish to kiss her?

She felt herself quiver at the thought. Somehow it was unbearable to think of Chuck's lips on Kate's full, red mouth. Kate would return his kisses, she thought. She would seek them greedily and graspingly, just as she gobbled up everything else which would give her hot, sensual body satisfaction.

172

"Did you not bring a *robe de chambre* with you?" Madame Bertin voice burst in on Zaria's thoughts.

"No, I'm afraid I didn't think of it," Zaria said.

"Then that had better be your first purchase," Madame Bertin said. "I have several of them here in washable cotton, very pretty, *très bon marché* and eminently suitable for a warm climate. *Voilà!* Here is one that will suit you, in soft pink with white flowers on it."

She drew it out of one of the cases lying open on the floor, and helping Zaria into it, wrapped it round her, and pulling the sash round her waist, tied it in a big bow.

"That is charming," she said. "You could not want anything prettier than that."

"No, nothing," Zaria agreed.

"And now you had better go to bed," Madam Bertin said. *"Vous êtes fatiguée.* I will look out all the things you want and the steward shall bring them to your cabin in the morning."

"Thank you," Zaria said, then added: "Thank you very much indeed. You have been so kind to me. I . . . I can never thank you enough."

"Pauvre petite!" Madame Bertin ejaculated. "You have suffered in your life, and you are suffering now. Do not be afraid. That stupid little Kate will not take him from you. She is nothing, that girl—just a body with an empty mind.

"He will find her out, as other men have found her out, and remember, a man never wants for long anything that comes too easily."

"Do you really think that?" Zaria asked.

"Je le crois bien," Madame Bertin said. "Men! They are all hunters at heart. They run after what they cannot get, and when they have got it—pouf!—

173

they don't want it. It is old, finished. They know it exactly for what it is."

"I wish I could believe you," Zaria said.

Madame Bertin smiled.

"Toujours l'amour," she said. "And love hurts so much! Yet that is the way one learns—by being hurt, by trying not to be hurt again, and by knowing that at the end it is so very worthwhile."

"Is that really true?" Zaria enquired.

Madame Bertin nodded.

"Thank you," Zaria said, and to her surprise kissed Madame Bertin on her cheek.

Then, to hide the tears that were welling into her eyes, she ran from the cabin towards her own.

She was tired and yet she did not go to bed. Instead, she sat in front of the dressing-table staring at her reflection, making no attempt to wipe away the make-up which Madame Bertin had put on her face or to take the mascara off her eyelashes.

She was studying herself perhaps for the first time in her life, trying to see her good points, trying to realise how she could improve and beautify herself— not for her own satisfaction, but for Chuck's.

She knew it was a hopeless dream, that he would never love her.

Yet she felt that just by being with him she could serve him and perhaps save him. From what she did not know. But she found herself thinking of all the ways in which she could assist him, she could lighten his troubles.

He needed money—she could give him some. That was the first thing and perhaps the easiest of the lot. But to do so she would have to reveal who she was and she shrank from doing that until the very last moment.

Yet to help him she would do anything, however

deep her embarrassment, however paralysing her shyness.

There might be more difficult things from which she must save him than merely the lack of money. She had not forgotten the sinister remarks made by Edie, the innuendo behind his words, the vague menace which lurked beneath every sentence.

Why they should want to get rid of Chuck she had no idea, and yet she was certain that they did. She must warn him and she must be ready to fight for him as she had fought tonight.

"I love you!"

She said the words humbly and felt almost ashamed of the deep, warm glow of happiness they brought her.

She was asking nothing in her love, only the privilege of being near Chuck for a little longer, of feeling his hand upon hers, the closeness of his broad shoulder, the calmness of his voice.

She remembered how he had said, "I love you," and how, for a moment, she had felt panic-stricken for she had not expected it. Now she dreamed, for a moment, that he said it to her in reality. And then, rising from the dressing-table, she laughed at herself.

How ridiculous she was being!

A different haircut, a new dress, didn't alter the fact that she was the ill-treated, undernourished girl who had come down, shivering with fright, from Scotland to learn that she had inherited a fortune. And when she had got the fortune, she didn't know what to do with it.

She felt again the agony it had been to enter the Cardos Hotel; how she had stammered and stuttered when she had asked the chambermaids to help her; how terrified she had been of staying there alone; and how, in desperation, she had taken Doris Brown's place and gone to Marseilles to board *The Enchantress*.

"She always enchants me!"

It seemed to her she could hear Chuck saying those words, and something within her cried out because they were not the truth but only a pretence and a façade to deceive the people who were listening.

It was Kate who should wear the word *Enchantress* emblazoned across her sweater. It was Kate, with her warm, red lips, who could enchant any man if she set her mind to it.

As if the whispering of her own jealousy were made aloud, Zaria put her fingers in her ears and walked up and down her cabin. Why should she mind? Why should she care? She had no right.

She and Chuck were only ships that pass in the night, as she had told him once; and although he had called her a mercy ship, it was she who had asked mercy from him, mercy to stay a little longer, to succour her a little further.

She looked at the electric clock on the cabin wall and saw that it was nearly one o'clock. Slowly she undressed, slipped into her nightgown and went to bed. It was no use waiting in the hope that she would hear the others coming below.

They were making a night of it, as Kate said, and nobody wanted her at that sort of party.

Suddenly her eyes filled with tears and resolutely she fought them away.

'I will not be sorry for myself,' she thought. 'Whatever happens, I have met Chuck; whatever the future holds, I love him, and I shall go on loving him all my life.'

She must have fallen asleep with that thought in her mind, for it seemed to her that the moment of sleeping and her dreams intermingled to leave her quite unsurprised when she opened her eyes and found Chuck sitting on her bed.

He put out a finger to lay it on her lips so that she should not make a sound. She only stared at him drowsily.

"We have got to be very quiet," he whispered, "in case the others hear us. This was the only way I could see you alone."

For a moment he seemed to be part of her dreams. His face was looking down at her and he had taken off his glasses so that she could see his eyes—those steady, grey eyes which seemed to look down into her very heart and see it beating there for him.

"Have you had a nice time?"

It wasn't what she meant to say, but somehow the words came to her lips, drowsily, warmly, happily as if it didn't matter because, after all, he was here now.

"I hated to wake you," he said. "You looked so young, so very young."

He spoke in a kind of wondering voice, and now at last she roused herself to look at the time and saw it was four o'clock.

"It's so late," she exclaimed.

"I didn't dare come before," he answered. "I thought they might still be awake."

With an effort she made herself remember what she had wanted to tell him.

"Listen," she began, and he bent his head until her lips were almost against his ear.

"Speak very softly," he said. "If they think I am here, they will either put a very unpleasant construction on it or think we are intriguing against them."

She told him quickly what she had heard while she was supposed to be asleep in Madame Bertin's cabin. She felt that it didn't surprise him, and when finally he raised his head and looked down into her eyes, she saw that he was smiling.

"You are not to worry yourself," he said. "Just leave everything to me."

"But, I do worry," she replied. "Supposing . . . supposing they do something to you?"

She paused a moment and then added:

"Perhaps it would be best, the moment we arrive in Algiers, if you slip away to find your mother."

It was the greatest sacrifice she could make, and yet, because she loved him, she made it. She was offering him a way of escape, a way out. She was suggesting that he should go away and leave her, at whatever cost to herself.

"Leave everything to me," he answered. "You are not to think about it. Just behave quite ordinarily, just be ready to act as secretary to Mr. Virdon."

"What about you?" she asked.

"I can look after myself," he said.

"And you will be . . . going away?"

"Not until I have to," he answered.

"What do you mean by that?"

"Let's leave it, shall we? When I have to go, I must go. Until then I shall be here with you."

"I don't understand," she complained.

"Does it matter?" he answered. "We are together— two of us against the rest. Isn't it that which is important?"

She knew it was and she knew he was right. Nothing else was of any consequence save the fact that they were together, that they could face things side by side.

"I'm afraid of losing you."

She would never have dared to say it in the daytime. Because she was drowsy, because it seemed so unreal to have him sitting there beside her on the bed, she said the words. In answer he put his hand against her cheek.

"You poor little thing," he said. "It is all very

178

bewildering, isn't it? And rather frightening, too. But don't you remember the story I told you about the stray dog? He picked me up and he was my dearest friend until he died. I have a feeling, Zaria, that you and I are going to be very great—friends."

She was not certain whether it was his words or the touch of his hand which made her feel almost lightheaded with happiness.

"All the same," she murmured, "I wish I understood what all this is about. I wonder why Mr. Virdon has such strange people around him? They are not good people, I'm sure of that."

"I'm sure of it, too," Chuck agreed. "Now I am going to leave you. All I want you to do is to go to sleep and not worry. Good night, Zaria."

He tucked her in as if she were a baby, then bent suddenly and laid his lips on her forehead. She wanted to say something, but he was too quick; he had gone from the cabin and the door had closed silently behind him before the words would come.

She listened to hear him go down the passage, but she heard nothing. And then she realised she was holding her breath.

He had kissed her! He had kissed her again and this time of his own free will.

Granted it was only the friendly, consoling kiss of a brother, but at least she had felt the touch of his lips again, at least she could believe he was sincere in the friendship that he had promised her.

"Oh, God! Thank you! Thank you!" she said aloud in the darkness, and felt the tears come into her eyes and, this time, start to roll softly down her cheeks.

They were tears of happiness—a happiness such as she had never known before. The happiness of believing that Chuck, whom she loved, was indeed her friend.

Chapter Nine

Zaria was awakened by Jim coming into her cabin with her breakfast. He set the tray down on the table beside her bed and pulled back the silk curtains from the portholes.

The sunshine came flooding in, touching everything in the cabin with fingers of gold. Zaria sat up and rubbed her eyes.

"Good morning, Jim," she said, and felt there was something strange.

For a moment she wondered what it was, then realised that the engines were silent.

"Why aren't we moving?" she asked.

"We're in port, Miss," he replied. "We reached Algiers at dawn this morning."

"I thought we weren't going to be there until eleven o'clock," Zaria cried.

"Oh, *The Enchantress* can put on a bit of speed if she wants," he answered. "Besides, whoever told you that Miss, must have been romancing. It only takes about fifty hours direct from Marseilles. Of course, we went out of our way to pick up *Madame* in Spain."

"But Madame Bertin said Mr. Morgan told her definitely we wouldn't be here until eleven o'clock," Zaria protested.

"I think Mr. Morgan had his reasons for saying such a thing, if you'll excuse me saying so, Miss," Jim said confidentially. "Well, here we are, and I must say it's good to see the old familiar landmarks. As I always says to the Cap'n, Algiers is one of the prettiest ports in the whole of the Mediterranean."

"I've always thought so, too," Zaria said absent-mindedly. She was thinking of Chuck, wondering what he was doing at the moment.

"I've got something here for you, Miss," Jim said with a smile.

He disappeared out of the cabin to return a moment later with his arms piled with clothes.

"*Madame* said I was to bring these in to you the moment you woke. There's another armful yet to come."

He set the clothes down on one of the chairs, disappeared, and re-appeared again with another pile.

"I'd better be bringing you some more coat-hangers," he said.

Zaria stared at the garments, taking in the colours—red, blue, green, white and a soft, silvery grey which must, she thought, be a travelling suit.

Now Jim was coming again with a box of shoes and a frothy nylon-edged petticoat which she knew was meant to go under the summer dresses with their brilliant, colourful patterns against a white or pastel ground.

"Getting quite a trousseau, aren't you, Miss?" Jim smiled.

For a second his words stabbed her. She was never likely to want a trousseau, she thought, and yet her thoughts were too busy to linger on her aching heart. She had other things to think about—for instance, what was going to happen to Chuck now they had arrived in Algiers.

"I must get up," she said impatiently.

"I'll start your bath running, Miss," Jim answered. "And by the way, the chef's compliments and he hopes you'll make a good breakfast."

181

He paused for a moment and then went on:

"We're all feeling very proud, Miss, that you're looking better. And, if you'll forgive my presumption, we all thought you looked wonderful last night."

"How sweet of you to say so!" Zaria blushed.

She remembered that she had noticed during dinner one or two faces peeping through the service hatch, but she had not realised that they were looking at her.

"The chef thinks it's all due to his broth," Jim said. "But I'm putting my faith in those pills of Mrs. Cardew's. There's no doubt at all, Miss, you're putting on a bit of weight."

"Oh, Jim, do you really think so?" Zaria asked, forgetting everything else for the moment in the sheer pleasure of receiving a compliment which she knew was sincere.

"Certain sure, Miss," Jim replied. "If you ask me I think we ought to get a weighing machine aboard and then we'll know exactly how much you're gaining every day."

"I think that would be a quite unnecessary extravagance," Zaria retorted, but she was laughing as Jim went from the cabin and she sprang out of bed.

It didn't take her long to bath and put on one of the pretty thin dresses which Jim had left on the chair. She felt a little shy of choosing one of the gayest of them, and instead picked out one of pale blue linen.

It had a short woollen coat to match in case the sunshine was offset by one of the chill little winds that so often blew in the Mediterranean.

She combed up her hair in the way that Madame Bertin had showed her, put a touch of colour on either of her cheeks, touched her eyelashes with mascara and, feeling strangely unlike herself, hurried out of the cabin.

It was only as she came up on deck and saw Mr. Virdon that she remembered that her first thought must be of him. He was, after all, her employer, and though she had done nothing to date to justify her salary, now was the moment when he might require her services.

"Good morning, Mr. Virdon!" she said. "Is there anything I can do for you?"

He gazed at her vaguely through his dark glasses as if, for a moment, he couldn't remember why she was there or why he should want her. Then, with a wave of his hand, he said:

"Find Edie. He was looking for you just now."

Zaria looked round the deck and saw, up in the prow, Edie Morgan and Victor talking with some important looking officials covered in gold braid. She hurried towards them. As she approached, Edie Morgan looked towards her with a frown between his eyes.

"There you are, Zaria," he said. "Try and make these men understand that Madame Bertin has already registered as a shopkeeper. They seem intent on believing we are merely tourists."

"Have you told them about Mr. Virdon?" Zaria asked.

Edie Morgan's eyebrows went up.

"About Virdon!" he said. "What about him?"

"That he is here as an archaeologist," Zaria replied.

"No, I hadn't thought of it," Edie answered.

Zaria turned to the two officials and speaking rather slowly, because her French was rusty, explained at some length who Mr. Virdon was and that it was his intention to start his explorations almost immediately.

As she had expected, the fact that he was both a genuine archaeologist and an American millionaire impressed them considerably. The officials were instantly all smiles and ready to help in every way they could.

"Mr. Virdon has brought Madame Bertin here as an act of friendship," Zaria went on. "She is a *couturière* of great consequence in Paris and her creations will obviously be of great benefit to the shopping facilities of the town."

Again there were smiles, promises of help.

"*Ma'm'selle* is obviously wearing one of *Madame's* gowns," one of the officials remarked with a gallantry that was characteristic of his race.

"Yes, that is so," Zaria agreed.

"Then we know that *Madame* will be sincerely welcomed by all the women in Algiers," the official replied.

Zaria smiled at him and explained to Edie, in English, that everything would be all right.

"The clothes, of course, must go through the Customs," she said. "But these kind gentlemen will see there is as little delay as possible. They would now like to make a small tour of the ship."

"A mere formality," one of the officials said, and Zaria translated this as well.

"Perhaps it would be best for the Captain to take them round," she suggested. "In the meantime, I am sure they would appreciate a cup of coffee or a drink."

Edie and Victor took the hint and hurried off to fetch the Captain and to order Jim to bring coffee and a bottle of cognac to the saloon immediately. Zaria explained what was happening to the officials.

"That is most gracious," they replied. "Is this *Ma'm'selle's* first visit to Algiers?"

Zaria shook her head.

"I was here some years ago," she answered. "But I have not forgotten how beautiful it is."

184

"You are to work with Mr. Virdon on the excavations?" the other official enquired.

Zaria nodded.

"If you will give me the passports, I will see that they are all checked and returned to you immediately," the official said. "It will save time, *Ma'm'selle,* and Mr. Virdon can be assured that every possible facility will be put at his disposal."

"That will be very kind," Zaria smiled.

She saw the Captain approaching, introduced him to the officials, then went in search of Edie. He was in the saloon having a drink himself.

"The officer would like the passports and he will get them all stamped immediately," she said. "Shall I collect them?"

"I'll do it, Miss," Jim said.

He had been hovering near the door obviously interested in what she had to say.

"Thank you, Jim," Zaria replied.

To her surprise she found Edie was scowling.

"Is that usual?" he said. "This passport racket?"

"But, of course," Zaria answered. "You can't enter any country without going through the Customs and the passport controls. What about getting Madame Bertin's luggage ashore?"

"No hurry for that," Edie snapped.

"But I thought you wanted to get to her shop . . ." Zaria began.

"I said there was no hurry," Edie snapped. "Take it easy, can't you?"

Zaria subsided into silence, feeling that there was no reason for him to shout at her, and at that moment Jim came back into the saloon with a pile of passports in his hand.

"I've got hold of everyone's, including yours, Miss,

185

with the exception of Mr. Tanner's," he said. "He will have taken his ashore with him."

"Ashore!" Zaria said quickly. "Has he gone ashore?"

"Yes, Miss. Went off as soon as we'd docked."

"Here, what's that?" Edie Morgan asked. "Who said anyone could go ashore? I thought nobody was allowed off."

"Anyone can go ashore, sir, as long as they go through the Customs office."

"Where's the damned fellow gone?" Edie asked. "He should have told me. No right to go rushing off like that. I don't like it. Where did he say he was going?"

"He didn't say, Sir."

"Did he tell you?" Edie enquired, glaring at Zaria. She shook her head.

"No, I had no idea that he would get the opportunity of going ashore. If you remember, last night you told Madame Bertin we shouldn't be in port until eleven o'clock."

"Did I?"

Edie asked the question unconvincingly and she had the feeling that he had known all the while that they would be in earlier.

"Anyway, he's got a nerve going off without a word to anyone," he continued. "I thought he was here to help you."

Unless Edie was a very good actor, Zaria thought, he genuinely had no idea where Chuck had gone and why he had left the ship. It was somehow consoling to know that he had nothing to do with it, and yet she could not help feeling anxious and worried.

Supposing Chuck had left her? Supposing, having reached Algiers, he had got exactly what he wanted and gone hurrying off to his mother without troubling any more about her or the strange people with whom they had been travelling?

She somehow could not believe that he would do such a thing, and yet he had gone without leaving a note or even a message for her. She could not help her spirits dropping and a feeling of depression seep over her.

At the same time, she told herself, he was bound to come back. She could not believe that he would just disappear like that for no reason.

The officials, having made a perfunctory tour of the ship, came in for their coffee and cognac.

Their English was very difficult to understand, so it was easier for Zaria to interpret any conversation Edie and Victor wished to have with them.

She was surprised that Mr. Virdon did not join them. He was still on deck doing, so far as she could see, nothing. And yet he made no attempt to come into the saloon.

'Perhaps he is shy,' she thought to herself.

Although he was rather morose and spoke very seldom, she did not feel that his reticence was due to shyness. He was a strange man, she thought, and she did not understand him. It was stranger still that he never seemed to give an order himself but always left everything to Edie.

The officials rose to leave. With much politeness and bowing they went from the yacht, taking the pile of passports with them.

"Well, let's hope that's all O.K." Edie said doubtfully, turning to Victor.

"They certainly didn't seem to pick on any snag," Victor answered.

"Is that the last of these goddam'd snoopers?" Edie asked.

He had hardly said the words when he seemed to realise that Zaria was there, and turned upon her quickly.

187

"Run down and tell Madame Bertin to come up if she's dressed." he commanded.

"Very well," Zaria replied.

She went from the saloon, but as she shut the door she heard Victor say:

"You preach to us, Edie. Getting to be a bit indiscreet yourself, aren't you?"

What was all the mystery about? Zaria wondered, and she went below and knocked on Madame Bertin's cabin door.

"Entrez!" Madame's rather thick voice called, and Zaria entered to find her sitting in front of the dressing-table making up her lips.

"Bonjour, ma chère," she said. "Let me look at you this morning."

She turned round to face Zaria in the sunlight coming through the porthole.

"C'est charmante!" she exclaimed. "But you are still a little pale. You need a little more rouge. Just a *soupçon,* but enough to give your cheeks the colour they should have when one is as young as you are. And that dress, it is *délicieuse,* so simple, so fresh. Nothing could be more suitable. Turn round!"

Zaria did as she was told.

"Ah! There is no doubt I am a genius when it comes to creating the clothes for the sunshine," Madame Bertin went on. "The clothes for the cold weather— *hélas!* then I am not so good."

"I think the clothes you have chosen for me are lovely," Zaria said. "But I haven't had time to look at them all. I didn't expect we should arrive so early."

"Nor I," Madame Bertin replied. *"Mais je suis contente.* What is happening on deck?"

Zaria told her about the officials who had been so polite and offered to help in every way.

"They are impressed by Mr. Virdon," she said.

188

"They are delighted when American millionaires visit Algiers. They think it brings money into the town and if his excavations are successful there will be more money still—tourists and other archaeologists flock to look at a new find."

"You sound very enthusiastic, *ma petite*," Madame Bertin remarked. "Do you really enjoy this—what do they call it?—digging?"

"It is very exciting," Zaria said.

She hesitated and then she said:

"I only wish Mr. Virdon seemed more enthusiastic. We haven't yet had a talk about what he is going to do. He doesn't seem to want to discuss it somehow."

Madame Bertin turned round again to her dressing-table.

"*Ne souciez pas!*" she said consolingly. "I expect he will be keen enough when the time comes."

She picked up her big pearl ear-rings and screwed them into her ears.

"What are the plans for today?"

"I have no idea," Zaria answered. "I thought that Mr. Morgan would want to get your clothes ashore, but he said there was no hurry."

"No, of course not. There is no hurry," Madame Bertin said. "I will view the shop first and see that it is ready for my beautiful creations."

"I hadn't thought of that!" Zaria exclaimed. "Of course, Mr. Morgan is quite right. If the painters have not finished and if there are any other alterations to be done, the clothes are much safer where they are."

"*Je suis prête,*" Madame Bertin said. "Get me my scarf from the cupboard—the blue one which matches this dress."

Zaria did as she was told and then, following in Madame's wake, went up on deck.

It was the first time that she had been able to have

a look at their surroundings. There were ships of every size and description in the beautiful semi-circular harbour, and behind it the white, flat-topped buildings rose tier upon tier towards the great fortress where the old bronze cannons still watched over the harbour.

Zaria knew the fort was where the old Beys had lived. But it wasn't only the beauty of Algiers which seemed to catch at her throat.

It was almost like coming home to feel the memories of when she had been here last crowding in upon her—the sand, getting into one's clothes whatever one did; the sound of workmen singing as they dug, the pieces of pottery being assembled in the sunshine; the breathless moment when a new find was unearthed.

She could remember it all, recalling only the happiness of it rather than the moments when her father's rages distorted everything into a nightmare of unhappiness, violence and cruelty.

She could remember the little donkeys she had fed and petted, the women she had talked to—shrouded and mysterious with only their eyes showing above their yashmaks until they drew them aside to show the high cheekbones, the blue-black hair and the kohl encircled eyes of one of the Ouled Naïls.

How exciting it had all been, and now her heart was beating faster again because she was back.

She didn't realise that she was standing alone on deck. Madame Bertin had left her and gone into the saloon. On the quay a little crowd of Arabs, children and ragged beggars were staring at the ship.

She was lost in a fairyland of her own and saw nothing but the sunshine and the great stretches of empty desert winding away into a cloudless blue sky.

This was Africa—a land which until this moment she had not known was so much a part of herself.

It was then, almost as if he were part of her dream, she saw Chuck coming up the gang-way. For a moment she could only stare at him, and then with a little cry of joy she sprang forward to run towards him.

"Oh, Chuck, where have you been? I was so worried, I was so afraid you would not come back."

"Did you really think I would do such a thing?" he asked.

"I . . . wasn't sure. Why didn't you tell me you were going?"

"I guessed you were asleep," he answered. "And, besides, I didn't particularly want to advertise my intentions. I had to go ashore."

"Edie's angry," she said.

"Is he?"

Chuck merely looked amused.

"They are in the saloon now," Zaria went on. "He found out you had gone when the officials asked for our passports."

"Is there any trouble about them?" Chuck enquired.

Zaria shook her head.

"Not that I know of. They haven't come back yet."

"Well, mine has been passed at any rate," Chuck said. "So that needn't worry anyone. And now, what are the plans?"

"I don't know," Zaria answered. "Madame Bertin is talking of going ashore to see her shop. I offered to help Mr. Virdon, but he didn't seem to want me."

"I shouldn't be too insistent," Chuck suggested. "He will start working in his own time."

"Yes, I suppose so," Zaria answered humbly.

"And now let's face the headmaster," Chuck said with a twist of his lips.

He walked across the deck and opened the door of the saloon. Edie looked up and said angrily:

"Ah, here you are, Tanner. Where the heck have you been?"

"Ashore," Chuck answered. "Any objections?"

"A great many. Why didn't you tell us you were going?"

"I really didn't think of it," Chuck answered. "As a matter of fact there was somebody I particularly wanted to see."

"Who?"

The question rang across the saloon like a pistol shot.

"Just a friend," Chuck answered. "No-one of any consequence. Just a friend, and if we'd got in, as you told us we were going to, at eleven o'clock, we should have missed each other!"

"Who was it?" Edie asked.

Again the question sounded almost menacing as if it came from the point of a gun.

For a moment Chuck didn't answer. Then he said in almost a deprecating manner:

"Excuse me if I seem to hesitate. As a matter of fact it is rather a personal matter. The friend I wanted to see was . . . well . . . a lady."

It seemed to Zaria as if Edie relaxed. There was even a hint of amusement in his eyes as he said:

"So that's why you were so mysterious?"

"Exactly! You must see that you are making it rather embarrassing for me," Chuck replied.

"If you had been open with me, I shouldn't have been curious," Edie said. "But let me make this quite clear. No-one on this ship is to go off or move about without asking my permission. You and Zaria are employed to work for us, and now we are at Algiers there's a lot to do."

"Would you like us to engage transport and work-men to help with the excavation?" Zaria asked. "It is best to book them as far in advance as possible, otherwise the best are always snapped up by some-one else."

"Well, I think that's quite an idea," Edie said. "You and your young man get busy on that at once. Or, rather, on second thought, let Tanner do that. I think I shall want you, Zaria, to do a little in-terpreting for me."

"Yes, of course," Zaria said trying not to sound disappointed that she shouldn't go with Chuck.

"You get busy then, Tanner, and make all the ar-rangements," Edie said.

"It sounds all right," Chuck answered, "but wouldn't it be a good idea if Mr. Virdon told us where he wanted to go and what he was actually planning to do? It's quite a wide field, you know."

Edie scowled at him.

"The trouble with you, Tanner, is that you ask too many questions," he said. "You get the diggers—or whatever they are called—and leave the rest to Mr. Virdon. By the way, where are these people found?"

"I'm told there is a bureau which deals with them near the Sidi M'Hamed Mosque," Chuck answered. "I will go there and see what I can do."

"Wait a few moments and I'll come with you," Victor said.

"That will be fine," Chuck answered.

Zaria saw a look pass between Victor and Edie. She did not understand what it meant or what they were trying to convey to each other. She had the strange feeling that they were waiting for something, just sitting around playing for time.

Yet there didn't seem any sense in such an idea because they had wanted to come to Algiers and here they were.

"What about a drink?" Edie said.

Madame Bertin, who had been sitting in a chair staring at her fingernails, replied:

"I want some coffee, black coffee and—*ma foi*—see that it's hot."

Edie rang the bell and when Jim appeared gave the order.

"Would everybody like coffee, Sir?" Jim enquired.

"I'll have some," Chuck replied, while the others seemed uninterested except Edie who added:

"And a bottle of Scotch, and make it snappy."

'Why were they so jumpy and on edge?' Zaria wondered. And then as Jim went from the room, she heard the low voice of a sailor speaking to him outside. He came back into the saloon.

"There is a man here, Sir, who says he has a message for Mr. Morgan."

"Show him in. Show him in at once," Edie said, springing out of his chair and seeming galvanised into life.

There was a pause and a silence in which no-one spoke, and then into the saloon came a small, thin little man with a fez on his head and a peculiar, half Eastern, half European get-up which ended with his feet being encased in brown boots.

"A message for Mr. Morgan," he said in a singsong voice, smiling at the assembled company.

"Give it to me," Edie commanded.

He took a piece of paper out of the man's hand, read it, then said abruptly:

"There's no answer."

The little man with the fez still stood waiting expectantly.

"I think," Chuck said in an amused voice, "the messenger is expecting to be rewarded for his services."

"What's that?" Edie enquired. "Oh, give him a dollar, if anyone's got one."

"I have some French money," Chuck said, and threw the man a hundred *franc* piece which he caught in the air and with a salaam vanished through the cabin door.

Zaria could see that both Madame Bertin and Victor were watching Edie. And then, while they waited for him to speak, she felt Chuck's hand on her arm.

"Come with me," he said quietly.

The other people in the saloon made no attempt to stop them as they went. Chuck led her across the deck until they were out of earshot.

"What's it all about?" she asked.

"I don't know," he answered. "And I don't want you to get mixed up in it either. I am wondering if it would be better for you to come away with me now, at this moment."

"Come away with you? Leave the ship?" Zaria asked. "But, why? I can't do that."

"But I am worried about you," he said.

"There is no need to be," Zaria answered. "I know they are strange and extraordinary people and I think they are doing something which is wrong, although I am not certain what it is. But you are the only person who is in any danger. I think if anyone ought to go, it should be you."

Even as she said it she realised what it cost her to say the words, to tell him to go away, to ask him to leave her alone.

"I can look after myself," Chuck answered. "And I will look after you if it's humanly possible."

"What are you afraid of?" Zaria asked. "Chuck, please tell me, tell me the truth. What do you think these people are doing?"

"I can't tell you that," Chuck answered. "Just trust me to try and do the right thing."

195

"What about your mother?" she asked.

"My mother is much better," he answered quickly. "I telephoned her when I left the ship this morning."

"So that's what you went to do," Zaria said.

She hadn't realised until that moment how the thought of another woman—Chuck's lady friend—had been weighing heavily on her thoughts. Now, suddenly, it was as if a little cloud sped away in front of the sun and everything was golden again.

"Of course," he answered, "but I couldn't tell them so, could I? I have a feeling they wouldn't like me to have relations in Algiers."

"They are mysterious, aren't they?" Zaria said. "I wish I knew what was behind it all and why Mr. Virdon is so peculiar."

"Don't worry," Chuck said. "I have told you before, leave the worrying to me. And now I am going off to get some porters, as soon as Victor condescends to be ready."

Almost as if his thoughts had communicated themselves to the people inside the saloon, as he spoke the last words the door opened and Victor put his head round.

"Tanner!" he shouted. "Tanner! Where are you?"

Chuck walked back towards the saloon followed by Zaria. They had left three people silent, inactive. Now all three seemed to be filled with impatience and a desire to get going.

"Tanner, you and Victor get off at once about these porters," Edie ordered. "And on the way drop Madame Bertin at the shop. Zaria, you are to come with me."

Edie seemed almost like a general deploying his troops, and there was no question of the fact that they were ready to obey him. Chuck, Victor and Madame Bertin set off at once, while Edie went round to the other side of the yacht to look for Mr. Virdon.

Zaria ran below to get her coat in case it was cold, and as she came on deck again, she heard Edie saying:

"For Pete's sake look interested even if you're not. There's a hell of a lot to do and we can't afford to slip up having got as far as this."

"I can't see why you want me to come along," she heard Mr. Virdon say. "There's nothing I can do."

"For crying out loud!" Edie sounded angry. "You can look the part, can't you . . ." He stopped suddenly as he saw Zaria.

"Hurry up," he said as if she had kept him waiting. "We haven't got all day to waste."

They went ashore, hailed a taxi and drove away from the harbour. They travelled through broad streets crowded with traffic until they came to the entrance to the Kasba, where they dismissed the taxi.

Here the narrow winding streets shaped like defiles, dark and frequently vaulted over, climbed aimlessly up-hill. There were sinister windowless houses, mysterious doorways and an incongruous medley of stalls.

The people were moving so closely together that it was hard to get through the crowds. There were shouts, smells, noise. Moorish cafés with men sitting outside playing chess, craftsmen embroidering leather, cobblers, women pounding coffee with heavy lead pestles in stone mortars, weavers working on low-warp looms.

Merchants were also selling strange foods which made Zaria long to stop and stare.

On one stall small spits full of liver, kidneys and little red sausages sizzled on an open-air stove. On another an old man struck with his knife on the edges of a great iron plate laden with pastry and called in a high shrill voice:

"La calentita! La calentita!"

It all seemed to Zaria like a picture from the Arabian Nights as they walked down first one alley and then another, seemingly to lose their way in the labyrinths of a human-filled maze. There were booths glittering with native jewellery, others hung with rich silks and brocades.

There were dark eyes which stared at them from behind yashmaks and little boys who ran beside them crying for alms.

Still they moved on. She thought at first that Edie, who strode ahead, was walking at random, and then she realised that he had a piece of paper in his hand which he consulted every now and then. On one occasion when he stopped she drew near enough to look round his shoulder. When she did so she realised that the piece of paper he had was the same one that the messenger had brought him. It was not a message but a map. Made by hand, it was in fact little more than a rough drawing.

Zaria longed to ask Edie about it, but Mr. Virdon, trailing behind him, said nothing but merely walked with his hands deep in the pockets of his white trousers. Somehow she felt it was presumptuous for her to ask questions if he was prepared to accept Edie's leadership without comment.

Still they went on—another twist, another turn— and now they stopped in front of a low booth which displayed innumerable slippers of tooled leather.

There were also bags and belts and anything which could be ornamented with the elaborate designs of the native craftsmen.

The merchant—an Arab—wearing elaborate native dress, bowed low.

"You require shoes, very beautiful shoes for the lady, for yourself?" he asked in English. "I have many to show."

Edie did not reply, but just gave him a glimpse of the piece of paper that he held in his hand. The man glanced quickly up and down the street behind them and then beckoned them into the booth.

It was nothing more than a tiny room made of curtains. The shopkeeper pulled aside a hanging of ornamental leather and Zaria saw that behind it was a door studded with nails.

There was a moment's pause and then the door swung inwards.

"Quickly! Do not delay," the merchant entreated.

Bending his head, Edie went through the door followed by Mr. Virdon.

Just for a moment Zaria hesitated. Then she looked up at the Arab. There was a smile on his lips but his expression made her suddenly afraid.

Greed and avarice were written vividly and unmistakably on his face as he watched the unconscious backs of the two Americans passing through the small dark door.

Chapter Ten

Zaria bent her head to pass through the door and to her surprise found herself in a little courtyard.

It was not what she had expected, but now she remembered that so many of the Arab houses had them and this must have originally opened on to the street before the shoe booth was placed in front of it.

There was a tiny fountain spraying its water high in the air and the dark green leaves of palm trees waved against the arches and mosaic ornamented balconies which overlooked it.

But the high houses surrounding the courtyard seemed, with their shuttered windows, to be curiously like blind people and the shadows were very dark in contrast to the golden patches of sunlight.

"Make haste!"

The words were spoken in Arabic by their guide. Zaria pulled herself together and realised that while she was staring about her Edie and Mr. Virdon were waiting for her under a pointed archway.

"The man says 'make haste,'" she translated, feeling that it was somehow unnecessary, for the very tone of the Arab's voice was enough to tell them what he had said.

"Then for Pete's sake come on!" Edie ejaculated, and she saw, to her surprise, that he was nervous.

He was looking apprehensively over his shoulder. His dark, suspicious eyes were searching everything, even the roughly plastered ceiling above them.

"He wants you to follow him," Zaria said indicating

the Arab who was standing with outstretched hand pointing the way through an iron-studded door.

"I can see that," Edie snarled and, almost beneath his breath, asked:

"Do you think it's all right, Corny?"

In answer Mr. Virdon shrugged his shoulders and Zaria thought he was the only calm person amongst them.

'Why is he involved in all this?' she asked herself. 'Nothing seems to worry him or affect him in any way, and yet he allows all these things to happen, as it were, in his name.'

She wished she knew the answer to the problem, but there was no time for speculation for they were moving forward. The Arab disappeared through the doorway, Edie followed and Mr. Virdon walked after him without any pretence of inviting Zaria to go first because she was a woman.

She was thankful for their bad manners.

It gave her time to collect herself and wonder, as she had wondered before in Arab houses, whether they were being peeped at from behind the slatted shutters by curious, dark eyes.

The room in which they now found themselves was small and low and hung with silk rugs. There were several fat cushions arranged round a big brass tray.

Very little light was coming from the window, which seemed to be obscured by the palms and ferns outside, and there was the faint, unmistakable smell of musk and sandalwood and with it the inevitable fragrance of coffee.

The Arab salaamed.

"Pray honour this poor house, my masters, by seating yourselves."

Zaria translated the words and almost reluctantly, as if he felt he committed himself to something, Edie lowered himself on to one of the cushions. Zaria had a sudden desire to laugh. He looked so incongruous, so out of place.

She didn't know why, but it tickled her sense of humour to see Edie in these elaborate surroundings when he would have been obviously so much more at home propping up a bar.

Mr. Virdon, too, in his yachting clothes looked almost ridiculous and she wondered if she, too, appeared a figure of fun as she seated herself on a leather cushion tooled by a native craftsman into innumerable intricate designs.

"Do you think he is here?"

It was Mr. Virdon who broke the silence.

"He'd darned well better be," Edie answered. "After all the trouble we've had to get here."

"One never knows with natives," Mr. Virdon replied.

As if the waiting was too much for him Edie turned almost savagely to Zaria.

"Ask the man if the Sheik is here," he said.

"What is his name?" Zaria enquired.

"What's that got to do with you?" Edie retorted.

"I, personally, am not in the least interested," Zaria answered coldly, "but it is impolite to ask someone in Arabic without mentioning his name. They expect it, and you must remember the language is very flowery."

"Very well then," Edie said. "Ask for Sheik Ibrahim ben Kaddour. He arranged to meet us here."

Zaria turned to the Arab watching them from the doorway. He, too, was nervous, she thought, and guessed, though she was not certain, that he was not of much importance.

"The American gentlemen are asking when Sheik Ibrahim ben Kaddour is to delight them with his presence," she said in Arabic.

She was relieved to find that, though she had not used the language for so long, the phraseology and the words she required came easily to her tongue.

To her surprise the man seemed almost startled at her words. Bowing politely, with his eyes shifting from side to side, he hurried away.

"Perhaps he's gone to find him," Edie said.

"Who is the Sheik?" Zaria enquired.

"You mind your own business," Edie snapped, and then added, as if the thought had suddenly struck him:

"Everything that goes on here is of the utmost secrecy, you realise that? Mr. Virdon is paying you for your loyalty. You are not to breathe a word to anyone of what you hear or what is said. Is that understood?"

Instead of being frightened Zaria merely felt rebellious at the way he was speaking to her.

Perhaps it was her new appearance which made her so brave; perhaps it was because she was feeling well fed and better in health than she had been for years.

Yet she was almost astonished to hear her voice so defiant and firm as she said:

"Loyalty is not a thing that can be bought. At the same time, I should not think of discussing Mr. Virdon's private affairs with anyone so long as I am in his employ."

To her utter astonishment Edie crumpled up.

"See here, Zaria. We're friends, you know that. We don't want no trouble, any of us—isn't that right, Corny?"

"I think Zaria is being very helpful," Mr. Virdon said in his quiet manner. "You jumped down her throat, Edie, when she asked you a simple question, and nobody cares for that sort of thing."

"O.K. I apologise," Edie said hastily.

There were footsteps and they all stiffened and looked towards the door, but it was only the same Arab returning, this time carrying three cups of coffee on a tray. He offered them round with much ceremony and then sprinkled rose water on their hands.

"It's the custom," Zaria said quickly in an aside to Edie, who looked suspicious and obviously wished to refuse the pleasantry.

"What's the delay?" he asked. "Can't you ask him that?"

"Nobody ever hurries out here," Zaria answered. "The Sheik may be waiting to impress us with his importance, or he may have other reasons. They are always slow. Time does not count."

"Hell's bells! To the devil with them!" Edie ejaculated.

Zaria had the impression that he was more frightened than angry and his voice lacked substance and emphasis.

They sipped their coffee which Zaria thought was rather nasty, and then, through another entrance to the room which had been hidden by a curtain, an Arab entered. They all turned to face him and Edie sprang to his feet.

"Sheik Ibrahim?" he enquired eagerly, but the man shook his head.

He was young and rather good-looking. His golden skin was an effective contrast to his white robes and black burnous. His eyes had that strange, alert brilliance which Zaria had noticed before was characteristic of the Arabs who lived in the desert and who did not indulge in the debilitating riotous living of the town.

"My cousin very sad . . . unable come," the newcomer said slowly in broken English.

"Then when can we see him?" Edie asked.

"He not . . . come here," was the answer.

The Arab seated himself on a cushion, clapped his hands and almost like magic another cup of coffee was brought to him.

"You have . . . nice journey from . . . America?" he enquired politely.

"Let's get down to business," Edie said sharply. "I want to see your cousin, Sheik Ibrahim. He promised to meet us as soon as we arrived. Why is he not here?"

"My cousin send greetings, but . . . him not enter town . . . not safe!"

"But, that's ridiculous!" Edie exploded. "Unless, of course, you are going to manage his business for him."

"No business . . . without cousin," the Arab answered.

He sat there smiling as if he found the situation amusing, and Zaria suddenly had the feeling that he was playing a game, that he was matching his wits against Edie's and, as far as she could make out, winning.

Edie suddenly brought his fist down with a crash on the brass table, making the coffee cups jump and clatter.

"This is no time for playing about," he said. "I insist that the Sheik meets me immediately, or else the goods we have brought him go back to America."

The Arab looked puzzled.

"Please, I not understand."

Zaria translated the words quickly. She hesitated for a moment over the word "goods," wondering if the Arab would understand. But it was obvious from the expression on his face that it meant more to him than her.

"My cousin very pleased you come," he said. "But everything difficult, very difficult."

"Ask him what he suggests then," Edie said impatiently to Zaria.

She put the question to the Arab and it struck her that this was what he had been waiting for.

"My cousin suggest you come Timpassa," he said. "Plenty places dig there—very interesting. Very fine new temple. Bring goods with you."

Edie's eyes narrowed.

"Tell him I may be a fool," he said to Zaria, "but I'm not such a damned fool as that."

Zaria looked at him helplessly.

"I can't translate that," she said. "Besides, it sounds rather rude."

"I mean to be rude," Edie answered. "Now, tell him to get this straight. We don't move out of this town until the proper arrangements are made. He'll know what I mean."

Zaria repeated his words. The Arab bowed his head almost as if he was defeated, and then he said:

"I tell my cousin. You come tonight . . . Salem's House . . . see dancing girls. You get message there. Not safe . . . come here."

"O.K.!" Edie said rising to his feet. "But tell the Skeik if he doesn't want what I have brought, there are plenty of other people who will take them. He's not the only pebble on the beach."

"Please, I do not understand."

Again Zaria translated Edie's words but much more politely. Again the Arab bowed and she had the impression that he was enjoying this exchange of wits and that things had gone exactly as he had expected they would.

"And now let's get out of here," Edie said.

He turned towards the door by which they had come in.

"No, go other way," the Arab said. "We very careful. Perhaps the police and soldiers watch!"

He made a signal to the Arab who had originally shown them into the room and the man led the way through the curtained aperture through which the Sheik's cousin had entered and down a narrow, twisting passage that was almost dark.

They then passed through another courtyard where no fountain played, but there was only garbage left lying about beside unattended plants and bits of broken furniture.

Here there was a door in the wall and almost before they knew what was happening they had passed through it and it was closed behind them.

They were in a narrow alleyway, dirty and empty, leading, for perhaps fifty yards between the high, windowless houses until it came to a flight of steps.

These plunged downwards until, twisting and turning, Zaria saw ahead the closely packed crowd and the brightly coloured booths.

Neither Edie nor Mr. Virdon said anything until they had all managed to extricate themselves from the jostling mob and emerged into one of the main streets of the town. Then they hailed a taxi and, getting in, told the driver to take them to the port.

"Phew!" Mr. Virdon took off his yachting cap and wiped his brow. "It was hot in there."

"Damned waste of time," Edie said angrily. "Dragging us all that way to tell us precisely nothing."

"I am afraid you will always find the Arabs are like that," Zaria explained. "They seldom come to the point and wouldn't think of doing business the first time they meet you.

"To them business of any sort is an intricate, amusing game—it occupies hours, days and sometimes weeks of everybody's time to buy the simplest thing.

They don't want to be hurried; they don't even want money if it means having to scramble for it."

"If they think they are going to play us about, they are very much mistaken," Edie said savagely.

"It's no use working yourself up," Mr. Virdon said. "You can't alter the whole nation, Edie—if that's the way they want to play the hand, why kick against the pricks? We're in no hurry."

"I am," Edie said briefly.

"Well, as Zaria says, you're not likely to get anywhere. They want to do it their way."

"You'd think the damned fools would be only too eager . . ." Edie began.

Then seemed to remember that Zaria was present and stopped abruptly.

"O.K.!" he said. "We'll go to this place tonight. If Sheik Ibrahim isn't there, I'll take the roof off."

Mr. Virdon suddenly bent forward and closed the glass window behind the taxi driver's back.

"I've an idea it would be wiser not to mention names," he said.

"The Sheik you are seeking may have quite a wide reputation in the town. Wouldn't it be wiser to find out something about him?" Zaria asked.

Edie turned on her at once.

"Will you shut up?" he said. "You're here to translate what we want to say, not to make suggestions. And, remember, you're not to mention anything that's happened to anyone—and that includes that young man of yours."

"You can trust Chuck," Zaria answered. "He also is working for Mr. Virdon, as I am."

"Not as far as I'm concerned," Edie answered. "So we're trusting you, and you're not to tell him nothing."

Zaria wanted to argue, but the taxi was already

pulling up at the quay. They got out. There was a sailor on duty at the gangway and she remembered that the Captain had said that in harbour they had to guard against pilferers and thieves who were ready to take anything from an expensive looking yacht, however trivial, however useless to themselves.

The sailor saluted smartly.

"Mr. Jacobetti back?" Edie enquired.

"Yes, sir, he's in the saloon."

Edie turned immediately towards the saloon and Zaria followed him. She wanted to see Chuck. She wanted him with a sudden longing which told her that whatever was happening, however dramatic or eventful things might be, part of her mind was with him—thinking of him, loving him.

She knew now, with a sudden constriction of her heart, that she was half afraid that he would not be there. Supposing something had happened to him? Supposing they had "dealt" with him? It sounded so ridiculous and dramatic and yet she was afraid of Edie—afraid both of him and Victor Jacobetti. She had a feeling that neither of them would stop at anything which interfered with their plans.

But Chuck was sitting in the saloon beside Victor. As Edie entered, he got slowly to his feet.

"Well, we've ordered all the stuff," Victor answered. "It's going to cost a pretty penny, I can tell you that. Tanner insisted on having the very best. He said it came cheaper in the end."

"The end of what?" Edie asked sourly, pouring himself out a large whisky from a bottle which stood near Victor.

"How did you make out?" Chuck asked, as Victor did not seem inclined to answer Edie's question.

Edie took a long drink and then he said:

"I want to speak to Victor alone. Can you and

Zaria make yourselves scarce? You've an office in which to sit."

"But, of course," Chuck answered easily. "I apologise if we seem to be in the way."

"And there's one more thing," Edie said. "Neither of you is to go ashore without my permission."

Chuck's eyebrows went up.

"Any reason for that?"

"I don't intend to give you one," Edie answered. "That's an order, by the way."

He hesitated for a moment and added:

"From Mr. Virdon, of course. He's your boss."

"I don't quite understand," Chuck said. "It sounds rather as if you are keeping Miss Brown and me prisoners."

"We pay for your time," Edie answered. "Well, you're required on board. Is that clear?"

"Absolutely!" Chuck said sarcastically.

"Very well. As I've said, that is an order, and I suggest you obey it," Edie said.

"Otherwise I suppose we'll be cut into small pieces and dumped in the sea—having been carefully weighted down, of course," Chuck taunted.

Edie rose to the bait.

"Now, look here, big boy!" he shouted. "I've told you once before that you weren't invited on this trip, and you'll do as we say or it will be the worse for you."

There was so much venom in his voice that Zaria instinctively put out her hand and laid it on Chuck's arm.

"Don't argue," she said.

"But, of course not," Chuck smiled. He looked across the cabin at Edie. "Sir, we are but slaves to obey your slightest command."

He bowed in a manner not unlike that in which the Arab in the Kasba had bowed, and if Zaria hadn't been so frightened she would have giggled. And then, taking her by the arm, Chuck led her outside the door of the saloon and shut it behind them.

"Come down below," he said, leading the way; but when she would have gone towards the office, he shook his head.

"Too dangerous," he whispered. "Let's go into your cabin. That's safe, as far as I know."

She did as he suggested and he shut the door behind them and then had a quick look round as if in search of microphones.

"They can't be listening, can they?" Zaria asked.

"One never knows," he answered cheerfully. "In a moment we'll go into the office and I will show you some of the equipment I've bought. I made Victor pay a great deal more than he intended. It was quite amusing really. I kept saying,

'Mr. Virdon will expect to have the best.'

"As everybody in the shop seemed to have seen the yacht in the harbour, they were only too willing to agree with me."

"Will he want the best?" Zaria asked.

"Yes, of course," Chuck answered quickly.

"He doesn't seem to be in much of a hurry to start digging, does he? I don't understand," Zaria said. "It's been such an extraordinary morning. I must tell you . . ."

She stopped suddenly.

"What's the matter?" Chuck asked.

"Edie told me I wasn't to tell you anything," Zaria said. "I had almost forgotten."

Chuck took her hand and led her across to the bed. They sat on it side by side.

"Listen," he said in a low voice. "I don't think you owe these people much. To begin with, they haven't paid you any salary yet. Secondly, I don't think they

211

are the sort of people for whom you should be worrying. Virdon's the best of them—but that's not saying much. If you ask me we're in a bit of a spot—both of us."

"Why don't we go to the police?" Zaria asked.

"If you really consider it, what have we got to say?" he answered. "That we think our employers are a bit peculiar—that they're certainly not what one could call ladies and gentlemen in any language—and that they are running round the town trying to contact some Sheik or other."

"How do you know that?" Zaria asked. "I didn't tell you."

"No, I put two and two together with a little bit of information I got out of Kate. Does that make sense?"

"Yes, of course," Zaria said. "But . . ."

"There are lots of buts," Chuck said. "The point is we haven't got a really good story to interest the police, or anyone else, at the moment. So we've just got to be clever, you and I, and find out what is happening. I have a pretty shrewd idea."

"Please tell me," Zaria begged.

Chuck shook his head.

"No, it's better that we work independently," he said. "I don't want to involve you in this more than I can help."

"I still think it would be better to tell the police that we're suspicious," Zaria said. "And, anyway, they could tell us about Sheik Ibrahim ben Kaddour."

She felt Chuck stiffen.

"Ben Kaddour! Did you say Kaddour?" he asked.

"Oh dear! I suppose I oughtn't to have said it," Zaria answered. "But you did seem to know, even though I hadn't told you."

"I didn't know his name." Chuck said.

212

He gave a little whistle.

"So that's who their contact is, is it? This begins to be interesting."

"Don't keep me in ignorance," Zaria begged.

"What's the plan? When are they going to see him?" Chuck asked quickly.

"Tonight I think," Zaria answered. "Edie has been told to go to Salem's House. The Sheik is supposed to meet him there."

"I bet you a thousand dollars to a dime he doesn't turn up," Chuck answered. "Well, it will be interesting to see what happens."

"Shall we be allowed to go?" Zaria asked. "We are to be kept prisoners here apparently."

"I'll find a way out somehow," Chuck answered. "Incidentally, I can swim quite well."

"You won't go away and leave me all alone?" Zaria asked anxiously.

He took both her hands in his.

"Shall I promise you something?" he said. "I will never leave you alone—not for long at any rate. And that's rather an important promise, if you but knew it."

"It's all I want to hear," she said with a sigh of relief. "I'm not frightened of these people when you are with me."

"So that's why you want me, is it?" Chuck asked. "A strong armed nursemaid! Is that the only reason?"

She turned her head away from him. If only she could tell the truth, she thought. If only she could tell him there were a thousand and one reasons why she wanted him and why every moment she was with him was a sheer delight.

She remembered humbly how unimportant she was—just an incident that had happened in his life—and warned herself she mustn't cling to him.

She was conscious that he was watching her profile, studying her little nose etched against the panelling of her cabin, the sudden wistful droop of her mouth.

"You are so vulnerable, aren't you?" he said quietly and unexpectedly. "You ought to have someone permanently looking after you."

"That's not very easy," she answered. "You see, I am all alone in the world now."

"No relatives?" he enquired.

"None that I know of," she answered.

"So that if you disappeared nobody would worry," he said reflectively. "For Heavens sake don't tell Edie that."

She looked at him wide-eyed.

"What are you suggesting?" she asked.

"Nothing," he said. "But don't volunteer information to that gang up above."

"I've no intention of telling them anything," she answered.

"Dear little Zaria!" he said softly. "You are so small and so fragile. If I touched you, I would be half afraid of breaking you, and yet I have the feeling that inside you are very brave—braver, perhaps, than anyone else I know."

"I'm not," she answered. "I'm a coward. I don't face up to things. I don't make decisions when I ought to make them. To tell the truth, I'm a failure and I always have been."

"Who told you that?" he asked with a little smile on his lips.

And then he said quietly:

"It is funny to listen to a woman these days running herself down rather than cracking herself up. The trouble with American women is that they are always trying to over-sell themselves. You are different—so very different."

"And I wish I wasn't," Zaria said passionately. "I want to be like everyone else. I want to feel sure of myself, to be confident, to believe that the world is there to have fun in and all I have got to do is to enjoy myself. I have never, never been able to feel like that."

Her voice broke suddenly, as all the indecision and misery of the past years came rushing back into her mind.

As she turned, her eyes brimming with tears, towards Chuck, she saw that he had pulled off his dark glasses and was looking down at her with a tenderness that she had never imagined possible in anyone's face.

"Some day I will try to show you that life can be enjoyable," he said softly. "Just for the moment we have got to think of how to get out of the mess we've got ourselves into without getting hurt in the process."

"You mean . . ." Zaria began apprehensively.

"I mean nothing," he answered. "Just take things as they come. I've said that you've got courage. I'm quite sure of that and so I'm relying on you. You won't fail me, will you?"

"I'll do my best," Zaria answered.

He raised her hand suddenly to his lips.

"That's all I ask," he said. "Just that you will do your best. It is so much better than anyone else's."

He stood up and pulled her to her feet.

"Come and look at the equipment," he said. "Be careful to say nothing that might be misconstrued by those listening ears which I feel somehow are all around us."

His hand was still on hers and she stood for a moment looking up at him. The cabin was very quiet. There was only the soft lap of the water against the sides of the yacht, and far away in the distance the bustle and turmoil of the quay. A ship hooted far away out to sea.

There was no other sound to break the sudden stillness that came between them.

Zaria's eyes met Chuck's. She had a sudden feeling that this moment was momentous. She drew in her breath. She felt some flame within herself leap into being. There was something in Chuck's cool, grey eyes that held her spellbound so that she could not escape from him.

She had the tingling awareness that he might kiss her, and yet there was almost no need for physical contact. They were so close that they were fused, one with the other. They were together.

Then, just as she would have taken a step towards him, just as she knew that in one split second she would have been within his arms and his lips on hers, a noise and a turmoil broke out above them.

There was Madame Bertin shouting for Edie. There were heavy footsteps thumping across the deck, there was a slamming of doors and a sudden uproar of voices raised in anger.

The spell was broken.

Suddenly shy, Zaria turned towards the cabin door and without a word Chuck opened it for her and they passed through it.

Outside in the passage they listened to the altercation above.

"Something has gone wrong," Chuck said.

"I expect it is her shop," Zaria said. "She thought it would be wonderful and I wondered if she might not be disappointed."

"She's certainly telling Edie in no uncertain terms what she thinks of him," Chuck said with a smile, as Madame Bertin's voice, shrill and strident, came to their ears.

"It is disgraceful! *Vous êtes un imbécile!* A fool! A crook! How dare you suggest that I should accommodate myself in such a place?"

Madame Bertin was shouting and Edie was shouting back. It also sounded as if Victor and Kate were joining in.

"When thieves fall out, wise men come into their own," Chuck whispered against Zaria's ear, and then he suddenly stiffened and Zaria beside him stared.

A few yards down the passage the door of his cabin was open and standing by the dressing-table were two French *gendarmes* staring into an open drawer.

They glanced up swiftly, saw Chuck and Zaria, and instantly one, of senior rank, stepped forward.

"You are Monsieur Tanner?" he enquired in French.

"I am," Chuck answered tersely in the same language.

Zaria realised that he was as puzzled as she was as to why the police were here.

The cabin had obviously been ransacked. Clothes were scattered everywhere, the wardrobe doors were open, the bedclothes turned back. But it was easy to see what was engrossing the *gendarmes*—a narrow, thin box filled with cigarettes, and beneath it two others exactly the same.

"What have you got there?" Chuck enquired.

The *gendarme* spoke almost before he had finished his sentence.

"These, *M'sieur,* are, I think, your property. We must therefore arrest you for being in charge of dangerous drugs."

"Dangerous drugs!" Chuck repeated in almost a dazed manner, and the *gendarme* answered:

"I need not explain to you, *M'sieur,* that marijuana cigarettes are not permitted to enter this country."

217

"I don't know . . ." Chuck began, only to be interrupted by a voice from behind him.

Both he and Zaria turned round. Edie was standing in the doorway and, as usual, he had approached them silently in his rubber-soled shoes.

"I'm sorry, Tanner," he said in English. "But I'm afraid I could not allow Mr. Virdon's yacht to be used as a cover for your nefarious trade. As I have explained to the officers, dope carrying is something from which Mr. Virdon and myself shrink in horror."

"But . . . but there must be some mistake," Zaria stammered, then realised that no-one was paying any attention to her.

All the three men in the room were looking at Chuck, who was standing there staring at them, his expression, it seemed to her, quite inscrutable.

"We must ask you, *M'sieur,* to accompany us to the *Sûreté,*" the *gendarme* said to Chuck. Zaria gasped out an exclamation of horror, but Chuck laughed.

It wasn't a loud laugh, just a chuckle of sheer, undiluted amusement. He turned to Edie.

"All right," he said. "You win. This was something I didn't anticipate."

And then, before anyone could move, he was gone. He slipped past Edie in the doorway without touching him, and there was the sound of his footsteps hurrying up the companion-way onto the deck.

"Quick, after him!" Edie cried. "He'll get away."

The *gendarme* shook his head.

"We have a car and two of our men on the quay, *M'sieur,*" he answered. "They are waiting at the gangway. I anticipated that something like this might happen."

He spoke in French, but Edie seemed to understand what he was saying. And then there was the sound of a splash.

With one accord everyone turned and ran along the passage and up on to the deck.

Zaria, being faster on her feet, was there first. She was just in time to see two other *gendarmes* come running aboard up the gangway, then turned to see Chuck's dark head bobbing amongst the small waves of the water in the harbour.

He was already some way from the yacht, swimming strongly and making, she could see, for the shore on the other side of the port.

"Goddam these fatheaded cops! Why didn't they stop him?" Edie snarled.

He stood helpless, staring at Chuck's swift passage through the water. It was a second or two later before he was joined by the *gendarmes* from below.

"Mon Dieu!" one gasped as he realised what had happened.

"Stop him, can't you?" Edie yelled.

There was a moment's hesitation while the other *gendarmes* from the car made exclamatory noises as if they felt it imperative that they must express their surprise.

"Stop him!" shouted Edie again. "You don't want him to escape, do you?"

The officer drew a revolver from his belt. It took but a few seconds to unfasten it from the smart leather case in which it was encased, but even as he touched it Zaria gasped:

"No, no! You cannot shoot! It is ridiculous, it is absurd! You cannot do such a thing!"

"You have got to stop him," Edie insisted as the *gendarme* raised his arm.

As he did so, Zaria forgot everything but her fear for Chuck and her anxiety for his safety. She flung herself upon the *gendarme*, holding on to his arm, and as she did so speaking rapidly in French:

"Non, non, M'sieur! Do not do such a thing. There

is some mistake, I promise you. You cannot shoot an unarmed man. Consider, I beg of you."

She was sobbing by this time and she could not resist or fight back as someone pulled her away, leaving the *gendarme* free to raise his revolver once more.

But it was too late. Chuck was out of sight, hidden from view by the many ships anchored on the blue water—yachts, sailing vessels, two or three liners and several tankers. He might have been behind any of them.

"You should not behave in such a way, *Ma'm'selle*," the officer said severely. "What is this man to you?"

"He is . . . my *fiancé*," Zaria sobbed, her breath coming in uneven gasps as she struggled against her tears and her captors.

"Votre fiancé!"

The French policeman's eyes met hers and instantly she was free. This was something they understood. Obstruction, passion, feminine emotion of all sorts could be forgiven if it was *pour l'amour*.

"Well, don't just stand there," Edie snapped. "Can't you go after him? He's got to get out of the damned sea somewhere hasn't he?"

The senior official gave orders and the two *gendarmes* who had been sitting in the car until Chuck had dived overboard saluted smartly. One of them ran off, obviously in the direction of a telephone. The other got back at the wheel of the car.

"We shall arrest him as he steps ashore," the senior official said soothingly to Edie, who was stamping his foot with anger.

He saluted Zaria and said:

"My sympathies, *Ma'm'selle,* but in another time you must not obstruct the French police in the pursuance of their duties."

Then he saluted Edie and walked off the yacht. It

was a very dignified performance and Edie clasped his clenched hands above his head in an appeal to Heaven.

"Idiots! Fools!" he stormed. "Do they imagine they can catch a man by such methods? But they will get him, you can be sure of that. They will get him!"

"And if they do, what then?" Zaria asked, her voice cracking a little on the words.

"Then he will get a pretty stiff sentence," Edie answered. "Dope smuggling is frowned on pretty severely, I can tell you that."

"I don't believe that he was smuggling those cigarettes," Zaria said. "I've never seen them before."

"I'm afraid your evidence will be too prejudiced," Edie replied with a sly twist of his lips.

He turned on his heel and walked away from her.

Zaria stood on deck, hesitating for one moment. She thought of running ashore after the *gendarme.* Then she saw that the sailor was still standing on guard and was sure that he had his instructions.

She wouldn't get far. Edie and his gang would catch up with her.

Then she looked across the harbour. Had Chuck got ashore safely she wondered? She felt the agony of frustration, the agony of not knowing. Was he safe? What would happen to him?

She stood looking out over the blue water until she could see it no longer because her eyes were blinded with tears.

"Oh, my love," she whispered. "God go with you!"

Chapter Eleven

The taxi deposited them at the end of the narrow alley-way. The only light apart from the moonlight was a blue lamp burning outside a door some way down it.

"Is this the place?" Edie asked.

"Salem's House," the taxi driver said pointing with a dirty finger towards the blue lamp.

"It looks a pretty ghastly place to me," Victor ejaculated.

Zaria felt too unhappy to say anything. She was concerned only with one thing—her anxiety for Chuck.

All the afternoon she had sat in her cabin wondering what she could do or how she could find out if he was safe. Yet she was also afraid—afraid that perhaps, after all, he had done something wrong and that even were she to escape from Victor's and Edie's vigilance, she would not be helping him by going to the police.

The first difficulty was, of course, that she was a prisoner.

It was obvious that Edie and Co. had no intention of letting her out of their sight; and because she felt both afraid and helpless, she had finally gone to her own cabin just to sit there staring into space.

"Chuck! Chuck!" she murmured to herself, feeling somehow that the mere repetition of his name brought her comfort.

Occasionally she got up and walked to the port-hole to stare out at the sea, almost believing that by some miracle she would see his head bobbing amongst the waves.

Had he got away? What had happened to him? She felt at times she would go mad if she didn't know the answer. Had Edie planted the cigarettes in his cabin? And, if so, why? Was that his way of "dealing" with Chuck?

She thought this must be the answer, but even so some tiny, nagging doubt remained in her mind. Perhaps, after all, Chuck had other reasons for coming aboard the yacht than the ones he had given her.

"What am I to believe? What am I to think?" she asked herself aloud.

Then she knew that whatever he did or whatever he had done she still loved him—loved him so much that even if the *gendarme's* bullet had wounded her instead of Chuck, she would have been glad to have been of service to him.

"I love him!" she told herself as she walked about her cabin.

"I love him!" she murmured into her pillow as she lay on her bed.

"I love him!" she said to give herself courage as, having been told that she was expected to be ready to go ashore at nine o'clock, she came up half-an-hour earlier for dinner.

It required all her courage to walk into the dining saloon and yet somehow it was a help to realise that the dress she was wearing became her and that she could hold herself proudly because of it.

There was no doubt that one gained courage from feeling well dressed and presentable.

Perhaps, too, love had given her a new attitude to life. She was not the shrinking, terrified girl who had crept into the train at Victoria, running away from her old life into strange adventures and a new one.

She was someone who was in love, and because of it she was prepared to fight for the man who held her heart whatever he might have done.

Wearing a dress of sapphire blue silk with a little velvet coat to match, she sat down at the dining-table and stared with hostile eyes at Edie Morgan. He was looking worried, she thought with satisfaction.

She thought, too, there was a somewhat apprehensive look on Mr. Virdon's face, while Victor was obviously on edge and drinking hard to conceal it.

Madame Bertin was not there. After her row with Edie she had retired to bed with a migraine which necessitated her taking a sleeping draught. Kate was there, but in a very bad temper and sulking so that she refused to eat although she continually had her glass replenished with champagne.

"I have told you, no! You are not coming tonight," Edie was saying as Zaria entered the saloon.

"And why shouldn't I come?" Kate answered. "I've been to worse places, as well you know."

"That's not the point," Edie answered. "We've got to take Zaria, she's the only one who can speak this hellish language. But we don't want to take any unnecessary risks. From all accounts its no place that a woman should go to anyway."

"You're chicken-hearted, that's what's wrong with you," Kate retorted. "Americans, if they've got money, can go anywhere these days. Nobody's going to kill the goose that lays the golden egg."

"I'm not arguing with you," Edie said. "I'll take you there tomorrow night, the night after or the night after that, but tonight, no!"

"Then I hope your plans all rot!" Kate exclaimed, and she hardly spoke again for the rest of the meal.

There were uncomfortable silences broken usually by Victor calling for another whiskey. Edie looked at

224

him disagreeably but did not protest; and Mr. Virdon, in his usual unhurried way, ate solemnly through every course and said practically nothing.

At nine o'clock Edie rose from the table.

"Are you ready?" he asked Zaria.

"Yes," she answered.

She slipped her bare arms into the sleeves of the blue velvet coat which buttoned from her neck to her small waist, letting her full skirts flare out beneath it. It was one of Madame Bertin's prettiest models and Zaria wondered if she should have called in to see the French woman before she came on deck.

But it was difficult to think of anything or anybody except Chuck. She knew now, as she followed Edie to where the taxi was waiting at the gangway, that deep in her heart she believed that somehow, in some manner of his own, Chuck would contact her during the evening.

It didn't seem feasible, it didn't seem sensible—and yet she still believed he would do it.

He would know how anxious she would be, he would know in what a dangerous position he had left her. Somehow he would help her, whatever the risks to himself.

She was sure of it, and yet her logical, common sense told her he would have fled to his mother's house and be hiding where the police would not think to look for him.

If the *gendarmes* had returned during the afternoon, she had not been told. She would have questioned Jim, but she heard from one of the other stewards who brought her tea that he had gone ashore early that morning as it was his day off and he was not expected back until after dinner.

'He would help me,' Zaria thought, but realised there was nothing she could do at the moment; and even though she contemplated speaking to the Captain, she was afraid to do so.

Supposing—just supposing—Chuck had been doing something illegal? She might make it worse for him.

When she was ready for dinner, she had slipped from her own cabin into Chuck's. It was not only for the comfort of touching things that were his—she felt, too, that it was wise to have a look round in case there was anything else there that might be incriminating.

But everything had been put back in its place. Chuck's suits were hanging up in the wardrobe. His pyjamas were lying on the bed ready for him to put them on. His dressing-gown was over the chair. Everything seemed normal and impersonal.

She opened a drawer. There were a few handkerchiefs, unmarked, two ties and a packet of ordinary cigarettes—American Chesterfields.

She stared at them for a moment, thinking of those long, thin boxes the police had found and being absolutely certain in her mind that Edie had put them just so that he could inform against Chuck and get him arrested.

Then, as she went to shut the drawer, she saw there was something at the back of it. She did not know why, but she put her hand in and drew it out.

To her astonishment it was a small bottle of hair dye.

For a moment she stared at it and then she put it back where she had found it and went from the cabin. But all the while through dinner she could think of little else. Hair dye! Dark hair dye!

That was why Chuck's hair seemed somehow an almost startling contrast to his grey eyes.

She had always thought that he didn't seem the dark type. His chin was never blue like Edie's; there was something a little unnatural about the dark waves which he brushed back so severely from his square forehead.

She felt the problem nag at her mind. Why was he disguised? Why should he want to change the colour of his hair unless he was hiding from someone? Was that one of the reasons why he wore dark glasses? Was his story about the weakness of his eyes totally untrue?

They didn't look weak, somehow. Piercing, grey and extremely perceptive, one certainly would not connect them with ill health or a frailty of any sort.

She made no attempt during the ride in the taxi either to speak or to notice in which direction they were going. It was only the length of the journey which told her they were travelling away from the town into the rambling suburbs.

Some of the streets were well-lighted and busy with traffic. But the alley-way up which they now walked was empty save for the lamp at the end. It was therefore a surprise when they passed through a heavy metal-studded door to go down steps into a big, rectangular shaped room and find it packed with people.

The walls were draped with coloured rugs and round the room there were low, tapestry-covered seats. There were also little tables on which there were a multitude of different coloured drinks.

It was obvious that they were expected, for an Arab led them immediately on their arrival to a small alcove at the side of the room. It was about a foot higher than the ordinary floor and draped with cushions so that they were partially concealed from the other customers who were all Arabs with the exception of one or two women.

The latter, gaudily dressed, fantastically over-painted, but quite obviously of a certain profession.

The waiter who had escorted them to the alcove put a bottle of whisky on the low table, added four glasses, then went away, still without saying anything.

Zaria stared around her. The Arabs, in their voluminous burnous and white head-dresses, were picturesque; and yet, at the same time, she felt there was something slightly menacing about them.

These were not the town Arabs who were prepared to wait subserviently on anyone who would pay for their wares. These were Arabs from the desert.

There was no mistaking their weatherbeaten skins, and the wiriness of their bodies, acquired from long hours in the saddle and endless journeys across the relentless sand. They had in their eyes a look of an eagle; about their lips an expression of toughness.

Zaria wondered for a moment what attracted them here, but as soon as she noticed the Arab musicians seated at the far end of the room, she knew the answer. They were all blind, and she remembered that it was traditional for the Ouled Naïl dancing girls to be accompanied by blind musicians.

The tambourinists in the orchestra began to beat out a pulsating rhythm. A flute and a rhaytor—the Arabic clarinet—joined in.

The music suddenly burst into an evocatory, melodic storm and a girl swept on to the dancing floor. She had the high cheekbones, the blue-black hair and the huge eyes of the Ouled Naïl.

She wore the glittering ear-rings and gold coin necklace which showed how successful she was in her profession.

Her bare feet began to move slowly in the strange, individualistic dance which made her hips sway gently at first and then move faster and faster until, almost without realising it, the onlookers' breath came quicker and quicker as if in time to the rhythm.

The dance was strange and violent, not beautiful, but it seemed to awaken the senses with its primitive directness and physical vehemence. Zaria found herself forgetting everything, even Chuck, as she watched. Her heart seemed to beat almost in time with the girl's strange provocative movements.

And then suddenly, when all eyes were on the dancers, a voice behind Zaria said:

"She is good, is she not?"

The words were spoken in Arabic. She turned her head to see black eyes glittering in a dark brown face, a white headdress framing a handsome, cruel face and a brown burnous pulled a little to one side to show the inevitable long-handled knife.

"Who are you?" she asked, knowing the answer.

She glanced towards Edie and Mr. Virdon who had just realised that they had been joined by someone else.

"You are Sheik Ibrahim ben Kaddour?" Edie asked directly, but was interrupted as a brown finger was laid against his lips.

"No names," the Sheik said in Arabic, "and speak low."

Zaria translated the words.

"Ask him if he has the money," Edie commanded.

Zaria asked the question simply. The Sheik nodded.

"It is in my saddle-bag," he said. "How many have they brought?"

Zaria translated his question and in answer Edie held up three fingers, then opened both hands wide. The Sheik nodded.

"Tell the Americans," he said to Zaria, "to meet me at dawn at El Kettar—the cemetery outside the town. *Inshallah.*"

229

"If God wills it!"

The whole fatalistic creed of the Moslem lay in that word. Zaria translated what the Sheik had said.

Edie looked reflective.

"Dawn is too early," he said in English. "Anyone about would think it strange if we started moving off the yacht at that hour."

"Not if you are going to dig," Zaria replied.

"No, I suppose not," Edie answered. "Tell him we'll be there, but say that nothing will be handed over until he's forked out the dough. And I want half of it now."

Zaria repeated what she had been told. The Sheik's eyes narrowed.

"Half?" he questioned. "Why should I trust them if they will not trust me?"

Edie knew by the expression on his face what he was saying.

"Tell him those are my terms," he said. "We've not brought the stuff all this way to have it pinched off us by a lot of black-faced gangsters."

"I can't say that," Zaria protested.

"Then tell him either he pays or gets nothing."

Zaria repeated the words a little uncomfortably. The Sheik did not seem surprised.

"Wait!" he said.

He moved swiftly through some curtains at the back of the alcove. It was obviously another entrance and a very convenient one for those who did not wish to be seen. No-one in the room had noticed the Sheik's arrival.

They were all too intent on watching the dancer, who was coming now to the climax of her dance.

There was great applause when she finished, but before it died away two other girls, not more than fourteen years old, were beginning "the Dance of the Daggers."

The slim slivers of steel in their hands gleamed and glittered as they slashed the air. Their small brown feet moved swiftly to a kind of almost monotonous rhythm. The music rose and fell, crashing sometimes as if it portrayed the tempest strumming through the palm leaves or rushing like a desert wind through the clouds of sand.

The girls were practically naked, but their sinuous small-hipped bodies seemed somehow divorced from sex. It was a ritual they performed rather than a provocative dance.

Zaria had little time to watch them before the Sheik was back again. He squatted down on his heels beside Edie and without wasting time in words began to pass something into his hands from beneath the shadow of his cloak.

Zaria could not see the notes, but she knew that Edie was counting them, and both Victor and Mr. Virdon seemed, too, almost hypnotised as they watched. So engrossed were they that she felt they had forgotten her presence.

She wondered whether it would be possible to slip away through the curtains and leave without their realising that she had gone.

She was half inclined to take the risk and then she remembered how far she was from the town. There must be a better opportunity to escape perhaps on their return to the yacht.

The last note must have passed and the Sheik rose. His burnous brushed against Zaria's cheek as he turned silently on his heels and disappeared as swiftly as he had come.

"The Dance of the Daggers" had finished and now

another girl slid on to the dance floor. Slim and naked, her body was a most beautiful colour.

The music was the crash of tambourines and under cover of their noise Edie got to his feet. He flung a *mille* note down on the table and then led the way through the curtains through which the Sheik had departed.

The others followed him. They were in a narrow, arched passage which at one end led back into the dance hall. At the other there was a metal-studded door. Edie wrenched it open. It led into the alley-way just a little further up from the door with the blue light.

There was no-one in sight. The Sheik had vanished.

There was not a sound of horses' hoofs. The place seemed deserted and out here they could not even hear the music played by the blind musicians.

Edie wiped his forehead.

"How the hell are we going to get a taxi?" he asked.

A small Arab boy appeared from nowhere.

"Taxi, Mister?" he asked, in quite intelligible English.

"That's right, a taxi, and quick!" Edie answered.

The urchin ran down to the end of the alley, put his fingers in his mouth and let out a shrill whistle. Almost immediately an old, rather dilapidated taxi came slowly up the road.

"Where to?" the urchin asked.

Zaria gave the name of the quay where the yacht was berthed. The small boy shouted it at the taxi driver, who was old and inclined to be deaf, but he nodded as if he understood. Edie handed the child a few cents tip.

"Thank you, Mister," he beamed. *"Merci beaucoup!"*

He held the door for them as they got into the taxi. As Zaria passed him he said something in Arabic.

For a moment she thought she could not have heard aright, and then she knew that this was what she had been expecting.

It was a short sentence, but it told her all she wanted to know. Translated roughly it said:

"Be ready to run when you get to the quay."

That was all. Only a few words, and yet she felt her heart turn over because of them.

Chuck was free! Chuck was thinking of her! Chuck was going to rescue her! She felt as if she could sing aloud because of her very happiness.

She sat down in the rickety old taxi beside Edie and felt it was a chariot transplanting her to Heaven. Chuck had not forgotten. She felt the tears come into her eyes with utter relief because she had been so afraid.

She knew now that her desperate anxiety had been not only for his safety, but also lest, having found security for himself, he should forget about her or think her no longer important to him. He had remembered!

She felt as if the secret she was nursing in her breast was worth a million times more than the money weighing down Edie's pocket.

What did anything matter except that Chuck was not a prisoner and that she would be beside him in a few minutes? As they journeyed slowly through the crowded streets, she began to plan how they would get away from Algiers. She would hire a boat if necessary.

She could make arrangements at the bank for them to cash a cheque for any amount. She would telegraph or even telephone Mr. Patterson. Chuck must be transported to safety. He must hide until they were ready to leave!

Then once they were in France, or back in England,

nothing would matter, because there would no longer be Edie to inform against him or the French police looking for him on what was obviously a false charge.

'I must be wise and clever,' she thought to herself. 'I have got to look after him. It isn't a question now of his looking after me. I must look after him.'

She felt her whole being yearn towards him. She felt her love reaching out, protective, almost maternal, in her anxiety that he should not be hurt.

"I love him! I love him!"

The taxi wheels seemed to be repeating those same words over and over again as they drew nearer and nearer to the quay.

She didn't know what to expect. She hadn't time to make plans. She only knew that Chuck had given her an instruction to run when they reached the quay. She was ready to obey him.

The taxi passed through the gates and drove down towards the yacht. It all seemed very quiet and peaceful. There were the lights of the quay and the glittering, reflected lights of the yachts and ships shimmering on the softly moving water.

The stars overhead and the lights of the town rising up to the old fort looked like something out of a fairy tale.

There was the scent of spices and pepper trees and also, it seemed to Zaria, the hot, furnace-like smell of the desert sand when it has been baked in the sun.

She felt suddenly wildly and ecstatically excited. It was because she was going to see Chuck. But at the same time, she knew it was the beginning of another adventure—greater and more thrilling than anything she had experienced before.

The taxi was slowing down. She could see *The Enchantress,* the beautiful, clean white lines of her shining even in the darkness. There appeared to be no movement aboard.

Edie got out first and with his usual lack of manners he made no attempt to help Zaria who followed him. He fumbled in his pocket and then turned to Victor.

"Have you got any small change?" he asked.

"I think so," Victor replied.

"I've got some," Mr. Virdon said.

They both put their hands into their pockets.

It was then that Zaria heard the whistle. It was faint and low and it came a little to the left of her from the dark shadows of a warehouse.

She waited no longer. She turned and ran with a speed of which she had not known herself capable, in the direction from which the whistle had come.

Chapter Twelve

As Zaria ran she heard a shout behind her. Just for a moment she felt as if she was in a dream, flying from some inexplicable terror with her feet growing heavier and heavier and slower and slower.

And then, even as she was overcome with a blind panic of fear, she reached the darkness of some buildings and felt a hand go out to take hers.

She knew who it was—knew though she could not see him—and felt like a drowning man to whom someone has suddenly thrown a life-buoy.

"Chuck! Chuck!"

She heard her own voice come sobbingly from between her lips, and then without a word they were moving together through the dark shadows in which Zaria could discern little while Chuck seemed amazingly sure-footed.

There were some more shouts and cries behind them now. Zaria could hear Edie cursing and Victor calling her name.

"Zaria! Zaria! Where are you? Come here at once."

It was a command with an undercurrent of fear behind it.

Suddenly Chuck stopped. Zaria's eyes were more accustomed now to the darkness around and she saw, to her surprise, that they were in the midst of a great number of barrels. Piled high on each other, but providing peep-holes through which anyone could see and not be seen, they made a perfect hiding place.

The ceiling above them was arched, but there

were no side walls and a little to the left of where they were standing Zaria could see *The Enchantress*, serenely beautiful in the harbour lights.

Edie was shouting now.

"Zaria! Come here or it will be the worse for you! Zaria! Zaria!"

His voice went echoing around the great, empty buildings and the echo seemed to come back at him.

"Zaria! Zaria!"

But Zaria was no longer listening. Chuck was close beside her and while her own breath came in quick gasps, he was calm and still. She was vividly conscious of his nearness. She could not see his face, she could only discern the square outline of his shoulders.

He still held her hand, and now, uncertainly, a little shyly, her other hand went out towards him, as if she must be certain that he was really there.

"You are safe," she managed to say at last. "You are safe. I was so afraid."

"I told you to trust me," he answered in his low, deep voice, and then there was no longer any need for words.

His arms were round her, he was holding her close; and knowing what he wanted, she lifted her face to his. It was the instinctive gesture of a flower turning its face towards the sun.

His lips found hers, the whole world fell away and she was lost in a glory and a splendour such as she had never known in all her small, starved existence.

She felt her whole being respond to him. She felt every nerve in her body pulsating and throbbing as if in a very paean of joy and gladness.

Just for a moment she thought she must be dreaming, and then the tingling thrill running through her body told her that this was no dream, but reality.

Chuck was kissing her. She was his. She belonged

to him. Her very soul passed through her lips into his keeping for all eternity.

"Zaria!"

Edie's voice was nearer and now, as if he awoke to the dangers of the situation, Chuck drew her down between the barrels.

"Keep very still," he whispered, and then, as they crouched there, they heard Edie's voice again:

"Come out, damn you! You'll suffer for this if you don't obey me. Come out!"

Zaria turned her face against Chuck's shoulder. The menace and danger outside did not seem real somehow. This was her world—this dark hole between the barrels with Chuck's arms round her, Chuck's lips close to hers.

This was reality; everything else was just a figment of her imagination, an evil which could not touch her in her utter and supreme happiness.

"Zaria!"

The voice was further away now.

"I love you," Chuck said suddenly. "I suppose you know that?"

"No," Zaria managed to say as she buried her face still further against his shoulder.

"You have been so brave," Chuck said. "So wonderful. And now it is all over."

"What do you mean?" Zaria asked.

"I will show you," he answered.

He drew her gently to her feet and then slowly, moving cautiously and in silence, he led her through the barrels until they were still nearer to *The Enchantress*.

Now Zaria could see the side of the quay quite clearly, the gang-way, and Edie and Victor walking slowly towards it. They were talking angrily together and for a moment Zaria could not hear what was said.

Then, faintly, she heard the word "torch," and guessed that they were going aboard to get a torch with which to search for her.

She was not afraid. She was with Chuck. Neither Edie nor anyone else could menace her when he was there. And she thought that strangely she was no longer afraid for him.

They could slip away into the town and who would find them there? There would be friends in the Kasba who would assist them; and, if that failed, there would always be the desert, where they could vanish for months, and even an army would be unable to discover their whereabouts.

'We are free and together,' Zaria thought to herself, and turned impulsively to Chuck to say so.

"Wait!" he said softly, almost before the words could reach her lips.

Because he asked it of her, she obediently watched Edie and Victor climb the gang-way on to the deck of *The Enchantress.*

They hurried towards the door of the saloon. They opened it. For a moment there was no sound, and then an outburst of noise. Voices were raised; there was a shout, something curiously like a scream, and then Edie rushed back on to the deck drawing a revolver from his pocket.

He fired, and the sound of his shot was followed almost immediately by several shots. It was like watching a film, Zaria thought, as Edie heeled over slowly and fell.

Men came running from the saloon—men dressed in the uniform of the French Army.

"But . . . but what is happening?" Zaria gasped as

Chuck turned and taking her by the hand started to retrace their way through the barrels.

"It's all over," he said softly. "Come along. There is no reason for us to stay here."

"But . . . Chuck, I don't understand," Zaria began.

But she realised that he had no intention of explaining anything to her at that moment and so she followed him in silence through the barrels, through the big warehouses crowded with many different types of shipment and outside on to the road where a car stood waiting.

There was no driver. Chuck opened the door and helped Zaria in and then seated himself at the wheel.

"I . . . I don't understand," Zaria started to say again.

Then Chuck turned and looked at her and in the light of the street lamp she saw his face.

She knew then that what he said was true. He did love her. She could see it there in his eyes, in the twist of his lips, in an expression of such tenderness that her heart seemed to turn over in her breast.

She had nothing more to say. This was all she wanted to understand. Why and how and when Chuck had begun to love her.

He bent his head swiftly and laid his lips against hers.

"I adore you," he said in his deep voice that was somehow curiously moved. "And now, hold on tight, because we are going very fast."

He started up the car and drove at what seemed to Zaria breakneck speed away from the harbour, through the lower part of the town and on to the road which led up to the wooded slopes which have, since time immemorial, made a perfect setting for the beauty of Algiers.

Zaria wondered vaguely whether they were going

out into the desert. She sensed that Chuck did not wish her to ask any questions and so she was silent. Besides, her breath was almost taken away by the speed at which they were travelling.

On, on they went until the houses were left behind and there were only wonderful gardens filled with orange and lemon trees and great palms waving their fronds against the starlit sky. It was all enchanted— a night which might have come from a book of fairy-tales.

They turned in at a gate, drove down a drive of lime trees and stopped outside a huge, white porticoed villa gleaming palely beautiful in the light of the moon.

"Why have we stopped here?" Zaria asked, a little frightened.

In answer Chuck got out and went round the car to open the door for her.

"Where are we?" she asked again, and he drew her down beside him and put his arms round her.

"I have brought you home, my darling," he answered.

"Home?" she questioned.

"To my home," he replied. "At least, as far as my past life is concerned. In the future we shall make a home of our own together."

"I . . . don't understand," Zaria began again, but he laughed and taking her face in his hand turned it up to his.

"Does it matter, my little one?" he asked. "Explanations are such boring things. I love you. Let's be content with that for the moment."

"But, I am," Zaria whispered.

He held her close, his lips becoming more possessive and passionate, until, with a sigh, as if he suddenly remembered the world outside themselves, he moved, with his arm round her shoulders, towards the door of the villa.

He opened it and they walked into a big, cool hall. It was lit only by lights glowing over the pictures, and they passed through it and entered a room.

It was ablaze with lights, gleaming on beautiful furniture, pictures and a profusion of flowers, and as they entered a woman rose from a low chair and gave a cry of welcome.

"Darling, you're back! I was getting worried."

She came towards them with outstretched hands and Zaria saw at once her resemblance to Chuck. There was no mistaking that they were mother and son.

Chuck bent to kiss her.

"It's all right, Mother. And here is Zaria. I told you I would bring her back with me!"

He looked down at Zaria.

"This is my Mother, my sweet," he explained, "the Comtesse de Chatelneuf."

The *Comtesse* smiled and Zaria thought that she was one of the most beautiful people she had ever seen. Tall and slender, with big grey eyes in an oval face, her pure white hair made her seem somehow younger than her years.

"So this is Zaria," she said softly.

"She's still a little bewildered by it all," Chuck explained.

"I can so understand that," his mother replied. "Come, dears, I have got sandwiches and drinks for you, unless you would like something more substantial."

"I think that will be all we'll want," Chuck answered.

The *Comtesse* led the way to the far end of the room where there was a table containing several delicious dishes and every possible sort of drink.

"I'm so glad you are here," she said to Zaria. "Since my son told me of the terrible people with whom you were associating, I have been worrying all the evening lest they should hurt you."

Zaria at last found her voice.

"I . . . I thought you were ill," she stammered.

Chuck laughed.

"Mother, I've got to confess to you that I've told quite a lot of lies," he said. "You know how desperate I was to get on the yacht, so I had to tell Zaria that you were ill—in fact I'm not certain I didn't say you were dying—and I believe I also told a few fibs about some wicked step-brothers who were trying to cut me out of your will."

"That was very naughty of you, darling," the *Comtesse* said in an affectionate tone. "You know how I hate lies of any sort. Couldn't you have told Zaria the truth?"

"If I had, I don't think she would have believed me; and what is more, I certainly don't think she would have befriended me as she did."

"Then the sooner you tell her everything now, the better," she said with an effort at severity. "And when you have done that, please go and wash that terrible dye off your hair: I can't bear to look at you with it."

She smiled at both of them and then, putting her hand on Zaria's shoulder, she said:

"I am going up to bed now because I know there are lots of things you want to say to each other. As a matter of fact, I have been ill and I have to take care of myself. My son will tell you all about it. But before I go I should like to say one thing; I have always wanted a daughter, and now I hope I am going to have one."

She bent as she spoke and kissed Zaria's cheek. And then, before Zaria could respond, she had moved

243

across the room, Chuck had opened the door for her and she was gone.

Zaria was conscious of the tears welling into her eyes. No one had ever been so sweet to her, so kind, so understanding.

Somehow she couldn't believe it was true. It was just a dream from which she would awaken to find herself unwanted, unloved, crying into her pillow as she had cried so often before.

Chuck came back across the room.

"How do you like my Mother?" he asked.

"She's . . . wonderful," Zaria stammered, with something suspiciously like a sob in her voice.

Chuck put his arm round her.

"Tears?" he asked. "There's nothing to cry about, Zaria."

"There is," Zaria answered. "I am too happy. It can't be true. I must be imagining all this."

In answer Chuck poured out two glasses of champagne.

"We are going to drink a toast before we do anything else," he said. "Pick up your glass."

Zaria obeyed him. He raised his.

"To our enchanted future!" he said quietly. "And may the past be quickly forgotten."

He sipped his champagne and Zaria did likewise, and then he drew her down to a wide, cushioned windowseat in front of a big window which opened into the moonlit garden.

"Shall I start from the beginning?" he asked. "Because I know you are dying of curiosity."

"I don't think I am really," Zaria answered. "Not now. I am too happy to think of anything but the present."

"That is what I wanted you to say," he replied. "Oh, Zaria, I love you so much! You are full of surprises, full of so many things which delight and intrigue me. And yet, at the same time, you always do the right thing, the thing which makes each moment we are together perfect."

"It frightens me when you say things like that," Zaria murmured. "I am so afraid that you will go away and forget me."

"I shall never do that," Chuck answered. "Because I'm going to look after you, I'm going to make you happy, I'm going to wipe away those dark shadows under your eyes, that look of fear on your face. Sometimes it breaks my heart when I see your lips droop and eyes go dark and miserable because of what you are remembering. The nightmare is over, Zaria. Ahead lies sunrise for both of us."

The tears in Zaria's eyes welled over and ran down her cheeks.

"I am crying because I'm so happy," she said. "So utterly and ecstatically happy. I never knew that love could be like this."

"This is only the beginning," Chuck answered. "We have got so much more to discover, so much more to dig up together." His lips twisted a little. "I am really an archaeologist you know."

"Are you? Oh, I'm so glad," Zaria cried.

"We will go digging together," he said, "as soon as we are married. Will you be happy to spend your honeymoon with me like that?"

Zaria didn't answer for a moment and he added anxiously:

"You are going to marry me, aren't you?"

"Are you really asking me?" she enquired.

"I've never wanted to marry anyone before," he answered. "I shall never want to marry anyone again. You are the person I have been looking for, Zaria."

She bent her head suddenly and laid her lips against his hand. He snatched it away almost fiercely and swept her into his arms.

"Oh, darling, darling!" he cried. "Don't be humble. If you knew what you are giving me. If I could only tell you what it means to be loved for myself."

She did not answer him because his lips were on hers and she was quivering and trembling in his hold while a flame within her leapt vivid and fiery through her body.

After a long time he released her again and lifting her glass of champagne put it back into her hand.

"I must send you to bed," he said. "But before you go, I want to tell you about everything, because otherwise I am afraid you will lie awake asking yourself questions to which you won't know the answer."

"There is one I must know," Zaria said. "Why did you dye your hair?"

"Haven't you guessed that?" he asked.

She shook her head.

"No."

"I dyed it for the same reason I wore my dark glasses," Chuck answered. "Because otherwise I thought I should resemble too closely for comfort the gentleman on the yacht you knew as Mr. Virdon."

"Resemble him!" Zaria exclaimed, wrinkling her brow a little. "But why? Is he a relation or something?"

Chuck laughed and shook his head.

"He is an actor," he said. "A rather clever young actor who always, for some inexplicable reason, looked very much like me."

His eyes watched her bewildered face and he added:

"Haven't you guessed yet, darling? I am Cornelius Virdon!"

Zaria stared at him open-mouthed.

"You don't mind, do you?" Chuck asked taking her

hand in his and stroking it gently. "You see, darling, I was so afraid, if I didn't make myself out poor and impoverished, that you wouldn't help me to get aboard the yacht. So you have got to forgive me for lying to you, when actually I'm 'the rich Mr. Virdon.' "

He made the last three words seem somehow absurd, but Zaria couldn't laugh.

"But why, then, was that other man pretending to be you?" she questioned.

"That is what I am going to tell you," Chuck replied. "You see, darling, Edie Morgan is a very wicked man. Apparently he is well known as a gun-runner on the other side of the Atlantic; and having made the South American coast, and a great many other places, too hot to hold him, he thought he would try his hand in Europe."

"A gun-runner!" Zaria ejaculated. "But where are the guns?"

"In Madame Bertin's luggage, of course," Chuck answered. "Only the first consignment, of course. Having once made contact with the Sheik, Edie intended to make a regular business of running guns across the Mediterranean. So, for an *apéritif* he brought with him three machine guns of the smaller type and ten Tommy guns, all nicely dismantled and packed into false bottoms with Madame Bertin's most fabulous creations on top of them!"

"Oh, Chuck, how awful!" Zaria cried. "But what will happen to Madame Bertin?"

"I am afraid she'll get a prison sentence," Chuck answered. "But not too harsh a one. The French are always kind to a woman. And Kate, I expect, will get away with it completely."

At Kate's name Zaria turned her head away for the moment and looked out into the garden. Chuck's eyes were on the delicacy of her profile and the sudden little droop of her lips.

"You aren't jealous of her, my darling, are you?" he asked. "I'm terribly flattered, but you needn't be."

"But you seemed to like her so much," Zaria said accusingly.

"I know," he answered. "I was trying to get some very useful information out of Kate and the only way it was possible to obtain anything was by playing on her vanity. I'm afraid I've behaved rather like a cad. But the Kates of this world are so tough that they must expect people to be tough with them."

"Then you didn't like her?" Zaria asked.

Chuck smiled.

"Shall I tell you something?" he questioned. "I knew a secretary would be waiting for me at Marseilles, and as I flew the Atlantic and made my plans, I hoped she would be the sort of girl who would help me. But from the very first moment that I walked into your bedroom and saw you there, I knew you were the person I had been looking for all my life."

"You couldn't have thought that," Zaria replied. "You couldn't. I looked so terrible."

"You looked very young, very pathetic and very badly treated," Chuck answered. "But you couldn't look terrible. Have you any idea, Zaria, how lovely you really are?"

"It isn't true," Zaria stammered, while the blood mounted to her cheeks because of the look in Chuck's eyes.

"I shall convince you in time," he said softly. "But now I must go on with my story."

"But how did you come to Marseilles in the first place?" Zaria asked.

"That was just what I was going to tell you," he said. "I had arranged to charter the yacht because I had planned not only to visit my Mother, but to do some excavations on a new site that I had heard of to the North of Algiers. I made all my plans to leave America, and set off with my luggage from my apartment in New York.

"As my taxi turned into a side street leading down to the docks, two men got in during a hold up in the traffic and proceeded to set about me. The taxi driver must, of course, have been in league with them, for he made no attempt to stop even when I shouted for help. They hit me on the head with a rubber truncheon."

"So that's how you got the bruise," Zaria said quickly.

"Exactly," Chuck answered. "Fortunately I had done a Commando course in the army. I knew that when one was up against insurmountable odds it is best to feign a complete collapse to avoid further punishment. I slumped down on the seat and in falling caught my ear, which started to bleed profusely."

Zaria remembered the patch that had been on his ear when he had come into her room in Marseilles. Looking closely she could still see a scar on the lobe.

"An ear bleeds pretty freely," Chuck went on, "and one man said to the other,

'Hold it! Edie didn't want any marks on the body. He's out.'

"Mercifully, they didn't hit me again, and though my head was throbbing abominably I was able to feign unconsciousness while being very much aware of what they were doing."

"They might have killed you!" Zaria exclaimed.

"They intended to do that later," Chuck answered. "They stripped me of my clothes, dressed me in a ragged torn suit they had with them, and then, taking me down to the water's edge at a deserted part of the river, pushed me in."

"Intending to drown you!" Zaria cried in horror.

"Yes, that is what they intended to do," Chuck said grimly. "I don't know how many suicides are fished out of New York harbour every year, but it runs into some hundreds. I was to be one of them."

"What happened?" Zaria asked breathlessly.

"I swam below water until they were out of sight," Chuck answered. "It was a very unpleasant experience and my lungs were nearly bursting when finally I came up for air. By that time they had disappeared. I then managed to get back to the apartment of a friend of mine who is a police officer, and tried to find out what it was all about."

"Why didn't you have them arrested?" Zaria enquired.

"Well, to begin with they had already sailed," Chuck answered. "And, secondly, my friend made a number of enquiries and what he learned intrigued me. I was determined to fly to Europe and catch the cut-throats redhanded."

"It sounds terribly dangerous," Zaria said.

"I'm afraid that was what attracted me," Chuck answered with a smile. "What my friend told me was that Edie was a really evil man who had been too clever up to date to be picked up by the police on any really serious charge.

"They knew about him; they knew what sort of racket he was operating, but they just couldn't catch him. It wasn't only gun-running—that was bad enough—but he was also dope peddling."

"That was why he had those cigarettes," Zaria said.

"Exactly! Mister Edie Morgan was out to make money wherever he got the opportunity."

"They might have killed you for finding out about them!"

"There was always that risk," Chuck smiled. "But this was the biggest operation they had undertaken and it seemed a pity to make a move before they had really got the noose around their necks."

"But how had they ever thought of it in the first place?" Zaria asked.

"I don't know except that the papers were always writing me up as a recluse who liked travelling alone. They knew I never took a valet with me. They knew I intended to make this trip to Africa for the purpose of digging. The trouble with the Press is that they are always too free with their information."

"So they decided to impersonate you?"

"Yes! You see the thing that they wanted was a yacht, and it was no use their trying to hire one without credentials. By getting rid of me and hoping that my body would be unidentified, they would have provided themselves with the one thing that was essential if they were to get the guns to Algiers."

"How did they get hold of the actor who pretended to be you?"

"Dope, I think," Chuck said briefly. "He is a rather stupid young man who has got into Edie's clutches and who, in return for the small amount of dope that was doled out to him, has to pay for it again and again.

"As soon as I saw him on board, I realised who he was. I had seen him act once in a small part on Broadway, and several people had remarked on his likeness to me."

"But you had dyed your hair before that," Zaria questioned.

"Well, I didn't want Edie, or anyone else, to recognise me," Chuck explained. "You see, the newspapers are rather fond of putting in my picture."

"I don't believe I shall like you with any other sort of hair."

"Then I shall have to go on dying it," he smiled, "but it would be an awful nuisance. Besides, people might accuse me of being vain."

Zaria laughed.

"I found the bottle in your drawer and couldn't understand why you had it."

"I expect it made you even more suspicious of me," Chuck said. "My poor little sweet. I have tried you very high, haven't I? And yet you have gone on trusting me."

"I was rather suspicious at times that you had done something really wrong." Zaria replied honestly.

"I'm not a bit surprised," Chuck told her. "But you do see that I didn't dare make you too suspicious of Edie and Victor and all the rest. If they had thought you were wise to their game, they wouldn't have hesitated to bump you off and dump you overboard.

"They are really dangerous. There's half-a-dozen murders which ought to be laid at their door and which have never been rightly proved."

Zaria shivered.

"Oh, Chuck! Supposing they had found out that you were spying on them?"

"I had to take that risk," he said. "I must say, it was a double risk having to protect you as well."

"But who was buying the guns?" Zaria asked. "Why did Sheik Ibrahim ben Kaddour want them?"

"That is an easy question to answer," Chuck replied. "The Sheik is one of the chief rebels who are making a terrible nuisance of themselves to the French authorities. They were just as anxious to lay hands on him as the American police were to get hold of

Edie Morgan. That was why I didn't dare do anything until the Sheik had appeared.

"The military authorities picked him up, by the way, when he left the Salem's House this evening. It is the first time they have been able to get within a mile of him."

"I suppose that was why you didn't let the authorities arrest Edie Morgan beforehand," Zaria said perceptively. "After all, they could have found the guns in Madame Bertin's luggage as soon as we arrived."

"You're quite right," Chuck agreed. "And that was also why I couldn't let the police arrest me on Edie's trumped up charge of dope peddling. You see, I had not been in touch with the civilian police at all. I had been working with the military authorities, and you know how everything travels round like lightning in a native country. We didn't dare breathe a word to anyone in case ben Kaddour got to hear of it and slipped away into the desert."

"They might have shot you when you were swimming from the yacht," Zaria said accusingly.

Chuck shook his head.

"They are not particularly good shots, and I'm a very strong swimmer. It was a risk I had to take. I didn't dare stand up to them, just when I knew there was likely to be a showdown tonight."

"Then it was the military who were waiting on the yacht and who shot Edie," Zaria said.

"I told them to be there and to keep hidden," Chuck answered. "But I wasn't going to have your life risked in any way, and when people start shooting it is often the wrong people who get shot."

"How clever of you to think it all out," Zaria said.

"I had some good brains to help me," Chuck told her modestly. "But I'll tell you one thing. I am likely

253

to get the *Légion d'honneur* for this. Will that make you proud of me?"

"I am proud of you without that," Zaria answered. "So very, very proud."

He took a deep breath and looked down into her eyes.

"I hope you will always go on being so."

"The only person I'm unhappy about is Madame Bertin," Zaria said. "She was so kind to me and took such trouble over choosing me some clothes."

"She's rather a bad old girl, as it happens," Chuck answered. "She can't help spending money and she's an inveterate gambler. That's why she's hard up. She should have made a fortune by this time with her designs, but she keeps getting into debt and so she fell into Edie's clutches. He promised her not only a large sum of money, but to finance her new venture out here if she would carry his guns for him."

"Poor Madame Bertin!" Zaria sighed.

"Well, I'll tell you what I'll do," Chuck said soothingly. "I will talk to my friends about her. We may be able to prove that she was forced into it by Edie, more or less at the point of a pistol."

"Yes. Please, please do that," Zaria pleaded.

"And if I do that for you, what will you do for me?" Chuck asked.

"What do you want me to do?" Zaria enquired.

He drew her a little nearer to him.

"I want you not only to tell me that you will marry me at once—tomorrow or the next day, just as quickly as we can—I want you also to tell me something that you haven't told me yet. Do you know what that is?"

"Y . . . yes, I think so," Zaria murmured, blushing. "But you know it already."

"I want to hear you say it," he insisted. "I love you so much and yet I know so little about you—in fact, nothing except that you are the most adorable, wonderful person I have ever met in all my life."

At his words Zaria suddenly looked guilty.

"I have only just remembered something," she exclaimed.

"What is it?" he asked.

"I had really forgotten it myself," she said hastily. "Chuck! My name isn't Brown at all."

It was his turn to look surprised.

"Then who are you?" he enquired.

"I am Zaria Mansford," she said, "and my father was Professor Mansford—you may perhaps have heard of him."

"But of course I have heard of him," Chuck answered. "I read that last book of his only just before I left New York. Why the masquerade? Don't tell me you were mixed up in anything shady?"

"No, not exactly," Zaria answered. "But, you see, I . . . own *The Enchantress.*"

Chuck stared at her incredulously for a moment, and then he threw back his head and laughed.

"The new owner!" he exclaimed. "Jim told me about her. Miss Cardew's niece, whom none of them had ever seen and they all wondered what she would be like."

"It was stupid of me," Zaria confessed. "It was just that I was frightened, and Doris Brown chucked the job at the last moment, after the solicitors had engaged her for you, because she was going to be married. So I took her place."

"We'll send her the most wonderful wedding present that any girl has ever had," Chuck said. "Because if it hadn't been for her, we should never have met. Blessings on Doris Brown."

He raised Zaria's hand to his lips and then he added:

"And so, darling, you are not the penniless little

waif at all. You are a rich young woman, the owner of *The Enchantress*."

"Oh, Chuck, don't let it spoil things. Please don't let it spoil things," Zaria pleaded.

"Nothing you could do could alter or change my love for you," Chuck answered. "Whatever you do, whatever you say, however unkind you may be even, you will still enchant me. You are my sweet enchantress for all time. And now, my darling, tell me what I want to hear."

Just for a moment Zaria hesitated, and then, with the colour coming into her face, with her eyes flickering a little because of the fire and triumph in his, she whispered, as he took her in his arms:

"I love . . . you. Oh, Chuck, with . . . all of . . . me. I love you . . . so much."